COLD WATER BURNING

COLD WATER BURNING

100

"STRALEY'S DONE THE IMPOSSIBLE:
HE'S REINVENTED THE PRIVATE EYE NOVEL."
—*The Denver Post*

BANTAM BOOKS

D0034895

JOHN STRALEY

AWARD-WINNING AUTHOR OF *THE ANGELS WILL NOT CARE*

Don't miss
JOHN STRALEY'S
other
CECIL YOUNGER
novels

THE CURIOUS EAT THEMSELVES

THE MUSIC OF WHAT HAPPENS

DEATH AND THE LANGUAGE OF HAPPINESS

THE ANGELS WILL NOT CARE

Available from
Bantam Books

BANTAM BOOKS

ISBN 0-553-58076-0

US $6.50 / $9.99 CAN

9 780553 580761

50650

The Angels Will Not Care

"Straley brings to his work a passion, intellect and artistry rare in popular fiction. . . . A born storyteller who laces his work with just the right amounts of humor, suspense and excitement, wisdom and poetry."
—*The Denver Post*

"What makes Straley's latest Alaska mystery a must is—as always—the sheer beauty and energy of Straley's writing."
—*Chicago Tribune*

"Straley's novels are often compared to bestselling Tony Hillerman, but it's not a valid comparison; Straley is much better and much deeper. He's one of the field's greatest unrecognized talents, an oversight which should be corrected."
—*Boulder Planet*

"Ingenious . . . original."
—*Ellery Queen Mystery Magazine*

"A well-written book . . . Will definitely make you want to turn the pages to see what happens next."
—*Rendezvous*

"Pure delight."
—*Milwaukee Journal Sentinel*

"Straley transcends the genre with his finely crafted prose. . . . [He] has created satisfying thrillers that also explore human failings and the conflicting nature of a state whose majestic beauty is threatened by unbridled greed. . . . Readers won't be able to abandon ship in this first-rate work."
—*The Tampa Tribune*

"Astonishing . . . no less than a meditation on death itself . . . remarkable."
—*Houston Chronicle*

Death and the Language of Happiness

The Music of What Happens

Cold
Water
Burning

John Straley

BANTAM BOOKS
New York ◆ Toronto ◆ London ◆ Sydney ◆ Auckland

COLD WATER BURNING

A Bantam Book

PUBLISHING HISTORY
Bantam hardcover edition published January 2001
Bantam mass market edition / November 2001

Excerpt used as epigraph from THE ESSENTIAL HAIKU: VERSIONS OF
BASHO, BUSON & ISSA, EDITED AND WITH AN INTRODUCTION
by ROBERT HASS. Introduction and selection copyright © 1994 by
Robert Hass. Unless otherwise noted, all translations copyright © 1994
by Robert Hass. Reprinted by permission of HarperCollins Publishers, Inc.

Library of Congress Catalog Card Number: 00-42924

ISBN: 0-553-58076-0

Published simultaneously in the United States and Canada

Bantam Books are published by Bantam Books, a division of Random House,
Inc. Its trademark, consisting of the words "Bantam Books" and the portrayal
of a rooster, is Registered in U.S. Patent and Trademark Office and in other coun-
tries. Marca Registrada. Bantam Books, 1540 Broadway, New York, New York
10036.

PRINTED IN THE UNITED STATES OF AMERICA

10 9 8 7 6 5 4 3 2 1
OPM

Naked
on a naked horse,
through pouring rain.—Issa

TRANSLATION BY
ROBERT HASS

Cold Water Burning

Chapter One

The storm had passed, Toddy was dead and I was clinging to the overturned hull of my yellow skiff. I pulled down the hood of my rubber survival suit and looked up to see gulls circling the tangled mess my life had become. There was no help, and there wouldn't be. Light dazzled on the tip of every gray-green wave, but there were no ships. I was wide awake in the empty sea wishing I could go back in time, back to the dock before I had pushed away, back to the unsolved homicide, back to the recurring nightmare of murder, gasoline and children screaming.

It could be argued that being a private investigator in a small Alaskan town is one of the worst career decisions a person with a high-school diploma can make. But there's lots of opportunity for free time. In that regard, the summer started off well. I had spent six wonderful days catching a few of the early king salmon, all thanks to the money I'd made working for a rich herring boat captain who had crushed some fool charter fisherman's face in a bar brawl. The case was my dream come true: a rich client with serious felony charges. The summer was looking up, but summers are short here. The skipper settled his case long before trial; I had spent most of his money on bait and boat repairs before September came around.

I would never have gone out into that storm willingly. The weather radio had been tracking two low-pressure systems on a collision course in the north Pacific. If the systems joined forces it would become the kind of storm that would crack the limbs off alder trees and churn the shoreline white. I still remember the feeling of those few days as the storm moved in: black clouds like bags of anvils rolling up over the horizon, and the trees along the beach standing motionless as if they were trying to hide from what was coming. I remember the expectation and the dread before the storm hit.

It was two days before the peak of the storm when Patricia Ewers walked into my office and asked me to find her husband Richard, who had gone missing with fifty thousand dollars of their money. Richard Ewers's case may have been my greatest success as a defense investigator. Three years ago he had stood trial on four counts of first-degree murder and one count of arson, and had been found not guilty.

He had been accused of killing two adults and two children on board a fish-buying scow, soaking the deck with gas, and setting the whole mess on fire as he escaped in a red tin skiff. This was Richard Ewers. My client.

A five-month murder trial is an ordeal that forges loyalties that only come out of combat. All the subtle conflicts boil down to "us" against "them." I thought of Patricia Ewers as an old army buddy. Captain of the "us," Patricia provided the strength and calm presence during the wildest part of the ordeal. All through the halfhearted police protection, the ugly phone calls and the reporters digging through her garbage, she never wavered in her support of Richard. She and her parents had stood by him; they had lost both their houses and their savings accounts to legal fees. The not-guilty verdict was some vindication, but nothing could pay them back for what they had been through.

When I saw her walk up my stairs unannounced three years later, I knew something more serious than a multiple murder count had to be bothering Patricia Ewers.

"Cecil, he's gone. I think they killed him this time."

I put my hand on her back and moved her to my sagging couch near the woodstove. "He took the money. In cash. A large amount of cash," she said as she flopped herself on the old couch. Dust rose up in a plume. "I told him not to take it."

"What money?" I asked her as I offered her a towel to dry her hair, for she had been caught in a rain squall walking to my house.

"The tabloids. They kept offering Richard money for his story. I told him not to take it. We were through the worst of it. We had made it through the trial and things were beginning to calm down. But they kept offering more and more money. He's had trouble finding work, you know; no one would hire him in the fishing industry. Anyway, when they finally offered a hundred thousand dollars for an article, book, and film rights, he told them he would take it."

"One hundred thousand dollars?"

"We had only gotten half of it. There was fifty on signing the deal and the rest after he did the interviews. I know, we shouldn't have taken it."

"I wasn't going to say that, Patricia. I was just wondering if they wanted my story."

"Have you been found not guilty of mass murder?" She said it sarcastically.

"No," I said, "but I'm close friends with some people who were. That should be worth a couple of grand at least."

"You can have it, Cecil. I mean, jeepers, we have no control over the story. They could print anything." She held her hands up as if framing the headline in the air. "*MYGIRL* MURDERER BEATS THE RAP." Then she buried her head in her hands.

I could understand her concern. Richard's story had everything for the tabloids: drama, sympathetic victims, terrific color photographs. It had everything except a killer behind bars.

The murders occurred in late August of 1995. The *Mygirl* had been anchored in Kalinin Bay just north of Sitka. It was just after dark, past midnight on that Alaskan summer evening, when a man got into a skiff and pulled away from a conflagration. He left behind the bodies of a father, a mother, their nine-year-old daughter, and a teenaged boy who had been visiting the scow.

The parents, Charlie and Edna Sands, were each shot once through the chest before the fire started. Their daughter Tina had been clubbed over the head and almost surely died in the blaze while she was semiconscious. Albert Chevalier, the fourteen-year-old visitor, was shot repeatedly, in the arms and legs and once through the skull. His body was the most charred because the arsonist had doused the boy's body with gasoline before spreading the accelerant throughout the rest of the scow. The two Sands boys escaped the fire. The boys told investigators they had heard a commotion up in their parents' quarters and just as they went to investigate, the scow burst into flame.

Across the bay, Albert Chevalier's brother Jonathan had seen the first signs of the fire, rushed over in his skiff, and pulled the Sands boys off the burning scow.

Later, in trial, Jonathan Chevalier swore he saw someone leave the *Mygirl* in one of the scow's three tin skiffs. According to Jonathan, whose little brother, Albert, died that night, the driver of the tin skiff "could have been" Richard Ewers.

I've been asked dozens of times if I thought Ewers was guilty of four killings, and I always say the same thing. "I don't know who killed those people." But the truth is I believed wholeheartedly in Richard's innocence. I just couldn't prove it.

Ewers was the only hired crewman on board the *Mygirl*. Richard had been hired by Charlie Sands off the docks in Ballard, Washington. He had worked the Alaskan fisheries and Charlie needed a seasoned hand to help bring the scow up the coastline. It seemed incontrovertible that seconds after this mysterious man who could have been Richard Ewers pulled away from the *Mygirl* in a skiff, the scow went up in a bonnet of flame. Most of the usable evidence was lost in the fire and almost everything else of forensic value was washed overboard as local fishermen battled the fire.

A day and a half later, heat and smoke shimmered off the

charred remains of the beached scow. There was little in the *Mygirl's* hulk left to tell the story of the four murders. Because of that lack of evidence, a major crime investigation was based only on fragmented witness statements. All the investigators were left with was grief and a collection of wispy memories.

Richard's memory was bad. Particularly bad when he was first interviewed and he couldn't quite decide where he had been or what part he had had to play in the fire. Finally he confessed to stealing some money from Charlie Sands's till that night and heading to town in the scow's skiff. When he left the *Mygirl,* Richard said, everything was quiet and everyone on board was sleeping soundly. This was his final story and he stuck to it.

His clothes bore some trace elements of gasoline, but he said he'd had to pour gas into his fuel tank from a jerry jug. This was a reasonable story. But the fact that all three skiffs from the scow were accounted for, plus his guilty demeanor when questioned and the theft of the money, made Richard the trooper investigators' only viable suspect.

I liked Richard Ewers. I had sat with him through some of the worst days of his life. I was with him when children spat on him while walking to court, and when each day's mail brought new death threats. I never saw him bristle or clench his fist. In short, I never saw the kind of explosive personality it takes to commit these kinds of killings. Or so I thought. As has been pointed out to me many times, I don't have a large pool of people to compare him to. How many mass murderers does anybody get a chance to know?

"He took half of the tabloid money. He said he was going to end this whole thing one way or the other," Patricia told me and started to cry. "He was coming up here. Ketchikan first, then Sitka. It's been a week and I haven't heard from him. He hasn't called. He always calls, Cecil. You know that. He always calls."

She looked up at me with pleading eyes as if my just acknowledging the truth of that would bring her husband back.

"He always calls," I repeated lamely. I had been getting

dressed to go out the road on a job when she arrived. I looked at this woman who had done so much to calm everyone else during her husband's trial. Her hands were cupped around her nose and mouth and her collar was wet where tears soaked it.

"It's going to be okay," I said, and I winced at the insincerity of my voice. "What was he going to do with the money?" I asked, trying to cover for myself.

"He wouldn't tell me," she said, wiping her nose on her sleeve, as I reached for a napkin that was inexplicably resting on the banister. "All he would say was he was going to straighten some things out. He said not to worry about taking the money from the tabloids because we weren't going to keep it."

I sneaked a look at my watch. I had to get out on the road. I had been offered a ride, but I had just missed it.

"Did he ever take large sums of money before?" I asked while putting on my coat.

"No, no, he didn't." She was breathing hard now, no longer weeping but on the verge. "I don't think he was being blackmailed, Cecil. I don't know why, but it seemed like he wanted to do something with the money. He didn't act angry, like he was being forced. He was acting relieved."

"Why do you think someone has killed him?" I asked her. She would not look at me.

"Oh . . . I don't know really. It's all this . . . mess." That was how Patricia had always referred to the trial, the charges, the accusations of multiple homicide and arson: *this mess*.

"It was worse after he got some of the money. New people were angry and the old people—you know, the families—are furious now. We had calls. Mostly Richard hung up. But more and more he would talk to them. People saying he deserved to be shot and burned along with his blood money. Cecil, you know how people are."

How people are. Every time I begin to think I know something about how people are, I find out I am wrong.

My stomach hurt as I watched her because I knew she was right. The list of people who had wanted Richard Ewers dead was extensive. What concerned me most was that some of those on the list were quite capable of making it happen.

"Cecil, I want you to find him. I want you to start right now. I want you to go out to see some of those people in the families. I want you to ask them point-blank what they've done to my husband." The families she was referring to were those of the victims, the Chevaliers and the Sandses. Her blue eyes brimmed with tears and she stared at me as if there was something I could do.

"I will, Patricia, but first I've got . . . I've got a job to do for a person." I backed away from her and put my work gloves in my coat pocket.

"Cecil, we've got to start on this now. I can pay you, for gosh sakes." She dug into her zippered jacket pocket and fanned out some twenty-dollar bills. "I want you to start now. Please."

I said nothing. I wasn't going to tell her who I was going to work for, because I knew just saying his name would send her into a rage.

"Listen," I said as I fussed around with my work gloves and keys, "you can stay here. I'll ask a few questions around town and then I'll be back, okay? You just make yourself comfortable here. I'll be back tonight and then we'll get started looking for Richard."

Patricia stood up and without speaking walked down the stairs to the street. She slapped her money against the banister as she walked. "I can't believe you're making me go to the police," she hissed as she slammed my door. After she left I straightened a picture on the wall in an effort to assert the correctness of my actions.

I walked out into the street and smelled the storm sulking off the coast. It was still the early part of September and the fireweed in the ditches was frothing with its soon-to-be-airborne seeds. Dozens of humpback whales lolled on the surface out in Eastern Channel, and the hours of daylight were shrinking down to that intense window of opportunity that can drive a depressive to drink.

I walked along my street in this little island town wondering how I could tell Patricia Ewers that I was going to work for George Doggy, the police detective who had persecuted her family through the investigation and the trial. To Patricia Ewers, George Doggy was the author of her family's misery, the captain of "them."

A fishing boat eased in past the breakwater, probably looking for its berth before the storm hit. The sun had cleared the mountains of Baranof Island, lighting them like a bad religious painting. The flat water in the channel sent the light rippling lazily up the sides of the old wooden buildings on the waterfront. Gulls worked the air and a few eagles sat perched on the Forest Service building as I walked to the only traffic light in town, jaywalked across Halibut Point Road, and wandered backwards on the edge of the pavement with my thumb out.

I had stood next to Patricia Ewers three years ago when the jury foreman read the not-guilty verdict. We had hugged each other and cried while the rest of the world looked at us in scorn. For some reason as I walked down the road now I felt a strange certainty that Richard was dead, and I didn't want to be the one to find him. I think I was getting tired of murder.

Harrison Teller had been Richard's lawyer. Teller was confined to a wheelchair these days, yet he was still a formidable figure. Every gesture, every nuance in the courtroom was charged with an instinct for communicating his client's case to the jury. When a sniper's bullet had paralyzed him from the waist down on the banks of the Nenana River in Fairbanks, Teller recuperated for a year. Then he found a way to work his newly limited mobility into his law practice. He had said to me, "Younger, I would give anything to walk again, but this goddamn wheelchair makes for great theater in court."

Teller also would have been furious if he had known I was working for George Doggy. But I needed the money. I was a parent now. Of course that wouldn't have mattered to Teller. He had kids and he hadn't lost his belly for murder. I was getting soft and worn out. He had said as much to my face.

When our daughter finally pushed through the birth canal amid all the breathing and stifled screams, I got the impression she was traveling light: her fists were clenched, her tiny walnut face enraged at the world's intrusion into her life. She was as naked as grief or joy, and when the doctor laid her in Jane Marie's arms and she settled to her mother's breast, I felt that aching sadness I encounter when confronting great beauty. It's a sadness that says no matter what you do from that moment on, nothing will ever be the same. Maybe Teller had been right. Maybe I had lost my stomach for murder.

I was thinking about this when a sleek sedan with a rental company sticker on both bumpers wheeled by with country music thumping from behind the closed windows. Patricia Ewers was driving. She flicked her hair in my direction and pinched her cigarette tightly between her lips. I looked at her as she made the turn, and although she looked back at me, her stare was dead.

In a moment, the rental car was gone and only a puff of exhaust remained, the engine's breath hanging in place above the pavement. I stepped through it, then resumed walking backwards, thumb out.

I didn't blame her for hating me. It's been said that I'm not much of a private investigator, even though I had done good work for her husband. Teller and I had torn the state's evidence apart until there was nothing left. But we hadn't been able to put their life back together. Or find the real killer.

I'm a good PI for the real world. I can wear blinders and I'm as steady as a tractor. But the fact that I don't save the day by finding the truth is not all my fault. People don't really want to know the truth, no matter what they say. I meet most of my clients after they have been arrested for a crime. Guilty or innocent, they want the same thing: they want whatever bit of their innocence is left intact. They want me to re-create it for them. That's all Richard Ewers had wanted, and that's what Teller had paid me for.

I'd been walking ten minutes when a rusted Chevy truck pulled over twenty yards down the road and Gary Gouker heaved open the passenger-side door. Gary was my gym partner and I knew why he had stopped.

"C, man, where you been? Have you been to the gym? I kind of slacked off after you didn't show up those times, Cecil."

"I'm going to cut wood for Doggy," I said, as if that explained everything in my life.

"Cutting wood's good," Gary agreed. I jumped onto the bench seat, which sagged badly to the outside of the vehicle.

"I can't drive you out there. I've got a guy coming in with a job. He's been on me. I mean *on* me! Sent his kid to drag my ass out of the coffee shop. He's probably up at my shop right now. I'll drive you to the corner."

I looked through the cracked windshield. The corner was some hundred yards away.

"Yeah, good," I said and slammed the door. Gary was a machinist and a blues harmonica player. His father had been the mill manager here for years and Gary had worked there too, but that was long ago now. The mill was closed, his dad was dead, and Gary's real love was the blues harmonica.

"What d'ya think of getting Cary Bell up here for Alaska Day? If not him, I'm pretty sure I could get Paul deLay. What d'ya think?"

"Perfect," I said. "Get them both and promise to take them fishing. I'm sure two great blues players would give anything to play Sitka, Alaska."

That was all the conversation we had because we were at the corner already.

Gary let me off and drove away quickly with a wave. There was a three-legged dog sniffing the stop sign by the funeral home and when he peed on it I noticed that he swung around so he didn't have to worry about lifting a leg. "Convenient," I thought, and stuck out my thumb. Only five miles to go.

I hadn't thought of the *Mygirl* killings since our daughter had been born three months ago. I hadn't had many coherent thoughts since I saw her push her way out into the light. She had been blood-slick and angry. We had decided to name her Blossom and despite my smile in the hospital room I had hated the birth experience with all the screaming and the blood. It reminded me of a bar fight without the drugs and the music. When the nurse started to hand my daughter to me, my first reaction was to shy away, thinking that this creature who had just bullied her way out of my lover's stomach must be some sort of enraged snapping turtle. I wasn't sure her name fit her.

The three-legged dog sniffed my leg. He was some kind of lab-husky-terrier beast, friendly, and I was sure he had an empty bladder. I thought of Blossom and wondered if we would get another dog for our house. My roommate Todd had a Staffordshire terrier named Wendell who seemed fine, but many of our friends were almost hysterical with anxiety over having Wendell around the baby and had tried to convince us to take Wendell out into the woods for a long dirt nap. I've noticed that we parents can justify almost anything in the name of protecting our children. Anything, including executing other people's dogs, or even their children if necessary. I had sided with the Staffordshire terrier. "How soft is that?" I wanted to ask Mr. Harrison Teller, with his belly for murder.

Bob Rose stopped in his coughing VW van. He was off to Sandy Beach to check the surfbreak. He told me Nels, Mark, and Steve were going to meet him there because a swell was running from the storm. The break "should really be working," he said. Bob had curly red hair and wire-rimmed glasses. He was wearing a thick wet suit pulled off his shoulders as he drove, and although he seemed interested in the surf, he wasn't stoked. When we got to the beach, none of his friends were there and the waves looked puny. Bob didn't seem to mind. He took a thermos out from under the seat and watched the waves intently as he poured himself a cup of cocoa. "Wait for the tide a bit," he said to himself, and I got the idea that this ritual of watching and waiting was as much part of the surf scene as actually getting wet.

I got out of the van and saw Jude and his sister Rachel standing by the rail watching the sun come up and pointing out the eagles to a woman standing between them. Jude waved me over and introduced me to his mother. Jude is a lawyer and has helped me out over the years, so it paid for me to be civil. Jude is handsome and funny and fairly successful, but in spite of all that he's a decent guy.

"This is my mother, Jammikins," he said, and I looked at him evenly because I never really know when Jude is joking. When I shook the woman's hand she smiled pleasantly and didn't appear to be laughing, so I said nothing about her name.

"Cecil is a detective," Rachel said brightly.

Jammikins looked at me with some vague tourist-like interest. "Really?" she said as she scanned my clothes: torn wool jacket, dirty purple scarf, and tattered canvas pants. I looked more like a Siberian street urchin than I did James Bond.

"I'm cutting wood today," I explained, then shook hands all around and walked out to the road hoping to get a longer ride to my job, but there were fewer cars coming this far out. I was past the big grocery store, and the liquor store at the far end of the road had shut down years before. If a ferry was coming in there was hope, but I couldn't remember the ferry schedule. Once again I stuck out my thumb, thinking that, like prayer, it couldn't hurt.

Teller thought I'd lost my belly for murder because I had stopped drinking, and had turned away from the intense comradeship forged in ugly murder trials. Teller liked to drink. Drinking with his investigator was the one form of comradeship he could tolerate.

But I had stopped tolerating it. The drinking and the lawyerly comradeship that had always been as thin as stone soup. Trial lawyers love their investigators the way bird hunters love their dogs: their affection is heartfelt and intense at the moment, but it's understood the hunter will eventually get another dog.

I remember when I stopped drinking. I remember the moment but not the exact place. I was in a bathtub in a strange hotel room. It was a tiny plastic tub with a thick ring of gray-green soap scum. The bath water was cement gray and cold. The skin on my feet was soft as a sea anemone's. I held the barrel of a revolver in my mouth and propped my elbows on the islands of my knees. I remember how the front sight rattled against my teeth, how the gun oil tasted metallic on my tongue and slicked my lips.

I pulled back the hammer, then eased it down. I stepped out of the tub and toweled off. I knew I wanted a drink but I also knew I wasn't going to drink anymore. I don't know why. "Some haystacks have no needles," William Stafford wrote somewhere, and maybe he's right.

Only three cars had passed. None stopped. I looked up the hillside and noticed I was near Sean and Kevin Sands's trailer. I thought about calling George Doggy and telling him I was still on my way. And I *should* stop and talk to the Sandses. For one thing, I could get Patricia Ewers off my conscience. And for another, in the last few months I had tried to befriend the younger Sands brother, Sean, and had promised I would drop by but I hadn't yet. Sean's brother Kevin didn't like surprises of the "just dropping by" variety, but I now could use the excuse of needing to use their phone to justify my visit. If I walked quickly, I could manage to get to Doggy's in twenty minutes or so, even if I didn't get a ride.

Doggy would understand. Besides being a retired police detective, George Doggy was an old family friend who had offered to pay me to help him put up firewood for the year. George was the retired head of the Alaska State Troopers. He had been a hunting companion of my father's and a confidant to several governors all the way back to territorial days. Doggy was a man who had lived the Alaskan life before jet service and during the era of steamships and dog teams. He had run things, and would come into service if a commissioner or governor asked nicely.

Doggy had been shot several times in his duties, once while working a case I had gotten him mixed up in, and more than any person in my life he was invested in shaping me up. I have to say that he had grown more relaxed in his semiretirement and had taken on the kind of philosophical laissez-faire that some people can accommodate if they've outlived most of the people they ever loved, which meant George's lectures were getting shorter and the war stories longer. At least Doggy was talking to me. Harrison Teller had dropped out of sight after Richard Ewers's trial ended.

In the last six months Doggy had grown noticeably more irritable. He appeared more distracted; he would sometimes pause a long time to find a word and would snap at anyone who tried to supply it. I think he was getting to be an old man, and it bothered him.

Doggy has suggested that I was trying to take Sean, the younger Sands brother, under my wing solely out of the guilt I felt for what I had done to free his family's murderer. That's not entirely true. I had always liked Kevin Sands as an alternative suspect during the Ewers trial. He had the profile, repressed hostility and explosive temper. He had a history of violent arguments, some with his own father. Unfortunately for my theory Kevin also had two alibi witnesses: his brother Sean and Jonathan Chevalier. Sean swore consistently that when the shooting started on the *Mygirl* Kevin had thrown him down on the floor and hidden him under the bunk until Jonathan Chevalier broke through the door and got them out of the fire. Jonathan backed this story up. Teller could possibly have sold Kevin as a murderer to the jury but could never have broken down his two witnesses who had both lost family members themselves and were unshakable in their testimony.

But I had always looked for something in Kevin, something that might tell me more about who had done the shooting on the scow. That . . . and my concern for his little brother made me stay close to the both of them. Even before the murders on the *Mygirl*, the Sands brothers were seriously troubled young people. But afterwards they consistently got into trouble and needed legal help. I had worked their cases for free. But it's true I couldn't shake the image of the dead bodies in the burned-out scow. Kevin Sands was so hardened I suspected I wouldn't glean any new information from him. But Sean was different. If Richard Ewers wasn't the killer and Sean knew it, I suspected he would someday have to let it slip. That was part of the reason I wanted to help him. That, and the fact that I wanted some tiny new bit of information that might change the plotline of my own nightmares.

George Doggy had tried to warn me off helping Sean Sands. "Forget about it, Cecil. That boy's damaged too bad. He'll do life in prison on the installment plan," Doggy had told me.

Sean Sands was twelve and Kevin was twenty-one that September, and by that time I had worked for Kevin's lawyers on at least ten different cases. Kevin had been tough even before the murder of his family. As a juvenile, Kevin had lit fires, broken into schools, and been accused of killing pets. Now he bullied people for money and, I was told, expedited various criminal activities. As far as I knew, he had avoided the more obvious forms of vice like drinking and drugs. I figured Kevin liked the buzz he got from being in the atmosphere of violence.

Someone once told me that because God did not abide in time the way human beings had to, He could prevent suffering that had occurred in the past. I stopped and fished a pebble out of my shoe and watched a raven watching me from a wire. I wondered if it were possible for God to prevent the pain the Sands brothers had felt in their lives.

If God could relieve suffering in the past, why wouldn't He do it for the Sands brothers? Maybe they had to be more deserving. Certainly Kevin hadn't made it easy. At every juncture in his life he seemed to lead with sullen rage. He was keen with attention, as if his hungry eyes could suck up light. His little brother, Sean, was a dreamy boy. He had been held back a grade in school, so I think he felt awkward and too big, but he could show sensitivity. He had become a fat kid who liked camping, and his eyes held some sadness and empathy that couldn't be detected in his brother's.

I looked out toward the bay and beyond to the Gulf of Alaska. Up the hill the daylight had spread through the forest. The sun seemed to illuminate each needle of every hemlock and spruce tree. To the west, the breeze freshened and the black clouds edged a little closer. I was struck by a feeling that I urgently wanted to remember this moment all my life, but at the time I had no idea why.

I had decided to see if there was anything I could do for Sean because I knew I hadn't really helped Kevin by assisting him in his criminal cases. In his last case, Kevin had slashed a young fisherman's forehead with a hunting knife so deeply that the flap of skin hung down over the fisherman's eyes. Even when the stunned fisherman held up the flap of skin, the flow of blood blinded him so he had to be led by hand up the harbor ramp to the waiting ambulance.

Kevin was thin and blond, with strange, vacant good looks. When I talked to Kevin in jail and asked him why he had slashed the man, he shrugged his shoulders and said, "I don't know. He just kind of pissed me off." He was wearing a green prison jumpsuit, and his doughy white face was as vexed as if he were waiting for the ferry.

As a defense investigator I am supposed to fill out my client's experience for the court. I am supposed to find all the complex mitigating factors that will help explain actions that might otherwise seem bizarre. But as far as I could tell, there really was no more to the story with Kevin. It really was as easy as that: the fisherman had "kind of pissed him off," so he cut his face. Maybe all the empathy he had ever felt for anyone had been burned on board the *Mygirl* along with his parents and little sister.

The psychiatrist from Chicago who shrank Kevin the last time didn't want to give us a written report, which is always a little worrying for a defense team. The doctor spoke slowly over the phone so we could hear him through the static. "There are some clients you can easily describe as delusional. They are experiencing a reality which no one else does, which can be very dramatic and fairly straightforward to treat, but this doesn't describe Mr. Sands. There are others you can say have a particular type of personality disorder resulting in enhanced psychosexual impulse problems. These clients are overcome with repressed rage and are unable to control themselves—Ted Bundy, perhaps, or Gacy. This does not really apply to Mr. Sands either. Others could be said to have character disorders which cause them to have eccentric or unique moral values systems. They simply believe different things and are acting in accordance with those beliefs. Even that doesn't apply to Mr. Sands, although he is close. He has some . . . humanity . . . let's call it—but it appears his ability to appreciate anyone else's suffering is . . . diminishing. This may be partially due to the posttraumatic stress he has suffered with the loss of his family, but that doesn't account for his condition. He is close to his younger brother but apparently not to anyone else. He has impulse control problems, which you might expect of a young man affected by his kind of stress. He's defensive and guarded, but my greatest fear for this young man is that he will become . . ." and the doctor paused as if he didn't really want to even say the words. "My fear is that Kevin Sands has turned into something very much like the person who stole his family from him. He may be becoming what could only be called . . ."—he coughed, then finished quickly—". . . a monster."

I thought of the inside of the scow as it had appeared in my dreams—iron decks, slick with blood and quiet, thick with gasoline fumes just as someone was striking a match. The doctor continued, "A person of this sort is sane and, in a sense, normal in most respects, but they like to cause pain—death even—out of the merest bored interest. A person like this will murder someone, will make them suffer, not out of some explosive rage, but out of some vague interest stemming from boredom. This person kills other humans the way you might eat one more doughnut, Mr. Younger," and he paused, "even though you know you shouldn't. This is my fear for Kevin Sands."

We got Kevin off on the assault charges. He had a plausible self-defense claim, and we were lucky the victim testified and Kevin never had to. There was no written psychological report; the shrink stayed in Chicago and never came near the courtroom. The lawyer's closing argument was a rambling flag-waver filled with non sequiturs about the Constitution and the right to bear arms, even sharpened fishing knives, and the jury was unable to reach a verdict. After a lot of bluster and bluffing the D.A. finally dismissed.

The fisherman with the cut face sat outside the courtroom after we all filed out. Kevin didn't acknowledge him sitting there. The fisherman shook his head and stared down at the floor. Kevin chuckled and blew him a kiss just as I pushed him into the waiting elevator.

The Sands boys had been the survivors in my most important murder case. Kevin Sands let me work on his cases even though he hated me, even though he knew I suspected him in the murder of his own parents, even though I had tried to befriend his younger brother, hoping that I might save him from becoming a monster, too. Kevin saw right through me but it didn't hurt my pride. I don't have much practice at doing good, so I hadn't developed that much of it—pride, that is. So little practice, in fact, that I had no words to reply to Patricia Ewers when she came to me again for help. In her eyes, just by talking to these boys, I was sleeping with the enemy. She might even consider me a suspect in the disappearance of her husband. I couldn't blame her.

I looked up at the trailer park where old cars lay near the ditches with their hoods open like dark mouths. Ravens picked apart the garbage bags piled near the firewood stacks. I suspected that Kevin was bullying or abusing Sean. I didn't even want to fully examine what I suspected, and as I stood there looking up at their trailer, I remember now that I felt a strange pain near my heart and some kind of pressure behind my eyes as if I might start crying. I wondered if, in the same way God could prevent things in the past, perhaps He could make someone experience future suffering. Maybe that was what I had been feeling ever since the Ewers verdict: suffering that sat inside me like a swallowed pin, inching closer and closer to my heart until finally I would not remember anything—the pin, the heart, or a fine, mild day before a storm came ashore.

When I looked out to sea the sun flared off a breaking wave, and when I looked back to the road the raven had tipped forward off the nearest corner of Kevin Sands's trailer house and landed right in front of me. The black bird cackled, then barked, and I shuddered as if ice had been dropped down my shirt.

Just then, Jane Marie pulled her old station wagon up next to me and honked the horn loud enough to save me from a bad case of the creeps.

"Hey, handsome, storm coming. I'd better give you a ride." She smiled, and I knew no matter how long I had to live, I was a lucky, lucky man.

Jane Marie was headed out the road to check out a potential garage sale. There were many new things I never thought we would need that were apparently necessities now.

"I saw in the paper they had baby clothes and a playpen. I know we don't need a playpen now, Cecil, but we will before long."

Blossom was in her carrier next to her mom, and I got into the backseat and warily fluffed up her downy hair.

"Can you drop me at Doggy's?" I said to Jane Marie while stroking our daughter's wildly flabby cheeks. Blossom raised her nose as she tried to get me in focus. She looked a little like Winston Churchill and I couldn't get over the feeling that she was going to snap at me.

"Sure," Jane Marie said, and she looked up in the rearview at me. "You okay, big guy?"

"I'm just thinking," I said, as we pulled away from the Sandses' trailer court and Blossom chewed on the callused tip of my finger. If I was struggling with my own attitudes, I knew for certain Jane Marie was tired of my life of crime.

George Doggy had bought a couple of adjacent lots at the end of a dead-end road near the boat repair yard. They must have cost a fortune, because both lots had nice waterfront houses. George lived in the smaller one nearer the bend in the cove, and he had converted the larger one into a bed-and-breakfast. Ever since Blossom had been born, Doggy had been offering to let me manage the B-and-B. He'd give us a place to live in a little cabin back behind the houses, and we could work cleaning and scheduling people in. I couldn't drive a car thanks to having had my license jerked during my drinking days, but I could certainly drive a boat to take visiting white men with thick necks out salmon fishing. I had passed on Doggy's offer repeatedly. Jane Marie made enough money to pay her expenses: the maintenance on her boat and the fuel to run it. She made enough money from her publications and selling photographs so that she could remain independent. She had never put pressure on me to earn more, even when we had been well short of money, and I loved her for that, but it had been dawning on me that we were running out of options on this island and maybe it was time for me to take Doggy up on his offer.

She stopped at the end of the road and pulled on the Subaru's hand brake. She turned and looked at me with concern. Jane Marie has black hair and sparkling dark eyes. She is truthfully prettier than any of the anorexic movie stars plying their trade today. If anything she most resembles Myrna Loy in the old Thin Man movies. Jane Marie has the hooded eyes and crooked smile of the perfect drinking companion. She is so pretty that I often can't pay attention to what she's telling me.

"Cecil," she said softly, "have you looked at our checking account lately?"

"Huh?" I said. "No . . . no, I haven't."

Jane Marie leaned her forearms above Blossom's carrier so her face was right in front of mine. All I could see was her.

"You know what I like least about being a mother?"

"Is there a quiz on this later?"

"No," she snapped. "What I'm trying to tell you is, you know, I always liked our lives. I liked that you did what you loved, and not having a lot of money felt like freedom to me."

"But now?" I offered her the opening. I looked at her and felt that pin near my heart.

Jane Marie stroked the top of our daughter's head and looked into her tiny face. "Now, our life feels too much like poverty. I hate that feeling, Cecil. I do. But that's the truth."

I had two hundred-dollar bills from the herring fisherman's case that I still carried around in my pants just to feel flush walking around town. I fished them out of my pocket. Jane Marie bit her lip.

"Don't get me wrong, Cecil. You've been great. You're not drinking or whatever." She leaned over the seat and kissed me. I could taste waxy lip balm and the coffee on her tongue. "But maybe it's time for something else, something that pays a little better."

I handed her a hundred-dollar bill and she crumpled it in her hand. Then she shoved it back at me.

"Forget it, Cecil. I can't do this. I'm not going to start down this road. You've done enough."

"Janey, I haven't done jack shit. You do everything."

She kissed me again, harder this time so I felt the cat-like roughness of her tongue. "You're here. You quit drinking. You walk with me and swim with me. That's enough, Cecil. Heck, if I could pay you to be my companion I would."

Blossom squawked, and I opened the car door.

"Male escort. That might pay better than private eye work," I said and frizzed Blossom's hair one more time and she bobbled her head around accusingly.

Jane Marie rolled her eyes at me and locked the car door. The baby made some little barking sound. I swear that strange little girl was growling at me.

"Go cut some firewood." Jane Marie smiled, then blew me a kiss.

After she released the brake she called out through the window, "Hey, I almost forgot. Patricia Ewers called for you, must have been just after you left. There was a message on the machine. She sounded sad. Said she was going to make the calls herself and that she was sorry for walking out on you."

I waved as if it didn't matter. Truthfully, I didn't want to think about murder so soon after kissing this beautiful woman.

"She's back in town," I told Jane Marie. "She got mad I couldn't do something right away. It will be all right. I'll talk to her later," I said, as I jammed the crumpled hundred-dollar bill back into my pants pocket. I turned and saw George

Doggy coming down the steps of his house putting on his leather work gloves.

"Bye, sweetie. Call me if you need a ride." Then she was gone. The wheels of the station wagon kicked up a few fallen alder leaves. The weather was a swirl of possibilities, but all of them called for change.

So here is the question I was posing to myself as I got out of the car: How much of this did I really need to carry with me during the day? In a story, you expect that every single person will be part of the plot, but how does that happen? If your life is a story, a story you revise over and over again in your memory, how do you choose the themes? How do you choose the people? Richard Ewers was missing but Bob Rose was surfing Sandy Beach by now. Jude and Rachel were most likely taking their tourist mother for coffee. Gary was fabricating a part in his machine shop. Paul deLay was probably playing the blues in Portland, Oregon. And I had made it to work with the help of a beautiful woman in the company of her cranky and unexpected baby. Kevin Sands's parents were dead. George Doggy had lived a long and productive life. And all of these people were part of my story this morning. But what to make of that? Every investigation, whether a murder or a shoplifting, begins with a swirl of unimportant facts. The trick is not to throw any of them away too soon.

I kept going back to that raven on the roof of the Sandses' trailer. I couldn't shake the feeling that God was reaching back from the future and showing me a clue, that the raven was telling me, "Right now! Pay attention. Don't throw this one away." Of course, it could all have been a trick of memory, or maybe this shudder I felt was just the storm pushing in, foam-flecked and howling, indifferent to any story other than its own.

Chapter Two

There has always been a certain kind of person at the top of the heap of blue-collar heroes. They are smart working people whose jobs involve getting important things done in an understandable way: tanker captains, commercial pilots, auctioneers, some clergymen and certain veterinarians. They have this quality of being both elite and common at the same time. Most simply have it and are generally unaware of it, but George Doggy, whom I had known from my childhood, had refined this presence into a valuable asset for police investigations.

Most of the criminals I've met wanted nothing in this life so much as the respect of these blue-collar heroes. Teachers and doctors could go fuck themselves as far as most crooks were concerned, but almost every pedophile, bar brawler, or opportunistic burglar would clear his schedule and put on a clean shirt to be invited to dinner by a coastal pilot or to stand at the bar with the chief engineer on a container ship. These were the guys who made the world work and asked for nothing but a fair wage, unlike the lawyers and government assholes whose authority infested the lives of the poor and unsuccessful. George Doggy had mastered the vibe of the blue-collar hero.

Doggy had found early on that men with horrible secrets would rather talk to other men they admired. He saw it in the interview rooms when young lawyers from the D.A.'s office pined and wheedled away for confessions, and blunt officers faked a cajoling tone, talking sports with a suspect for hours trying to build some kind of "relationship." Doggy had learned as a young man how to walk into an interview room with a suspect and take charge without ever saying a word. Everything—from his posture to his tweed coats to the calluses on his hands when he firmly gripped the witness's hand—bespoke this fact: here, finally, was a man who got things done. Here was a man you wanted on your side, a man to whom you could entrust a secret. He had found a way of becoming a father figure to men who had always hated their fathers.

Doggy had become a legend for his ability. He had more confessions than anyone else in the system. There was only one exception, and that was a sex cop up north who had a gift for breaking down child abusers, but the cop went over the edge himself and ended up charged, so the official record belonged to Doggy. There were many stories: the ten-second confession where the guy spilled in record time, the Moonlighter confession where the defendant spilled to four homicides in the Moonlighter Hotel and afterwards sent Doggy a thank-you note. But the one I had always been most impressed with was the young soldier out of Fairbanks who had picked up three girls on Fourth Avenue, killed them and buried their bodies out on Becker Ridge. Forensics had nothing and the other witnesses only tied this guy loosely. He had been interviewed twice and was leaving the country. The soldier was flying by jet from a base in Seattle on his way to Korea. He was drumming out and was traveling in civilian clothes. He had cashed out everything he had and was wearing twenty-five thousand dollars in the lining of his clothes. His plane laid over for an hour in Anchorage. Doggy went on board the plane and asked the soldier if he would like to have a soda with him. Doggy explained shyly that he had been given a free pass to the private boardroom at the airport. He was just thinking it would be a good opportunity to talk before the soldier shipped out, and besides, the pass might not be good all that long.

Before they called for the flight, the boy with a fortune in his coat and a confirmed ticket to a foreign country told George Doggy all about the killings and where to find the evidence the police had overlooked.

Doggy apologized when he snapped the cuffs on a little too tightly, and the soldier said, "That's okay, George. I understand." He did understand, probably right up until Doggy handed him over to the street cop who put him in the back of the cruiser. Then it dawned on him that he was not going downtown with his new best friend but was going to jail for the rest of his life.

That was the layover confession, and its myth had been told and retold many times by law enforcement types over the years. So many times, in fact, it didn't really matter anymore if it was true.

George Doggy had had only one failure that had entered into lore, and, like most blemishes on otherwise handsome records, I sensed that the *Mygirl* killings were the only thing George Doggy saw when he looked back on his career.

George Doggy had been at the peak of his fame when he became the chief investigating officer in the *Mygirl* murders. More than any other case in modern times, the *Mygirl* killings were all about missing evidence, and the most important thing missing from the *Mygirl* that night was a crewman who swore he'd gone off to town in a skiff to get drunk. This, of course, was Richard Ewers, and it had fallen on George Doggy to get a confession from him. Without it, the evidence was a mess of circumstantial facts that was thin at best, and mere gossip at worst.

At that time Ewers was twenty-five years old and a typical deckhand. He was from Ferndale, Washington, and had dropped out of high school to follow the Alaska fisheries. He was a pot smoker and owned a 9mm handgun. The 9mm showed up in the charred remains of the scow, but the bullet pathways and slug fragments from the bodies were inconsistent with having come from his handgun. Like everything else in this case, the ballistic evidence was inconclusive. The slugs were so shattered it would have been hard making a definite match even if they had had a known weapon to compare them to.

The most damning thing against Ewers had been his own attitude. Friends said he acted strangely after the boat fire, and some said he had been dissatisfied working on the scow. He had never had anything good to say about Charlie Sands as a boss or about Sands's family as human beings. Richard had been a complainer, which also didn't really distinguish him from any other deckhand. But no other deckhand was being accused of mass murder.

George Doggy had interviewed him twice, but apparently Richard Ewers had had a good relationship with his father because he would not confess anything to Doggy other than stealing some of the cash off the *Mygirl* before he went to town that night. He lied about it at first, but when a bartender from the Pioneer Bar gave a statement that Ewers had rung the bell above the bar and bought everyone in the place a drink to the tune of two hundred dollars with cash he had wadded up in his pants, Richard admitted to stealing the money off the *Mygirl*.

Harrison Teller, Ewers's lawyer, was the most fervent true believer in Ewers's innocence. Teller hired me, originally, to find the real killer. But of course I labored under the same burden as the official police investigators. There was no substantial physical evidence left. Teller had wanted to paint Kevin Sands as a suspect, but he hated the idea of tearing down Sands's kid brother on the stand. The kid brother who had lost his entire family and was a stand-up alibi witness for his big brother. Teller preferred the phantom robber or drug-dealer theory. Teller had fantasized that somehow we could bring this real killer into court and there he would apologize to Richard Ewers.

I had spent eighteen months working on Richard Ewers's case. I moved around the state and made contacts in the fishing fleet all up and down the coast from Valdez to Bellingham. I spent a year listening to bar talk and psychics. I traced down a man with a beard who had once been sitting next to a fisherman on a plane who had said he knew that the Sands family had welshed on a debt to a Canadian drug enforcer. When I did find the bearded man he looked at me as if I were asking about alien abductions and he told me he knew no such thing. Physical evidence is usually the fulcrum used to help pry statements out of people: show someone the bloody boots and he'll feel compelled to tell some story about them. But if you're empty-handed and he knows it, no one with any sense is going to tell you a story.

There was a singing psychic who would put her visionary predictions into operatic-style rhymed quatrains. She told me she had seen a helicopter landing near the *Mygirl* and men in dark hoods holding guns jumping out of it. She could see three of the numbers on the side of the chopper. Teller had told me to check out all the choppers on the west coast bearing these numbers, but I put my foot down.

By the end of the trial, the case file filled one hundred and five banker boxes. I had to make sure all of the interviews, expert reports, witness statements, previous testimony, and the hundreds and hundreds of motions, which Teller dictated in an almost endless stream, were kept in some kind of order. This fell to me because Teller's two secretaries were constantly on the verge of hysteria just keeping up with the typing and other casework that piled up as Teller devoted more and more time to Ewers's case.

I finally convinced Teller that we should stop trying to find "the real killer." If three law enforcement agencies and three million dollars of the State of Alaska's money hadn't done it, we weren't going to find anything more useful than they had. Teller dismissed this line of reasoning. But he listened to this: What, I asked him, would "the real killer" be doing right now? The real killer would be living his own life and watching with interest the prosecution of Richard Ewers for the crime the real killer had committed. What, I asked again, would the real killer have to say about the crime even if we could motivate him to talk? Say I had some small shred of evidence, a jailhouse snitch, or a written statement from a known drug dealer pointing the finger at the real killer. What would the real killer say if I could drag him into court? Teller waited for my answer as I stood in the shambles of his office.

"The real killer is going to look at the investment of time, energy and pure spleen the State of Alaska has put into their prosecution of our client, and the real killer is going to say Richard Ewers killed Charlie, Tina, and Edna Sands. Then the real killer is going to say that Richard Ewers killed young Albert Chevalier and poured gasoline on his body. The real killer is going to say Richard Ewers burned the *Mygirl*. That is the only reasonable thing for the real killer to say, this being real life and not a Perry Mason television show."

Teller stared at me. He had been holding a yellow pad in his lap. He dropped the pad off to the side of his wheelchair, rolled into his office and slammed the door. From then on we played a defensive game, tearing into all the police evidence, making it look mean and vindictive. We offered no solution to the four murders. We called no witnesses. And the jury acquitted Richard Ewers simply because there wasn't enough evidence.

George Doggy liked me in a long-suffering kind of way, but we never discussed the *Mygirl* killings, probably because Doggy never figured that work as a defense investigator was really investigative work. It was an amateurish kind of whoring in Doggy's mind. He had been trying to find me other work for years.

"Where's that pretty girl of yours?" Doggy said, as he walked briskly down the steps of his house making fists to stretch out his tight leather work gloves.

"She just took off." I nodded down the road.

"I don't know how a guy like you ended up with such a good-looking lady friend and a near perfect daughter." He slapped me on the back.

"I was born lucky."

"You ready to work, young fella?" The old workhorse shambled down the narrow trail, rolling his shoulders as he walked and smacking a gloved fist into his palm.

"Heck, yeah. I'm not, like . . . disturbing your television shows, am I, George? I mean, you don't want to miss any bass fishing or the soaps."

Doggy snorted. He hated television. He had once told

me that if I found him watching television during daylight hours I could shoot him through the brain.

He had hauled three logs up onto his beach that he planned to buck up into firewood for his house, his guest accommodations, the cabins and the sauna. Doggy had a mechanical splitter and another mechanical contraption that had been a conveyor belt for putting hay bales up in a barn. This was set up with one end near the hydraulic splitter and the other up the bank to where his woodshed was set back under the trees. George Doggy was a strong and vital man, but he used every mechanical advantage he could muster when it came to putting up his winter's wood.

The logs were old spruce trees cut long ago that had escaped from a log raft headed for the mill. The mill had been shut down for years, and there had been fewer and fewer of these logs to be found on local beaches. These particular ones hadn't rolled around in the surf for long, because a friend had hauled them off a steep beach with a tugboat and towed them to George Doggy's house. The spruce was straight-grained and dry. I had already cut up a cord and a half and piled it under the shed roof. George loved to use the fancy hydraulic splitter, but I still used a heavy maul and a sharp ax.

Today the hydraulic splitter was broken, apparently from some bad gas off the fuel barge that had fouled the plugs. I split by hand while George sat on a spruce round cleaning the plugs and absentmindedly fiddling with the motor. After the first ten minutes, I fell into a rhythm of splitting straight-grained wood: a swing and a chunk that let the faint turpentine smell of the tree come up to my face. I love the light sweat of working hard on a cool morning, and I love pausing to hear the gulls tearing the stillness apart as they wheel above the water. George and I worked steadily for more than an hour. There were some forty rounds already sawn off, so we had plenty to do before we had to start any engines. Off near Old Sitka Rocks I heard a loud exhalation of breath as a humpback whale broke the surface, pushing its way toward the outside waters. I turned and saw the veil of vapor hanging like a scarf in the air.

"They say it's supposed to storm like the dickens the next couple of days," George told me. "I listened to the marine forecast at six this morning and they say there's a heck of a low-pressure system coming in from the southwest. 'High probability of damage to life and property' is what they said. We better get this wood up off the beach or it'll be scattered from here to kingdom come by next week."

He wasn't looking at me but was staring out past the cove to where the black clouds seemed to be plugging up the horizon.

Then he blurted out what was really on his mind. "You've got to get yourself some security, son. You can't just fiddle around the way you have been. You've got that little baby girl to think about. You need to get serious now."

The whale blew again and a second one broke the surface beside it. This second one was a much smaller whale. Almost certainly a cow and a calf.

"Serious . . . I always have been serious, George. Hell, you always told me I was a serious boy ever since I was in junior high school and I wanted to be Vincent van Gogh," I said, and flexed my fingers to work the stiffness out.

"You were just plain goofy. I mean you need to grow up a little now, boy. You come to work for me full-time. Hell, there isn't anything in the investigations these days, is there?"

Both whales lifted their flukes some six feet into the air and eased down underwater. From where I was I could see the water blossom on the surface where the great tails churned their first stroke.

"No," I said almost absently. "No, there hasn't been much in the way of investigations."

"You've been hanging around that Sands kid and I'm telling you, Cecil, you steer clear of that family. They are a train wreck. I'm telling you, there are some people who will take a carrot and there are others who will only take a stick, and those brothers . . ." Doggy looked down at his boots. His voice softened with regret. "The Sands brothers have been hurt bad. They're bent up and they're only going to respond to the stick."

I supposed that was true. Nothing I did seemed to help Sean Sands. He was quiet and wore army fatigues all the time, even though he was only twelve. He loved guns more than comic books, and he would talk about explosives all day long but would never think of playing a musical instrument or even listening to one. Still, there was something in his eyes that seemed to be asking for help. But how could I know for sure? Sean never asked for anything, from me or anyone else as far as I could tell. It was as if the fire and the death of his sister and parents had somehow sealed him up. He faced the world with the stony face of someone who only seems to be thinking "You don't know. You'll *never* know."

Doggy's wife had passed away two years earlier. He had been typically stoic and matter-of-fact about getting his life going again after her funeral, but I had started observing the irritable signs of age increasing from that time.

"No. You come live out here with me, son. We'll have a real live lodge up and going this coming summer. You get your six-pack skipper's license and we'll spend the summer lying to tourists and catching salmon. What do you say?"

"You've been good to me, George . . . ," I said, letting the words trail off.

Sometimes I think fate speaks to me in a strange kind of gibberish. My father, who had been a stern judge and a practical man, died in a Las Vegas casino after one pull and a jackpot on a hundred-thousand-dollar machine. The woman who used to love me abandoned me for good reasons, and the woman who loves me now does so for reasons I cannot fathom. Friends have been killed by stray bullets, and great loves have come to me unbidden. There is no way to make sense of this. What I wanted to tell George Doggy was that no matter how hard I tried, I had grown up as much as I ever would, and that no matter how much I tried to be responsible, I could not change my luck.

I was thinking about Patricia Ewers and her hunt for her husband, and I knew I couldn't change her luck either. Maybe the old policeman was right and it was time to sit by the ocean and take insurance men out fishing. I was having a hard time picturing it, though. For what Doggy couldn't understand was that I would always be more like the Sands brothers than he liked to think. I was haunted by what had happened on the *Mygirl*, just as they were, and just as Doggy himself seemed to be but wouldn't admit.

The *Mygirl* was a steel barge that belonged to a Seattle-based fish company. It was eighty-five feet long, with freezers, ice-making machines, a small store for supplies, and living quarters up on the second floor. There was an open deck on the center of the scow where the hands could wrestle totes of ice around and there were large scales to weigh the catch the fishing boats brought in off the grounds. Up off the living quarters was a small deck with a barbeque where the Sands family would sometimes cook dinner on nice days. The kids played on shore when their father could spare one of the tin skiffs. The Sands family had run the scow for three years before the season that would turn out to be their last. It had been an idyllic life for them, spending the summers out in remote bays in southeastern Alaska. There were long evenings in narrow bays rimmed with ancient spruce and hemlock trees. It was the perfect life that everyone on board the *Mygirl* had dreamed of, right up, I suspect, until the fire.

After the killings and the trial, the two Sands brothers hardened into a dark kind of cynicism which seemed to focus their hatred on everything they saw. Sad or angry, their eyes cast shadows. I tried to help them and the fact that I worked for the accused murderer of their family hardly mattered to them. Their world was too dark for them to notice me much.

If the Sandses cast shadows, Jonathan Chevalier's eyes focused hatred like the sharp shaft of a laser. He could have done more in his testimony at trial to convict Richard Ewers, but he held firm. Jonathan would not positively identify Ewers as the skiff operator escaping the burning boat. He claimed the pictures in the lineup were confusing and that Ewers looked "similar" and "most like" the man who was operating the skiff. Jonathan got beat up by the lawyers on both sides but he would not budge. He was not sure.

There was one other tantalizing detail in Jonathan's testimony. He said that this mysterious skiff operator that night had been carrying something in his hand. He only got a glimpse. It could have been a fishing rod, or it could have been a rifle. No gun had ever been identified as the murder weapon. All the guns on board the *Mygirl* had been accounted for in the wreckage. The Sands brothers had identified each gun for the troopers. Doggy had always presumed Ewers had thrown the murder weapon into deep water as he ran the skiff to Sitka.

Jonathan Chevalier had been vague but credible. Too many details often bespeak a liar, at least in a jury's eyes. The troopers had beat up on Chevalier quite a bit to "remember more," and Harrison Teller tried to characterize him as a helpless victim of police overreaching. In the end, Chevalier just seemed sad about his murdered brother and wanted nothing more to do with the judicial system.

Jonathan was a fisherman and had rigged his wooden sailboat for salmon trolling. The boat was named the *Naked Horse*. She was a wooden ketch with heavy canvas sails and stays that seemed to sag from the top of the mast down to the chain plates. The *Naked Horse* appeared to be a loose-limbed runner, but under sail she tightened into the wind and took deep breaths with each swell she lunged through. Jonathan Chevalier had been an infantryman in the post-Vietnam army. After he mustered out, he had tried painting and then photography, but he had walked out of his only gallery show in San Francisco in 1985 and had come to Alaska to sign on with his uncle and younger brother in the last organized activity of hunters and gatherers: small-boat commercial fishing. Once it and subsistence hunting and fishing are gone, the last remaining trace of the Paleolithic age will have disappeared from North America. Jonathan Chevalier thought Alaska was the perfect place for an artist at the end of the twentieth century. He fished two years with his uncle and then bought the *Naked Horse* down in Port Townsend and sailed her up the coast.

Once, right after the verdict came back, I tried to offer my sympathy to Jonathan. He was standing just inside the double doors of the courthouse in Juneau. I put out my hand and said that I could understand if he didn't take my hand but I truly thought justice had been done. He looked at my hand as if it were a bowlful of snakes. Then I offered lamely, "I can't imagine how it feels to lose a brother. I'm sorry. . . ."

Jonathan looked up at me and said the words that the Sands brothers' eyes spoke: "You don't know anything." Then he turned and walked away.

Albert Chevalier had been fourteen years old when he died. He had been in some foster homes and we tried to get his records from Social Services but were denied. The prosecutors had blown up portraits of the victims for their closing statements to the jury. The lawyers had intended to play the strongest card in their circumstantial case: grief. But the effect of the huge portraits backfired. The pictures seemed like advertising: two adults, two children smiling into the camera lens. They were brief and beautiful, and they would have been great marketing tools, except the D.A.s had very little to sell: burned bodies and a couple of tentative memories was all, not anything approaching what was needed to overcome reasonable doubt.

Still, Albert's portrait lingered with me. The chubby face of a boy under a baseball cap, brown eyes slightly crossed, and the turned-down, rueful smile of a kid who had never considered that his life might be cut short.

In recent days Jonathan had been drinking in the Pioneer Bar and buying rounds for the house twice a night. He was running a bar tab that would eat a summer's wages in a week.

I knew Patricia Ewers was going to confront Jonathan and the Sandses. She would get nothing from them. I knew that. I screwed up my courage and spoke up as I pretended to be checking the handle on the splitting maul.

"George, Patricia Ewers is in town. She says Richard is missing. You haven't heard anything about that, have you?"

"Not a word" was all the old man would say. But he stared out at the water for a time. Finally he slapped a file down onto a stump and said, "Jesus Christ, Cecil, I told you . . . ," and he stopped, then looked out past where the whales had dove. "I told you I could give you a good job. I can give you security, for Christ's sake." George Doggy seemed pale and agitated. The spark plug he had been working on fell to his feet.

I was going to clarify my question. Then I noticed Doggy's hands were shaking and I held my peace.

"Cecil, listen to me. Stay away from those Sands brothers."

A murder of crows flapped down the beach and landed in the small crab apple tree above us. The crows brought ragged shadows and their voices rattled like stones in a culvert. I stopped my swing and held the splitting maul in my hands, shifting my attention from the noisy birds back to the old man.

His face was pale and George Doggy repeated, "Just stay away from those boys." As he said this, I heard the whales blow again, but this time farther out to sea.

Chapter Three

We chopped wood through the afternoon hoping to beat the rain. The sky had darkened as we worked through the lunch hour, and George had brought me a sweet roll and a hunk of sausage to eat between swings. Squalls rattled the trees and lifted a fine spray off the water. I turned my back to the weather and ate in a hurry. George tried to work through it, but bits of grit blew into his eyes and he dropped the plugs in a pile of seaweed. Even though he turned his back on the wind, he couldn't ignore it.

He gave me a ride home in his new pickup. George had a new truck and two new charter boats. He was living in a fine house on the water. He was a walking testament to a life of responsibility.

I have never owned a new truck and maybe for that reason George's truck seemed unreasonably large. The leather seats gave the cab the smell of a boardroom, and the scene through the windshield passed smoothly into my eyes like the large-screen movies I had seen at the World's Fair as a kid. This truck didn't just travel on the pavement but seemed to gather the road up behind itself for safekeeping.

Leaves blew across the road in skittering patterns like small animals fleeing from a fire. Trees waved their arms around in alarm. On my right, the waves were building and breaking white, and gulls bobbed in the air like kites. On my left and ahead of me, the mountains rose up from the sea in steep-forested slopes until they gave way to rock and ice. Up high on one of the peaks I could see a fine spume of snow lifting into the sky as the wind scoured the face of the rock.

Artists always make a lot of mountain peaks. I suppose I have always been a valley sort of guy. It never bothers me that something is taller than I am, and I've been content to let it stay that way. But when the light hits a peak, even if I'm watching it from the front seat of a tugboat-sized truck, something rises up in my chest. "You don't have to be here," the mountain says, and I know that's true and am grateful.

I was thinking this as a small skinny white girl ran in front of the truck and George hit his brakes hard enough to send me lurching into the dash.

"Jesus . . . Lord," George sputtered.

I couldn't see the girl in front of the truck and when I opened the door and stepped out, I still couldn't. Reflexively I looked under the truck. Nothing. I stepped around the front to see George Doggy stooping down and patting his hands over the pale cheeks of the girl who was standing stock-still not three inches from the grillwork.

"They're shooting people," the girl whimpered.

"Where, honey?" George said in a gentle, friendly tone as if he were asking about her puppy dog.

The girl lifted her right arm and pointed up the hill toward the trailer park.

"Has anyone called the police?" Doggy asked as his eyes followed her gesture up the hill.

"They are there. They are shooting people," the girl said. Now I noticed how her eyes were wide and blank with terror. She was trembling. She had a long smear of snot down her upper lip and across her cheek. George took out his handkerchief and first wiped his own hands and then wiped her face. Then he took her hand and we all walked to the side of the road.

Up the hill, two police cars sat outside the Sandses' trailer. Their light bars flashed quick patterns of red and blue onto the mossy, sunken trailers in the court.

Doggy started up the hill on foot. He turned to me.

"Take care of this girl and move my truck off the road." He didn't wait for a response. He didn't expect one.

I hadn't driven a car in a long time. I started the engine and when I gave it gas, it lurched an inch forward and the motor died.

"You have to take the brake off," the little girl sitting next to me said in the same zombie voice.

"Yes, of course," I said. "Now don't worry. I'm going to get you safely back to your folks." The truck lunged in front of an ambulance, which yowled its siren at me.

"Sure," the girl said. I was starting to not like her tone.

I made a left turn and lurched the powerful truck into a shallow ditch. The girl hopped out the passenger door and darted up a narrow gap between two trailers. Rain started pelting down like scrap hardware. A loose piece of roofing began beating in the wind, the sheeting screaming against the nails and flapping hard against a rotted two-by-two support.

I walked up toward the Sandses' trailer. Officers were running back and forth. One had a camera. The chief was kneeling in front of a young policeman slumped sideways in the front seat of a patrol car and was putting the young officer's service revolver in a plastic bag. The young man had his head buried in his hands and was breathing noisily. When the chief asked him a question, the young officer looked up and I could see a pained expression on his face that was both angry and remorseful.

Inside the narrow trailer, the damp mustard-colored carpet of the front room was littered with beer cans and magazines. Someone was taking flash photographs. Two cops were waving off the EMTs.

"No. No. No," one cop kept saying. The other said in a shaky voice, "At this stage, preservation of the scene is the first priority. You have done all you can. She doesn't need you guys now."

Two EMTs stood by the police officers. Two more uniformed EMTs stood just inside the trailer door stripping off their latex gloves, putting them in waste bags from their kits. The waste bags were marked with red stickers that read:

"BIOHAZARD, DO NOT BREAK SEAL ONCE CLOSED." The gloves were smeared with bright red blood.

There was a brief exchange of angry voices that I couldn't make out and a cop pushed one of the EMTs toward the door. As he did, they moved just enough so I could see a woman's arm on the floor. The arm was pale and thin as if it were a tree branch stripped to the sapwood. Another gust hit the trailer and pellets of ice clattered on the roof and against the aluminum window frames. Along the edges of the window frames was a film of mold, and water stains swirled down the thin paneling. The mustard carpet was clotted with dark blood and my stomach churned. The room smelled like a dirty butcher shop.

I stepped to the side and saw Patricia Ewers's body bathed in the unforgiving light of a fluorescent lamp that had tipped off the end table near the couch. The shade was cockeyed on the floor and threw glaring light directly on her face. Her eyes, which had been blue in life, now seemed to be a washed-out gray. She was still as a mountain peak. There was a large pulpy wound in the middle of her chest, and the bloodstain crawled slowly through the dirty carpet toward the tip of my leather boot.

A large hand clamped around my biceps.

"What the hell are you doing in my scene?" A policeman named Pomfret whirled me around. I was caught in the glare of his pale face.

"I asked you something simple, Younger. What are you doing contaminating my scene?"

George Doggy stepped out of the back room. "He's with me. We were just driving by."

Pomfret let go of my arm. Doggy was like Moses to these guys.

Doggy pointed. "Cecil, walk all the way around there. Lieutenant Pomfret doesn't need your shoe prints anywhere on the scene. But come back here a second, will ya?" Pomfret's mouth was open, and I could tell he was hurt that George Doggy had not chosen to speak to him more directly. Pomfret turned and went back to the door of the trailer, and I did as Doggy asked.

Cops were bringing in more lights. The shadows curled around Patricia's unmoving features. Tucked under her right elbow was a shiny semiautomatic pistol. Her hand was cocked awkwardly behind her. In the harsh light I could see that she had a chipped tooth. I couldn't remember if it had been chipped before or not. The roof leaked and a fat drop of rust-colored water fell from the stained ceiling tiles. The drop fell onto Patricia's opened gray eye.

The hallway of the trailer was dark and narrow. I could smell the powder from the gun blast still hanging there. Doggy motioned with his chin toward a room at the end of the hall, and I followed behind him without speaking.

The room's back window was broken out, with only a few glass shards inside on the sill. The room was a mess of papers and ammunition. Books and magazines were flung open on the carpet. On one page, a blond woman lounged on top of a red car hood. She smiled knowingly up into the overturned room. There were two automatic pistols on the floor and an upended card table in the middle of the room. "Drugs," George said. "You can bet on that." In the right-hand corner was a small floor safe with the door open wide. In the back of the safe sat a thin photo album. The shelves of the safe were scattered on the floor.

"I'm sure of it, Cecil. They were counting out back here. There was a fight and the police came. They sent Mrs. Ewers up front. I don't know if they gave her the gun or if it was her own idea. She must have gotten excited and didn't drop it in time and that dumb kid shot her." George pointed his index finger at his own chest. "Shot Mrs. Ewers right in the center of mass just like they taught him a couple of months ago at the academy." There was no sorrow in his tone of voice. Particularly when he used the words "Mrs. Ewers."

Doggy reached down to pick up the photo album and I heard the unmistakable clicking of a slide pulling a cartridge into the chamber of a cheaply made automatic weapon.

"Don't look at those things," a shaky voice called out from behind us.

I turned and saw Sean Sands holding a 9mm automatic

pistol, the kind that looks like it's made of plumbing supplies and then painted a sinister black.

"Put those things down. I don't want you looking at them. Get out of here or I'll shoot you. I really, really mean it. I will shoot you, you know. I don't care," Sean said, and his voice rose as if he were pleading. Behind his shoulder I could see Pomfret. His eyes were questioning and his hand was moving toward his belt.

"I won't look at those pictures, Sean. I promise you I won't. Just . . . let's talk about this. Can we go into your room? We have to get out of this hall. I'm telling you the truth."

My voice was a half step high and straining with fake assurance. George was nodding ever so slightly, motioning Pomfret to back up and give him some room.

Sean eased his shoulder against the flimsy door to his own room and stepped in, never letting his aim wander from the center of my chest. The opening at the mouth of the barrel seemed about the diameter of a pencil. I waved Pomfret off and stood directly in front of George. I knew Pomfret wanted to shoot Sean, but it was very tight and if Sean ducked or Pomfret missed, he might shoot me or, worse for Pomfret's career, he might shoot Doggy. I also knew they didn't want me to go into the room with Sean because that would be a classic hostage situation and the protocol for that is long and complex and, frankly, Pomfret wouldn't have the patience for it.

But they let me go. Maybe they hoped Sean would just shoot me and have done with it and then they could ventilate the entire trailer and save everybody a lot of time and legal fees.

The room was unexpectedly sparse. A military-style cot with a gray blanket neatly tucked in on three sides was against the wall under the window. There was a small boom box, a gun rack, a dresser, and topographical maps pinned to the wall at the foot of the bed.

"What's in that photo album, Sean?" I said with as much casualness as I could muster.

"You hadn't oughta look at those things," Sean said softly.

"I swear to God I won't, Sean, but . . ."

I stopped. I wanted Sean to ask me something. I wanted to get him conversing.

"But what?" the boy finally said.

"The cops might be looking at them right now."

A look of terror crossed his face. I was standing in front of the door. He motioned violently for me to move, but the space was too tight; there was no way for him to get to the door without putting himself within my reach.

The boy was crying now. "They better not. They sure better not look at those pictures, or . . . brother . . . I don't know . . . they just better not." His hands were shaking and great slicks of tears ran down his puffy cheeks. His index finger was through the trigger guard and was curved around the trigger. He had child's fingers, small chubby things that didn't show their knuckles.

"Let me get them back before they look at them, okay?" I asked. Sean nodded in agreement as he tried to suck back his tears.

I rapped on the flimsy door. "George," I said loudly. "George, Sean is doing okay in here. He just wants that photo album, and he doesn't want anyone looking at it."

"I understand that, Cecil," George said in a calm and almost breezy voice just on the other side of the door. "Sean, my name's George. You know, I think I've met you before. I know I've seen you around town. Well, anyway, I've got the album right here with me, Sean. I've wrapped evidence tape around it. You'll see no one's looked at it. Sean, can you hear me okay? No one's looked at it."

Sean was crying harder now and his puffy face contorted into a blotchy grimace. His cheeks were red and the snot running down his lips was mingling with the tears, but he did not loosen his grip on the 9mm, and his finger was still inside the trigger guard.

Doggy spoke matter-of-factly. "This album is obviously private property. The courts wouldn't allow us to look at it without your permission. It's yours. All yours. Now, we have all the time in the world for this. We are in no rush. But I can hand this album in to you if you like."

Sean nodded vigorously.

I cleared my throat. "Sean said he would like you to hand it in."

"All right. That's great. That's great, Sean. Like I said, we've got all the time you want. But I have to ask you to do something for me, Sean. Just open the door and let Cecil out of there and I'll hand the book in. It's really easy. You're a good brave kid. I've heard all about you from the guys at the gun range and the other officers. You're a good kid, and this will all be taken care of just as easy as pie as soon as you let Cecil come out of the room."

"Kevin. Where's my brother Kevin?" Sean said it loudly.

Doggy didn't answer for a moment. I could hear heavy footfall, leather utility belts creaking, and keys jangling on the other side of the door. Doggy cleared his throat. "Kevin's outside. He said he wants you to come out."

"You better hand me that book. You had better or . . . or . . . I don't know what." Sean's voice was broken, almost squealing. He was a scared child holding an automatic weapon and he sounded like one.

"Okay, Sean. I understand. I do."

I heard more heavy footfall. Doggy kept talking. "I know these are important and, like I said, no one has looked at them. I've got tape all around your photo album, so when you see your album it'll look a little different, but that's just to show that no one has looked at it. Okay . . . Sean?"

Sean nodded. I heard Velcro straps being pulled apart and a muffled clicking on the other side of the door.

"Sean," Doggy said, softer now as if he were pressing his head against the door and speaking just to him. "Sean, it's going to be fine. We'll do this. Just have Cecil stand with his back to the door and open it very slowly. That way we'll have no surprises. I'll just hand the photo album in to you. Okay now, Sean?"

Sean nodded his head. "Yes," I said. I put my back against the door and reached my left hand across and put my hand on the knob. I heard a tensing of leather on the other side of the door. I heard the slightest muffled clatter of a shot-gun shell being chambered. Sean did not hear these things. He had no idea what was about to happen to him, but I did.

I took my hand off the knob and yelled out, "George, I'm not doing this!" And the door splintered off its hinges. I was knocked down and pressed under the weight of the door and the bodies lying on top of it. I heard screaming, men's voices shouting, "Down! Down! *Down!*" Two shotgun blasts exploded in the room. The breath was being squeezed out of me by the two large officers on top of me, but I could still smell the powder from the shotguns. There was no rattle of 9mm fire. Sean was moaning from on top of his bed in the corner.

Men were shouting, "Clear! Clear! Clear!" and I started screaming, "Get the fuck off of me!"

Pomfret rolled off the splintered door. He was in full bat-tle gear and behind him was a thin cop holding a Plexiglas shield. Two officers with flak jackets and riot helmets and what looked like hockey pads on their legs were standing over Sean's body with shotgun muzzles to his throat. George Doggy grabbed me by the arm and helped me stand up.

I started in on him before I had my balance.

"What the fuck are you doing, George? You kill a child after . . . what? . . . three minutes of talking to him? You and the cavalry here just blow the kid away? What happened to *finesse?* What happened to your legendary goddamn skill at talking people out of everything?"

Doggy looked at me with a pitying expression but said nothing. I stopped my tirade and stood heaving my breath in and out of my chest. Then Doggy held a small cloth sack up in front of my face.

"Beanbags, Cecil. They shot him with beanbags. He'll be sore as hell, but he's not bleeding a drop. Would you prefer to have him shred you up with that popgun of his or would you rather we take him down with a couple of beanbags?"

I hate being indignant, but stupid and indignant is really troubling to me. But not enough to stop acting that way.

"Listen, George, I don't care if you took him out with

lemon cream pies. I was giving you some not-so-subtle messages that the time was not right, and I was the hostage, for Christ's sake."

"That's right, Cecil." George Doggy smiled at me and put his giant calloused hands on my shoulders as he moved me out of the way. "You *were* a hostage."

Doggy pushed me down the hall and the same EMTs who had been kept out before now pushed their way down the hall, full of new importance at being on a police scene and having a live person to work on.

Doggy had the photo album under his arm. It was in fact wrapped in brittle red evidence tape.

"What in the hell is in that photo book?" I asked, as we again walked gingerly around the body of Patricia Ewers, who looked even more lonely and remote now that everyone was walking past her toward the back bedroom.

"The heck if I know," Doggy muttered, as his eyes lingered on the dead woman's face for a moment. "I didn't look. I told the kid that."

The squall had passed, and the hail and rain had moved up the valley behind town. The blackness outside would have been complete except that every emergency vehicle in Sitka's history seemed to be lined up along the lane of this trailer court. Lights sputtered color everywhere, and there was the sizzle of police radios breaking the air. Two women in housecoats stood on the edge of the sea of cops. The women had their arms draped over the shoulders of boys in sweatpants and dirty T-shirts. The boys were maybe six years old and were bouncing up and down trying to get a view of a dead body or maybe of someone getting shot. One kid wore a Seattle Mariners shirt and the other's featured a human skull with snake heads squeezing out of the eye sockets. The women held the kids back, but were also standing on their tiptoes, trying to get a look at something dramatic.

A muscular young white man was bent over the hood of one of the patrol units. He was handcuffed and swearing, banging his chin on the hood and kicking at the tires with the pointy tips of his gray cowboy boots. George Doggy walked over to him.

The large police officer holding Kevin Sands down on the hood was not responding to the stream of invective coming from Kevin's mouth. Doggy gestured for the cop to let him up.

"You killed him, you son of a bitch. You killed him. I'm going to saw your fucking head off and . . ." Doggy held his hand up in front of Kevin's face, and the handcuffed man stopped in mid–death threat.

"They didn't kill him. I kept them from killing him. You understand me? Keep your foul mouth shut," George said, with more ice in his voice than I had ever heard there before. Gone was the breezy man of power and here was one thug speaking to another.

Behind him, the EMTs began carrying a stretcher down the stairs. On it, Sean was pale and his eyes were closed. A murmur went up from the trailer-court crowd, which was growing larger as more people came off their porches.

Kevin Sands spat at George Doggy and spoke with an icy voice of his own. "If he dies, you will never shut me up, you fucking piece-of-shit low-life."

George reached around behind Kevin and took the heavy black flashlight from the utility belt of the officer holding Kevin's cuffs.

"If he dies, you will never shut me up. I'll be—"

George Doggy whipped the handle of the flashlight down across the forehead of the handcuffed man. The blow cracked against Kevin's face and sounded vaguely as if we were back splitting wood. Kevin's face blossomed with blood, and he fell down on the wet ground as if he had been dropped from a plane. Only one small kid actually saw the blow; everyone else was watching them load Sean into the ambulance, hoping, I suppose, to see exposed wounds.

The large cop must have wrenched his back when his prisoner fell. He hadn't been watching either. The cop picked himself up stiffly and for some reason apologized to George Doggy.

"I'm sorry, sir," he offered lamely.

"That's all right, son." Doggy handed him his flashlight back. "He was just making a move for your weapon and I needed to get his attention. We don't have to mention it."

"Thank you, sir," the large cop said earnestly.

"Don't mention it," Doggy said with a smile. He turned away from Kevin and the officer, then spoke to me.

"What did you do with my truck? I hope to heck we can get it out of here."

I pointed mutely toward his red pickup down in the ditch near the bottom of the hill. Kevin Sands was moaning. Someone had broken the lining of a chemical ice pack, wrapped it in paper towels, and laid it on the hood of the car. The large cop jammed Kevin's face down on it.

The one little white kid who had seen the blow was staring at George Doggy with a mixture of fear and awe. Doggy waved to him and said, "Stay out of trouble now," and the wide-eyed kid nodded his head in absolute agreement.

"You need a ride from here or what?" Doggy said to me. His voice was strangely conversational, I thought, for a man who had just assaulted a prisoner.

"No, I'm fine," I lied.

He waved to me and ambled down the lane of emergency vehicles with the photo album, still wrapped in evidence tape, tucked under the arm of his canvas woodcutting coat.

Chapter Four

I followed George Doggy down the hill for three steps, then turned and doubled back. Two of the officers watched me intently as I walked toward the scene. They had loaded Kevin in the back of a cruiser. People, women and skinny kids mostly, were still loitering around. Some were standing on their tiptoes trying to peer over the cops' shoulders. I knew I couldn't be seen asking questions or Pomfret would hustle me away. I sidled into the group of gawkers and listened to their conversation.

From my eavesdropping I pieced together how the police had ended up killing Patricia Ewers. One of the neighbors had called in a domestic argument. Patricia was out of control. Kevin Sands started wrestling with the cops trying to throw them out of the house. At some point Patricia had a gun in her hand and the young police officer shot her. I was guessing that it would all be laid out neatly in the police reports: Kevin was going to be held for assault on the officers and for an assault on Patricia.

Back up the hill a phone rang and a tired voice called a woman's name. The cops slammed their car doors and the group of gawkers broke up and drifted away on the plank walkways sunk in the mud between their homes. I turned down the hill.

I walked the rest of the way home and crawled into bed without eating supper. Jane Marie looked in on me at suppertime but didn't try to get me up. After washing the dishes she put the baby in her crib and came to bed. She cradled her body around my back as we lay on our sides.

I had a hard time believing it. Lying next to my lover that night I couldn't help shivering. Why had Doggy talked about drugs? What was in the photo album that Sean was willing to kill me for? The night came on with gusts of wind rattling the upstairs windows. I heard an aluminum can rolling down the street.

As I drifted to sleep I thought I heard the hammer crack of a gun echoing around metal walls. I could taste gasoline in my mouth.

The morning came too soon, even though the sunlight did not. My family was "up and at 'em" before the fingers of the rose-colored dawn stretched over the wine-dark sea or however Homer had put it. It was early. It was dark. And it was time to hit the garage sales.

Going early to a garage sale had always seemed like checking into the hospital just before noon so you could get lunch. I could lie in bed all day long and not worry if anyone was going to get to those stacks of *National Geographic*s before me, but there was a new urgency in my family and it was impossible to sleep with the clamor of pre-bargain anxiety.

I was on push-up number one hundred and sixty-two when Todd came into my room and gazed down at me with a clinical look of intense interest, as if he were checking to see whether I was dead yet and he would have to pick my body up by himself.

"Cecil, I have been looking at the street map and considering how we might want to approach the order in which we attend the various sales. Of course, one factor is when we will be leaving. Do you know when you will be ready to go?"

Todd was asking this with no sense of peevishness. He was merely curious. I lay facedown on our bedroom carpet breathing hard. I was wearing nothing but my underwear.

"Fifteen minutes. Five for the rest of the push-ups, five to dress, and five to drink a cup of coffee," I said into the short nap of the rug.

"I see," Todd said, then closed the door.

Todd has lived with me for some ten years now. He is my age, and yet I am his guardian. Todd has been called everything from retarded to autistic to learning impaired, but none of those labels really gets to the heart of who he is.

Todd is a pair of eyes and ears; he is a human instrument that takes in data and processes it according to certain prescribed rules, and these rules are designed by him to help him perform his vital function: gathering information. The problem, or perhaps the magic, is that all this information, while stored, is not integrated into what most of us think of as "a personality." Todd forms attachments: to me, to his dog Wendell, and to Jane Marie, but only because he has memorized his part. He relates quite well to his dog, but he does not play with him. He feeds, speaks to and attends to Wendell, but he can't really play with the dog because "playing" has an abstract purpose Todd can't comprehend. Just as I cannot understand Arabic, he doesn't read the social signals other people try to send him. As far as emotion goes, Todd knows frustration and panic. He can sense his own physical pleasure, but for any of the other emotional sensations which are not directly related to his presence, Todd has to play-act. He has little or no genuine empathy, not because he doesn't recognize warmth in other people, but because he has nothing in his own heart to compare it to. This makes him by turns endearing and irritating. Todd is not so much a fish swimming in the river of this life as he is a net strung across it. He scoops up all the facts and makes his own idiosyncratic sense of them. Living with him is like living in an experimental theater production where a bad actor is playing the part of an affable middle-aged man.

Todd has serial passions, areas which grab his attention at the cost of almost all other things. Our house has revolved around caring for his dogs, studying photography, and building his vocabulary. But his newest passion is hunting for bargains, and he is aided in this endeavor by Jane Marie.

Todd takes lessons at a center for independent living where they stress the value of money management. When he discovered that there were people who were willing to part with items from their homes at well below the replacement cost, each purchase at a garage sale felt like pure profit to him.

Our house is now full of carnival glass and transistor radios, manual typewriters and downhill skis. We finally had to give Todd an allotment of space in his room and the shed. Todd now sells his treasures on the first weekend of each month just to make room for more stuff, and hence, we end up having garage sales of our own.

Todd has grown more discriminating and now specializes in technical gear: cameras, projectors, tape recorders and such. He has less use for sporting equipment and will not buy a gun even if it is offered at a steal of a price. Todd was once shot through the chest by a person who was aiming for me, and this has soured Todd on the investment value of firearms. Jane Marie buys clothes for all our extended family and has informants out in the community looking for baby gear. Our phone almost melted down with calls one Saturday morning when a used car seat in perfect condition and an antique bassinet were going for two dollars each at eight o'clock over at Coast Guard housing.

Today Todd heard rumors that there was a selection of super-8mm movie cameras offered up at a sale near the ferry terminal. Todd was very respectful of people who advertised "No early birds," but neither did he want to sit by and let the day waste away to nothing. The thought of seeing someone walk away with a box of super-8mm cameras before he had even had a chance to hold them in his hands irritated him; it was as if I, by doing push-ups in my underwear, was in fact holding his hand in a fire made of hundred-dollar bills.

So I stopped my push-ups at one hundred seventy-five and quickly got dressed.

Jane Marie was dressed and carrying Blossom in the crook of her arm. She handed me a cup of coffee. "Did

Patricia get hold of you yesterday, Cecil? She sounded pretty upset." I had not told Jane Marie about the shooting when she crawled into bed with me last night.

I sipped the coffee, stood close to Jane Marie, rubbed the top of my daughter's head and stroked my thumb on the tiny coin purse of her cheek.

"Patricia was shot dead by a police officer last night."

Jane Marie at first looked blank and then almost angry. She shifted Blossom to her other arm and curled her away from me as if she could shield our baby from the sadness of what I was saying.

"Oh . . . oh . . . oh . . ." was all Janie could say.

"Do you remember exactly what she said to you yesterday?" I put my arms around both of them. Jane Marie buried her head in the cleft of my neck and shoulder.

"She said she was sorry she had been rude to you."

I was about to explain more when Todd poked his head up the stairs that lead down to the front door on Katlian Street. "I don't mean to interrupt, Cecil, but I was wondering if it would be possible to drive out toward the ferry terminal now. This could be a very good opportunity to buy some rare cameras at a reasonable price, and while I know your time with Jane Marie and the new addition to the house is very—" I waved him off and looked at the woman who loved me and who suffered over every act of violence that came into our sphere. She nodded, managed a smile, and we went down the stairs. Todd would not have stopped nattering at us even if we had been weeping openly and smearing ashes in our hair.

To the veteran garage-salers, the entire town becomes a large party on weekend mornings, and the party, instead of moving from room to room in a house, moves from house to house depending on where the sales are. A conversation started over a box of cloth diapers on Wortman Loop could continue over a broken desk lamp on Edgecumbe Drive. The talk on this morning was all about the shooting.

There were various versions. One version had Kevin Sands killing a police officer, and another had a police officer killing a child. Many people knew that Patricia Ewers, the wife of the *Mygirl* mass murderer, was dead, and everyone assumed drugs were involved.

We ran into Paulla, a tireless garage-sale veteran. We were riffling through a box of paperback books, which turned out to be mostly Christian tracts and sci-fi fantasies, when Paulla tapped Jane Marie on the arm and told her she had seen a wonderful handmade quilt at a sale over on Jeff Davis Street. Paulla said she had almost bought it for Blossom but wasn't sure if we needed anything like that. Jane Marie thanked her and Paulla continued on quickly, "Did you hear about Patricia Ewers? I heard Kevin Sands killed her. Why would he do that? It was her husband he hated. That woman never did anything wrong . . . that I know about at least."

"Have you seen Jonathan Chevalier?" I asked.

Paulla was twisting the knobs of a handheld two-way radio that seemed to be dead. She said, "Dave told me he saw him outside the Pioneer Bar last night." She set the radio down and looked at it without speaking for a moment as if she were lost in thought. Then she looked at us and her face was tired and sad. "Someone should tell Jonathan, I suppose. He had no love of Ewers either."

Todd bought the entire box of super–8mm cameras and parts for six dollars. And although he looked happy, he wasn't satisfied, for now there was the fixing and fussing and trying to assess just what their true value would be. This is the soul of the garage sale: assessing value on the things we don't really want anymore. It's a hard thing to do. How do you know what a piece of your life is worth, even a small and insignificant piece? For most of us, it's really too painful to contemplate for long. We just sell it cheap and quickly turn away. But this was harder yet for Todd, because for whatever accident of neurological chemistry that had made him forever unique, Todd did not have a sense of his life the way we did. He would not cry over Jane Marie's death, as he would not really cry over mine. He would seek more information and try to stuff more things into his memory, but in the end there would never be a fully feeling human being there. I looked at him and, as I so often did, I wanted to cry. I wanted to reach into his head and make the tiny adjustments necessary that would allow him to love and play and even grieve. But I knew he never would. Todd possessed a fine collection of human qualities without ever having the chance to become fully human himself. It made me mad when I thought about it that way, which is why I rarely do.

Jane Marie bought some plastic baby cups and a chair that could hook onto a countertop. She bought herself a blue wool sweater. She got me six rusty salmon lures which were very much like the ones I used to troll for king salmon and two cushions for our skiff.

Jane Marie drove us home by eleven o'clock. I had a call on the answering machine to come to the hospital immediately to see Sean Sands. It was a nurse from the hospital who called. She was whispering, giving the impression she was making the call covertly. I had to hurry, she said. Sean was to be released this morning and she said I needed to see him before that happened.

I walked down my street. The sky was dark, but it was no longer raining. As I walked past some of the oldest houses on Katlian Street, some Native families were working on one of the clan houses. The Coho house was owned by the members of the Coho clan. One elder and his family were allowed to live there with all of the regalia that belonged communally to the Coho people. The word of a powerful storm was making its way around Katlian Street, and the Cohos were shoring up their house. Some young men were on the metal roof nailing along the edges, and some of the women were screwing shutters onto the front windows. A child on a bike lounged over the front of his handlebars and took in the entire scene. From the roof, Mark waved down. "Cecil, you better get that roof of yours nailed on tight. They say it's going to blow big time!" I waved at Mark and agreed. I knew he was right, but I had to go to the hospital before I could tighten up my house.

As I walked past, a gust of wind came unexpectedly from the west and the trees above the street churned and twisted.

A raven sat hunched on an abandoned truck waiting for the garbage cans to blow over. He said nothing to me as I passed him.

At the hospital, the nurse who had called me was waiting near the entrance. She ushered me in as if we were sneaking past the guards. She said, "Good, you made it. He's only got another half hour here. I think he really needs to talk to you."

Sean was sitting on the edge of his bed in his street clothes: black sweatpants and camouflage T-shirt. His hair was neatly combed. Under his shirt I could see the bulge of bandages across his chest. His stomach hung over his waist, and he had that melancholy expression fat boys sometimes have when they are sitting at rest: their cheeks hang down, pulling their eyes into thin crescent slits.

I shut the door before he lifted his head up and when he did, his eyes widened and his cheeks reddened.

"Where's that book? My picture book?" the frightened boy asked.

"A policeman has it. What's in that photo book, Sean?" I looked at him steadily, but he turned away.

"Just some stuff. Stuff that's private. Nobody's business. What policeman? Is he looking at it?"

"The old guy who was talking through the door—George. He took it. He said he wasn't going to look at it. He really did wrap it in tape, you know."

"Big deal," Sean snorted. Then he looked at me hard. "Kev says you dropped a dime on him. Is that true? You ratted Kev out?"

"Sean," I said, as I held my hands wide, palms open. I sat in a rocking chair at the end of the bed. "I don't even know what Kevin was up to. I sure as hell couldn't have ratted him out."

The boy swung his feet and banged his heels against the bottom rail of the hospital bed. He looked straight at the floor without speaking.

"Why don't you tell me what he was up to? I can help

him, you know. I've helped Kevin get out of jams before. I'll get him hooked up with a lawyer and I won't talk to the cops. Just tell me what he's up to."

"So who's got that picture book?" Sean swatted an invisible fly and asked the floor.

"I told you. That old guy. He's retired now but they still sort of let him run things. Listen, I'll get the book for you. Just tell me what Kevin was up to. What was in the safe?"

"I never saw no old guy," Sean mumbled. "Just saw shotguns. They said they shot me with beanbags. Is 'at right?"

"Beanbags from shotguns . . . that's what they told me too. They sure didn't use steel shot or I don't think we'd be chatting now. What was in the safe?"

Sean kept staring down at the floor; his right hand crept up and he lightly touched the dressing along his rib cage.

"Beanbags . . . cool," he said so softly I rocked forward on the chair to hear him.

Outside the hospital a crow hung on to a phone wire looping in a gust of wind. When the bird finally let go, it rose straight into the air and then swooped up and backwards in a barnstormer's stunt. On the sidewalk, a scatter of store receipts blew toward the street like a stampede of cartoon mice, and a woman with a torn paper bag was chasing them.

If the nurse had been right, that Sean had wanted to talk to me, he would. Perhaps all he wanted was that photo album, but if that was true then he would have thrown me out by now. I would wait. A squall gusted again, bowing the glass. The building seemed awash with hissing wind.

"Gonna blow," I offered. "The wind . . . it's going to blow."

"I suppose everybody's talking about us again," Sean said.

"People talk. Then they forget and move on to the next thing."

"What're they saying about me?" he said, almost in a whisper. And then, "Did they tear my room apart?"

"They tore your door up pretty bad, but I think that's it. As far as gossip, I haven't heard a thing. Everyone's talking about Patricia Ewers getting shot. They're talking about how they think Kevin is responsible for her death. And George Doggy says it's all about drugs."

"Jeese . . . ," the boy blustered and shook his head, "people ought to keep their mouths shut. It's none of their business. They could get hurt. . . ." The boy's voice drifted away. He was angry, I could tell, but scared, too, as if he wanted nothing more than to disappear.

He wiped his nose and looked straight at me. "There weren't no drugs. Kevin isn't into that stuff. That lady was crazy, yelling and waving a gun around. We didn't ever try and hurt her any. Who was she anyway?"

I stared at him, not quite believing he didn't know. But then Sean hadn't sat through much of the trial. He had never paid much attention to the official aftermath of his parents' murders. I doubt that he had ever read a paper or listened to a complete news story about the *Mygirl* killings.

"Her name was Patricia Ewers. She was Richard Ewers's wife."

"Oh." The sad kid shrugged. The syllable was a soft puff from his lips. He smiled a little bit, as if he were thinking of something mildly amusing that he intended to keep to himself.

Then he lifted his head up and looked at me again. His face softened, and it was as if a mask he was wearing was melting away. He looked scared.

"I'm no snitch. I can't. You don't get it. He'd kill me." The boy's voice broke slightly.

"You don't have to do this alone, Sean." I leaned toward him. "You don't have to be bullied. I can help you, and I can have the state troopers protect you if you want. We could even take off somewhere and let things cool. I'll take you on a trip if you want."

He snapped back into his soldier face. "Yeah, to the youth home or jail," he smirked. "I can do that. But I'm not talking to you anymore."

There was a knock on the door and the nurse poked her head in and told us the van and the escort from the youth home were here to pick Sean up. Sean snorted ruefully and slid off the bed.

"Just tell that old guy to give me my book back," he said
as he walked past without looking down at me in the chair.
He tried to swagger, but the injury to his ribs and his natural
short-legged gait made him walk flat-footed in a Groucho
Marx stride.

I stood outside the hospital and watched the wind bend
the alder trees above the ball field. There were still plenty of
leaves on the trees and as each branch swayed, the wind
stripped some off and carried them away. Someone bumped
the door behind me and I held one of the doors open for a
woman and a new baby leaving the hospital. She looked to
be a Filipino woman and held the baby casually, but when
anyone spoke to her she addressed each of her words down
toward her new child. Men ran around for cars and an older
woman snapped pictures, and I took off, not wanting to get
caught in someone else's precious memory.

I walked up over the hill and toward the trailer court.
There was something else in Sean's room, something Sean
had been worried about the police finding. If I was ever going to gain Sean's trust again, I needed to find whatever it
was before the police did.

The trailer door had a police-evidence lock over the
knob, but the back window only had plywood loosely tacked
over it. Using an old fuel tank from the creek to climb on, it
was easy enough to get through the window.

Inside the trailer it was cold. The smell of blood hung in
the air, making it feel like a dirty refrigerator. I peered
around in the gloom. I couldn't risk turning any lights on,
and since I didn't have a flashlight, I had to move slowly. I
took a careful look around in the shadows to see if there
were any boxes wired into the corners of the room.
Sometimes police put motion sensors attached to silent
alarms in secured crime scenes, but apparently the Sitka
P.D. hadn't bought those toys yet. In the room with the safe,
there was nothing to help me, but some of the "nothing"
was useful: there were no scales, no plastic bags, no mirrors
or knives, no razor blades, no handheld torches, no butane

canisters, no grow lights or plant food, phone lists or money scattered on the floor. There was nothing that made the scene look like a drug operation had been walked in on. There was just a bit of scattered ammunition and some newspapers from around southeastern Alaska. There was a business report on the charter boat industry in Sitka and a couple of glossy men's magazines. Nothing extraordinary for the room of a young man who had worked in the fishing industry.

The broken door to Sean's room stood propped up in the hall. His bed was overturned where the police had jumped on him. There were a few books, old picture books, for kids much younger than Sean. There was even *Goodnight Moon*, the familiar green, red, and yellow sitting on top of a stack of *Soldier of Fortune* magazines. Sean's clothes hung in almost military precision in his closet: T-shirts on hangers, an army fatigue jacket. The maps on his wall were of the local area. He had a topographical map above his bed with pencil marks drawn on it. I recognized the area where the elementary school had been built a few years ago. Someone had drawn in the school with trails leading up and into the woods.

A fat drop of water hit my neck. When I looked up, I could see water stains on the false ceiling. The storm had pulled back a piece of the roof and a leak had started. The ceiling tile was off-kilter in its aluminum frame and along its edges was a gap. I stood on the side of the bed frame and poked up at the tile.

Photographs fluttered down onto the bed like alder leaves. Kids' school pictures. Dozens of them. Mostly they were wallet-sized, but there were some portrait-sized photographs too. There were children from all grades: girls with stylish new glasses and faux pearls around their necks, boys with goofy haircuts and stiff smiles, Indian kids, and Filipino, a couple of black children, but most of Sean's schoolmates were white. There was no writing on the back of any of the pictures. I tried to imagine why these photos were hidden in the ceiling. I flipped through them. Boys in sports shirts and some in flannel hunting gear. One or two wearing ties. Girls in pink with frilly collars, but many girls in plain button blouses. Smiles and smirks, and closed-eye grimaces. School pictures. Why hide these? Then I lifted a couple of large pages stapled together. These were the photos of the entire class, where all of the shots of the individuals were collected on a single page with the teacher and the school principal's portraits in the top corners. There was a page representing all of Sean's classmates for each grade. There were heavy Xs drawn over several of the photos on each page. Some of the portraits were cut out. On each page, the principal was carefully X'd out.

Another drop landed on my neck, and when I looked up I saw the butt end of a rifle hung on a rafter above the false ceiling. I crawled up again and took it down. This was no cheap imitation, no fifty-dollar knockoff that would jam, but an authentic AK-47, well oiled and maintained. On the stock was a kid's sticker, the kind they usually put on skateboard decks. The sticker had a drawing of a wild-haired kid flying on a skateboard straight toward a brick wall. The lettering read: *No Doubt.*

There was a canvas bag that looked military in origin, olive green and heavily stitched. Inside it were three fifty-shot magazines for the AK-47. Each had been gently sanded along the edges, and two were taped end to end so the chamber end of the magazine where the cartridge would slip into the gun was easily accessible. This allowed a shooter to empty one magazine, and, without reaching away from his weapon, eject the empty and insert a loaded magazine quickly. It took some practice, but a kid could practice in front of his parents' bedroom mirror.

I heard the rattle of someone working the lock on the front door. I hastily wiped the gun down with the corner of the blanket and stuck it back above the ceiling along with the photographs.

The trailer's outer door opened and I heard someone take one step inside. The darkness of the stormy day crept inside too. I slid open Sean's window and wedged myself out as quickly as I could. But I paused before I dropped to the ground, looking for a police cruiser along my side of the trailer. I saw nothing, so I ran to the rear, hoping I could at least stick the plywood against the outside of the window before the cops made it to the back room. No such luck. I heard the front door slam and someone running down the stairs. I dove through a gap in the trailer skirting and crawled underneath, rolling over and over in the mud until I was wedged between the axles. I saw work boots. Whoever this was, he was alone. He kicked the plywood and started running up into the woods where I had been planning to go.

I waited. There had been a leak in the sewer line some-where, because the smell in the mud under this trailer was powerful. There was also the mildewed carcass of a cat and a bag of old traps tucked by the front stairs.

The work boots came back and paced back and forth. Finally he picked up the plywood and took it inside, and I heard him hammering it in place. I decided to get the hell out of there. The smell was about to make me sick, and I thought the sound of someone retching would have caused even one of Sitka's finest to take a closer look around.

I bolted through the gap and rolled through the brush under the broken window. I got to my feet and ran behind a trailer on the downhill side, where a Rottweiler started barking at me from the back bedroom. After that, my feet had wings. I flew across the soggy mud all the way down to the fringe of trees between the beach and the road, where I lay in the wet brush until I was sure I couldn't hear anyone coming for me.

I am the first to admit that I'm a lousy detective. I'm sure most of it has to do with the fact that I have spent most of my career trying to help people establish their innocence. Looking for innocence requires a larger view than looking for guilt; larger, and usually less satisfying. When look-ing for guilt, you only look at the things that you know are connected, and making connections feels like progress. When looking for innocence, you look at everything else, and it never feels like progress. But sitting there in the wet brush off the side of the road, it occurred to me that I wasn't making much progress, yet I didn't feel as if I was in the presence of innocence.

Today I had seen work boots walking around the trailer, broken glass, and a dead cat in the mud. I had seen windblown leaves and photographs of children, an automatic weapon with a kid's *No Doubt* sticker on the stock. I had riled a neighbor's already paranoid dog. I sat in the wet brush and tried to make some sense of it.

But I couldn't, and that doesn't really surprise me. It goes back to the first principle of defense investigations, which is this: There is no trail of crumbs that leads out of the forest, so there is no sense looking for one. What I have seen more often in my life is a snowstorm of crackers on a landscape dotted with hungry ducks. I tried to explain this once to a police officer when I had been pulled over for some offense or another, and it was from his reaction to my "crumbs and ducks" theory that I came to the conclusion I would never be much of a detective.

Gulls sailed and dove over the surfbreak. A few stragglers would bolt from their circle and carve large turns downwind, then labor to come back to where they had begun. I was wet and covered in smelly mud. I was so sure I wouldn't get a ride I didn't even put out my thumb.

The rain felt almost warm as it pelted down on the wind. I walked quickly and was soon able to see down the street to where my house sat over the channel. Workers from the fish plant nearest the center of town were walking out into the middle of the street, some still wearing their aprons and rubber gloves. One guy still had his long knife in his hand. The workers were all looking down toward the Pioneer Bar. I was cold and filthy and in no mood to watch some lunchtime bar brawl, so I jogged the last little bit of the way to my front door. As I started to push my way to my house, I couldn't help but peer up toward the bar. More and more people were walking down the middle of the street. I heard laughing and cheering now. Even in waterfront bars in Alaska they don't cheer for bar fights, not in the daylight anyway.

Suddenly there was a blur of dark hair and saddle shoes running toward me at waist level. I held my arms out and caught the girl before she ran me over. Her name was

Natalie, and I knew her from down the street. She was only four years old and held a fistful of money. Her eyes were as big as new quarters, startled and a bit frightened.

"Cecil!" she said breathlessly. "It's mine, really. He's just handing it out. I asked the grown-ups and they said it was okay. Really." She held the bills out to me without unclenching her fist.

"He's just giving them to people down there. You go. You go and get some too!" Her voice was a lively tune.

I opened her fist gently and I saw what she had: three one-hundred-dollar bills bearing Ben Franklin's smirky countenance.

"Who's giving these bills away, honey?" I asked.

Natalie looked up at me with wide eyes, happy, and scared too.

"That goofy guy who lives on that sailboat. Really, Cecil. I didn't steal it or nothing. The guy's giving it away."

Back up the street, men were yelling, kids were laughing. "Crazy, huh?" Natalie said with delight and ran down the street with a death grip on her bills.

Chapter Five

Jonathan Chevalier was standing in the bed of a rusted red pickup throwing money into a small crowd. In the background I could hear a police siren. About a dozen people gathered in the street, reaching up toward him. Jonathan was smiling broadly, like a politician at a whistle stop, reaching into the pockets of his wool halibut jacket and pulling out crumpled bills. The bills looked like freshly picked maple leaves, and as he threw them just above the hands of the people in the street he was laughing, shouting out, "Easy. Easy now. Don't hurt yourself. I have plenty more to give you."

A police car rounded the corner near the old post office in the center of town, and I pushed my way through the crowd and grabbed Jonathan's arms. People started booing me. I jerked Jonathan down and put my arms around him, leading him inside a coffee shop next to the truck. The coffee shop had a back door that led to long corridors in the building, which had once been a hotel. It was a fine place to shake off the police.

Jonathan's smile was beatific, and just touching him I could tell he wasn't drunk. In my experience, drunks have soft handshakes and their bodies seem soggy with melancholy. But Jonathan's body was taut and he moved quickly and easily. He was breathing deeply, and when I looked in his eyes they sparked with a wild energy.

"We are not greedy, Cecil. We are all just born naked into this world." He smiled up at me. His new, overly friendly behavior had me more worried than his usual icy stare. Jonathan looked at my filthy clothes with an amused grin. "You could use a change of clothes," he said.

I was about to say something when I heard doors slamming and police radios hissing. The crowd outside was hassling the cops. A boy of about twelve came barreling down the hallway and I turned to fend him off with my forearm, but Jonathan reached over me and stuffed some twenty-dollar bills down the front of the boy's blue coat.

The kid stopped short, stunned, because he had expected me to slug him, but instead found himself with a coat full of money standing before a wide-eyed fisherman with a rumpled wool jacket and a grin like a broken bottle.

"Hey, thanks, dude," the kid said, backing away suspiciously.

"Don't worry about it. Just blow that money, okay? Just blow it on something beautiful, all right?" Jonathan's voice was clear and the words unslurred.

"Yeah, sure," the kid sneered and bolted down the hall.

"Don't tell anyone where we've gone. We have to get out of here, all right?" I yelled after him, and the kid stopped once more and took a long look at us. Jonathan's long hair was tangled down to his shoulders. He hadn't shaved in days, and his eyes were rimmed red. He was muttering something under his breath.

"Take the elevator to the top floor," the kid said, deadly serious. "Stay there ten minutes. I'll tell 'em you went out the back door to the dock. Ten minutes, yeah?"

"Ten. Thanks," I said and tugged Jonathan toward the elevator.

"I'm telling you, Cecil, you never know how many friends you have until you start giving money away on the street," Jonathan was saying softly. The elevator door eased open and we traveled quietly to the third floor.

"Going up," I said, without knowing why. Then I added jokingly, "Have any of that money for your old friend Cecil?" Jonathan just looked at me with the same sweet smile and said nothing. I guess irony is not a two-way street within the soul of a blissful person, particularly when it comes to cash.

We stepped off the elevator and found a laundry room at the far end of the hall. I could see down to the street where people were walking back into the bar. Some were looking down toward the dock where the police had apparently gone.

"Jonathan, what are you doing?" I asked. He kept smiling at me with such intensity I had the urge to turn away from him for a moment.

"Cecil . . . I've had some amazing breakthroughs, okay? I know this seems extreme, but trust me, it comes naturally from my work. I've had some amazing breakthroughs. And it's clear to me that none of this . . ."—here he gestured around in a way that I was guessing took in the entire known universe—". . . that none of this is me and all of it wants something. Okay? So . . . I'm just giving it away."

"That's, well, that's good to hear," I offered. I looked out the window again and saw that the kid from the stairwell was walking slowly with a police officer by his side, the kid pointing away from our location with urgently over-acted gestures.

"Jonathan, why were you giving the money away?" I asked.

"It wasn't mine, Cecil," he answered.

"Whose was it?" I looked back at him, and he had the palms of his hands turned up and he held his arms out in front of him as if he were about to deliver a sermon.

But instead he said, "Okay . . . All right . . . Money is printed by the government. To hoard the money is to deny your own erotic life."

"I understand that," I lied. "These bills had been in a safe at Kevin Sands's trailer. You took the money from his trailer last night. Were these bills yours or were they Kevin's?" I was trying not to let my voice sound as if I were lecturing a child but I was having a hard time. The elevator bell rang and the door began to slide open.

I pushed Jonathan back against a doorway, out of sight of

anyone who might be in the elevator. Jonathan did not seem disturbed in the least. He pushed me away easily.

"That money wasn't anybody's, okay?" he said, and his eyes locked onto mine as if he were trying to meld our minds together. "All of that is a misconception. I've got stuff I have to do. I've got to give the rest of it away. I've got to put things back to where they belong, okay? I've got stuff I have to do, okay?"

No one was on the elevator, so I stepped back into the hallway. I took a deep breath and was trying to formulate my question to see just how much Jonathan knew about last night's shooting of Patricia Ewers, when he quickly stepped in front of me and squeezed through the closing doors of the elevator.

"Don't worry," Jonathan called out to me behind the metal doors. "Don't worry, okay, Cecil?" And his voice sank away through the floor.

"Yeah . . . okay," I said to the blank closed elevator doors.

It took me fifteen minutes to walk over to the jail. They checked me in without much of a hassle, thinking I was here, as usual, to work on Kevin Sands's legal defense. The duty officer looked at my filthy clothes and shook his head as if he knew the whole story of my pathetic career. I took a cup of hot coffee in a paper cup back to the windowless interview room. The tape recorder took up half the tabletop, and a television with a VCR loomed in a rollaway rack beside the two chairs. I sat sipping sour coffee and listening to the piped music in the hall. Kevin Sands was dressed in a green jail jumpsuit. Both his eyes were black raccoon bruises bridged across his swollen nose. He was wearing the slipper socks that are regulation back in the block. His fine blond hair was damp and combed back. He looked at me with a disdainful smirk, which was strangely mirrored in the smirk the woman jailer gave me as she turned to close the door. Her leather utility belt creaked loudly as she winked and whispered, "I'll just leave you two alone then," and she closed the door.

"Where is Jonathan?" Kevin blurted out as the door double-clicked shut.

"Hey, good to see you, Kevin," I said. "How's your face?"

Kevin took a can of tobacco out of his jumpsuit, rapped the lid, twisted it off and placed a pinch of tobacco in his front lip. "I want my fucking money, Younger," he said flatly. He put the can back in his front pocket. "And my face hurts like hell," he added, just to squelch any more polite conversation.

"Where'd you get that money, Kev?" I folded my arms and leaned back in my chair.

"It was given to me. You tell that crazy motherfucker I want it back. I'll give you and that old bastard two days to get my money to me."

"Which old bastard are you referring to?"

"Don't be cute, Younger. You're not Columbo, you know. Just find that nutbag and get my money back."

"Well, on that matter, Kevin . . . I think he's spent . . . well, I should say he's gone through quite a bit of the money."

"Younger," he sighed, as if I were a naughty child, "clean out your ears. Just go hop around town and get it. Christ, it's not like you've got a lot of important things to do, is it? Bring it back." Kevin leaned forward and I could smell the minty tobacco on his breath. His bulging lower lip showed red, matching the scar on his nose.

"How much money are we talking about, Kevin? I mean, how do I know when to stop gathering up all this money of yours?" I unfolded my arms and leaned forward until my nose was almost touching his. Kevin backed up quickly. I don't suppose he enjoyed my invading his personal space, but I'm pretty sure he didn't want me to bump his broken nose either.

Kevin took the coffee cup out of my hand and spat into it. He set the cup on the table between us. He crossed his arms and stared at me in silence.

"Come on, Kevin. How much of this money am I looking for?" I threw one of the hundred-dollar bills from my pocket at him.

Kevin wouldn't answer. I flicked the other hundred at him.

"That's it then, Kev. There's your hundred bucks. I got you your money back. Now tell me where it came from."

"There's more money, dickhead." He picked up my coffee cup and spat in it again.

"Tell me, Kevin. Patricia wasn't carrying a gun. She hated the things. So, how did she come to have a gun in her hand when the cops broke into your house?"

Kevin leaned back in the chair and tried to make his eyes go dead. "She was freaking out, man, screaming all sorts of shit. I brought the pistol out of the back and she calmed down a little. Then when the cops came and told her to step outside she flipped out again. She accused them of killing her husband. They told her they were going to put her under arrest and she really went nuts. She grabbed the gun and that's all I saw. I was pulling Sean toward the back of the trailer by that time."

He stared at me as if he expected me to speak. He cleared his throat nervously, then went on. "That's all I know about that, Younger. Now I want you to do something useful and get my money back. That's all that should concern you now. I know you and that old cop are tight. I've always known."

"Really?" I grabbed the cup back, then took a handful of Kevin's hair. I put my mouth down by his right ear and whispered, "Now you tell me," I said through my teeth. "Where is Richard Ewers? I really don't like acting like this, Kevin, but I think you've done something to Richard. I think you're responsible for what happened to Patricia. I know you didn't care for Patricia and Richard. You may have good reason. But they were friends of mine. Now please don't scold me any further and just tell me what you did with Richard."

I took two fingers and lifted his nostrils toward his scalp so I could feel the crunching of the broken cartilage in his nose.

Both Kevin's fists were clenched. His legs were straight out in front of him and he was breathing hard through his mouth. He did not move to hit me, but he wasn't starting a sentence either.

I let him go and he relaxed so quickly it was as if he had deflated. His face was pale like he was going to faint. I handed him the cup he had been spitting in.

"Coffee?" I asked.

Kevin looked at me with the loathing and pity you'd show for a Labrador puppy who had rolled in shit.

"Cecil, I don't know where Ewers is and the truth of it is, I don't know exactly how much money there was. I was counting it when all hell broke loose. I was counting it. Chevalier was there. He was nervous about the money. I figured he wanted it for himself. When things got wild he scooped it up and dove out the window."

"Where'd it come from then?" I set the coffee cup in the wastebasket and pushed the basket in front of Kevin, who was now sitting slumped over with his elbows on his knees.

"I can't tell you, Cecil. If I tell you that, I'm just as fucked as if I don't have the money. Just get as much of it as you can. There was somewhere around forty grand. As far as where it came from, you should be talking to George."

"Doggy? You want me to give the money to the cops?"

"If that old bastard wants a cut, that's fine with me. You can get it to him, all right? But Jonathan's gone nuts. He says he wants no part of the money. . . ." Kevin rolled his eyes. "Yeah, he says he doesn't want anything to do with the money and then he fucking *takes* it from me. There's no fucking telling what he's going to do now. If I were you I'd get that money all squared away or. . . ."

Kevin's eyes were beseeching me. Deep in those red-rimmed eyes, I almost saw a flicker of the humanity the doctors said couldn't be there.

"Or what, Kevin?" I reached out and touched him on the knee as the door rattled open and banged against the TV cart.

"Cecil, you scamp!" Pomfret stuck his party-balloon-sized head in the room. "You better get out of here now. This is supposed to be a legal visit, and I've just been informed that you do not work for Kevin's legal representative. So you better shove off." Pomfret grabbed me by the elbow, and before I could say a thing to Kevin, I was propelled out of the room and down the narrow hallway to the front desk.

"Get a letter of introduction from an attorney and you can come back," the cop said, as I was launched into the first doorway past the bulletproof reception window. Just past the corner near the detective's desk, I saw George Doggy sipping coffee out of a ceramic mug with the Alaska state flag on it. He waved, then held his fist to his ear mimicking a telephone, mouthing the words "Call me later," just as I felt the skillet-sized hand of Officer Pomfret between my shoulder blades and heard the solid click of the reinforced door swinging shut.

I was out on the street again. Wind blew a sheet of newspaper down the street toward the elementary school and a paper cup chattered down the pavement as if it were frantic to be somewhere. Up on the mountain above town, the snow was still lifting off the ridges in an icy spume and a raven was stalled in midair with wings spread in flight. I had nothing more to do than try to gather up thousands of dollars of what was surely stolen tabloid money.

As I walked away from the jail, I saw Patricia Ewers's parents walking toward the courthouse. They must have flown up from Seattle on the early morning flight. I'm sure they were headed to the magistrate's office to process their daughter's death certificate. I changed direction in the middle of the street. I had met Patricia's parents during their son-in-law's trial. The old man had been a logger on the Washington coast. He walked with a stoop to his back and a limp, but his body was rock hard under his western dress shirt. His wife wore a print housedress and held a tissue to her mouth. I walked toward her with my hand extended and the old man stepped in front of his wife. He was frowning. He looked at me for a moment as if to take my measure. Then he opened the door to the courthouse, ushered his wife inside and shut the door firmly in my face.

A prisoner on the street was washing a police car behind me. He was wearing a red jumpsuit and slip-on rubber boots. The raven I had seen stalled in the air was now sitting on the dome lights of the car. The prisoner reached into his pocket and threw the bird a soda cracker. As I crossed back to the other side of the street, the raven landed on a light standard overlooking the elementary school. The black bird held the square of white cracker as if it were a folded thousand-dollar bill. Then without reason, he dropped it. I turned and walked down the street toward Jonathan's studio.

Jonathan Chevalier rented a storage loft in an old warehouse above the water. With the tolerant indifference of his landlords, he had turned the loft into a studio apartment. The warehouse was built out on an old wooden pier that stood on pilings encrusted with barnacles and sea anemones blossoming white into the shaded water at high tide. At low tide, the anemones hung limp on the pilings near the spidery red forms of sea stars and the occasional abalone. As I stepped onto the pier, I heard a heron yawping under the dock, and I watched it lumber into flight, pumping its body along the surface of the channel near the float-plane dock.

I watched the stairs to Jonathan's apartment, thinking there might be police interest in Jonathan's place, but after twenty minutes I'd seen no one come or go so I walked up the outside staircase and swung open the thin plywood-framed door, which was standing ajar.

I flipped on a light switch just inside the door. A folding chair was turned on its side in the middle of the plank floor. A collection of overstuffed and broken office furniture was pushed against the walls. One bare bulb hung in the center of the room. The windows were draped with black plastic that was sealed around the edges with silver duct tape. A mattress was slumped against the wall near the bathroom. An aluminum hot pot was plugged in and cooking the air. The pot was so hot I could smell the paint burning off its outer surface. An old record player was set up in the shadows of a corner, and the needle skipped relentlessly on the record still circling there.

Stumbling around in the gloom, I was able to unplug the hot pot and then looked around for another light. On the back wall I saw dozens of lamps, all set up so their hollow-mouthed shades pointed toward the opposite wall. I found a power strip with extension cords snaked to it and when I flipped the switch, all the lamps spat light at once.

The back wall held a massive canvas smeared with paint. This surface was perhaps fifteen feet tall and twenty feet wide. Some of the paint had been applied with a roller; some looked as if it had been thrown directly on the smoothed canvas surface. One bright crimson swath looked as if it had been swabbed on with an old-fashioned floor mop.

This paint was a mess, but not necessarily chaotic: reds and blues arching up higher than my head and sweeping down broader than my arms could reach. Some of the painted forms could have been running horses or waterfalls, but there was no real clue to the logic other than the paint itself.

Back in the shadows, a cat jumped down from the overturned desk. A saucer of sour milk splashed on the plank floor. Then the cat curled up on a stack of slide projectors. This was Jonathan's cat, Jackson.

I lifted the cat easily off the top projector. As soon as I curled Jackson into my arms, he started to purr. I switched on the projector and saw more of Jonathan's artwork.

There on the wall was a black-and-white photograph of Jonathan's brother Albert. The projector's fan whirred and I had to adjust the focus on the image. Albert looked to be about ten years old. He'd been dead at fourteen. The photograph showed Albert squinting up into the sun, standing on the deck of a fishing boat, his hands blurred and coming up to his face, perhaps to shade his eyes. The camera caught him smiling and unaware, a young boy with memories ahead of him. Jonathan had not been coloring in the image but was painting on top of the projected image. The image gave the impression that the ghost boy trapped in the projected beam was being consumed in light and color. The image was a jumble of hot and cold colors, as if the boy might burn or drown. Grass-green swirls looped around his face. Ice-blue arrows pushed down toward his eye sockets. Above him, orange and red feathered to the top of the frame. I turned on the next projector and the wall filled in with a color photograph of a sailboat, the *Naked Horse,* floating on a tranquil sea. The image of the boat floated through the squalls of red and orange, suggesting the *Naked Horse* rolling through an eruption.

Jackson purred in my arms. He felt warm and comforting, for now the wall looked frighteningly cluttered and disordered. Too much paint and too many ideas. This was the muddy adventure of an artist chasing genius without much success, and it made a sad artifact. The colors, as they had flowed to the bottom of the wall and across the floor, combined to make a murky diarrhetic brown. I put Jackson down and he curled against my leg, still purring.

There was a clatter in the back, and a wedge of light stroked through the room as the door opened. George Doggy came in and slapped his ball cap against his leg.

"Criminy Jane . . . Look at this mess," Doggy exclaimed, then turned and looked at the jumble of images on the back wall.

"Oh my Lord! Don't tell me this is supposed to be a piece of art." Doggy kept slapping his leg with his hat and squinting at the images.

"I'll tell you one thing, boy," the old man mused, "this guy's not much of a painter. I wouldn't have him paint my shed even."

He put his hat on his head and looked at me squarely. "So, you find any of that money?"

I stepped over to the old record player and put the needle on the third cut. The music of Art Blakey and the Jazz Messengers squeezed through the tiny speaker behind the old portable's tweed fabric.

"It was the money Kevin wanted to talk to you about, wasn't it?"

"Just whose money is that, George?" I asked, then turned the volume down so I wouldn't miss a syllable of his answer.

"He say anything about where it came from?"

"Kevin told me to ask you about the money, George."

"You're going to be a pain in the ass about this, aren't you, Cecil?"

Doggy set the chair upright and sat down in it like an old man resting after two rounds of golf. "You know, Cecil, every cop, I don't care who he is, starts out with some sense of fairness." He waved his hand as if swatting flies. "Oh, I know there are some kids who get into police work for dumb reasons: the guns, the cars . . . the power, of course. But almost every cop has some basic sense of fairness, like scales he uses to sort of weigh out his conscience as he does his job. Some work harder at tuning those scales up. Some work harder at how much they pile on each tray, you understand what I mean? But all of 'em got *something*." He was holding up both hands as if he were adjusting a balance.

"Every once in a while there's a case that just screws things up," Doggy said.

Art Blakey rode the high hat behind Freddie Hubbard's horn. A light wind found its way through the walls of the warehouse and swirled tiny dust storms across the floor.

"You and I don't ever talk about the *Mygirl*, do we, Cecil?"

I shook my head. A gust of wind rattled the metal roofing on the warehouse. I could hear water slapping on the beach below the floor.

Doggy wasn't looking at me; he was staring at the images on the back wall. "I worked the *Mygirl* scene, Cecil. I helped them pull those dead children out of the boat. Richard Ewers was laughing and throwing money around in the bar while that boat was still burning. They say we lost or mishandled all the evidence. Weak circumstantial case. Ewers's lawyers walked away from the jury and that sniggering little bastard walked out on the street."

I watched Jackson staring at a dust mote caught in the light of the projector. His eyes were focused and intent, then he leaped toward the painting, clawing the air.

"Why were you so certain Richard Ewers had done the killings on the *Mygirl*?" I asked Doggy. "The evidence just wasn't there in the trial. You have to admit that. Did you have illegal wiretaps on him, something substantial you couldn't use? There had to be something that made you so sure it was Ewers."

George Doggy looked at the cat jumping at shadows and he smiled sadly.

"Cecil, you haven't worked many bodies, have you?"

I shook my head. I had been a defense investigator and as such I had never showed up in time to try to save a life. I dealt in the stories people told after a murder, all the different versions. George Doggy had spent more time in blood-spattered rooms than any other man I had met. He had held children in his arms as they closed their eyes and stopped breathing. He knew the details of crime personally; I had only imagined them, or else tried not to.

"The *Mygirl* killings were like nothing else. This was a person who had killed his friends, a woman and little children. He had to stand so close to them they could have touched him as he put the last bullets into them. This was a world-class brutal murder, not some anonymous drive-by or a drunken dispute spun over the edge. The person who did this executed people he cared about at close range, and he incinerated their bodies . . . all for money."

Doggy seemed older now than I had ever thought he could be. He bent over and made an odd cricket-chirping sound by rubbing his fingers together. Jackson stopped stalking phantoms in the shaft of projected light and moved cautiously toward Doggy.

"You wear a murder like that, Cecil, for the rest of your life. No one walks away from that clean. I don't care what the shrinks say. I don't care how cynical a world you think we live in. A person wears a murder like that."

Jackson curled around Doggy's leg and the old policeman lifted the cat into his arms. "I interviewed Ewers. You know that, you saw the transcript but you couldn't know that Richard Ewers wore those killings on his body. He wore them over his hunched-up shoulders and down deep in his eyes. He wore those killings as if they were his shadow and he knew I knew it."

Jackson purred and I could hear his sound churning along with Art Blakey. "So what was it that kept him from telling you?" I asked the master interrogator.

"Two things. The investigation had gone on too long.

The defense lawyers were right about one thing: we'd wasted too much time chasing after crazy leads. We wasted time looking like we were doing everything right. We should have focused on Ewers all along. Thrown everything at him. Ewers knew too much about what we had been up to and he knew we didn't have anything on him."

"And the other thing?" I asked.

"This is just my own personal theory, but I believe Richard Ewers was dead by the time I got to him. I think he was dead down in his bones. You know what I'm saying? He knew he was going to die for this crime and there was no reason to tell anybody anything. He was just biding his time before that shadow he was wearing swallowed him alive.

"Most guys confess because they want forgiveness. It's the urge that moves them to spill their guts, and I do everything in my power to be the man who can offer them that forgiveness. Ewers knew there was no forgiveness for this killing. He also read in my eyes that I wasn't ever going to offer him anything, and that's how I blew that interview."

Wayne Shorter and Cedar Walton scampered around inside the tunes coming from the old record. Jackson jumped down off George Doggy's lap and went back to stalking phantoms.

Doggy took off his hat and patted it against his legs. "Did Sands ask you to find the money?"

"Yeah, he did."

"Then I think you should," Doggy said.

I took two steps closer to him. "George, tell me what's going on."

"Let's just say this case is still open."

"Which case? The *Mygirl* killings? Patricia Ewers's death? Or Richard Ewers's disappearance?"

Blakey rollicked around his drum kit, and Jackson started licking sour milk off the planking.

Doggy said nothing.

"Can I ask you some more questions?" I said, as the needle hit a scratch and one phrase of Wayne Shorter's saxophone line repeated over and over again.

"It will cost you." George Doggy stood up and walked

toward the door. "It will cost you about fifty thousand dollars," he called out over his shoulder. "Fifty thousand in blood money."

The plywood door flapped in a gust of wind, letting milky daylight into the room. Jackson stopped purring as he stood in the middle of Jonathan's studio and stared after George Doggy. I took the needle off the record, turned off all the lights, and went home to take a shower.

Chapter Six

Ineeded to follow the money. This is a maxim for most
investigators but it was a new experience for me. Most of
my clients were either too poor or too unsuccessful as
thieves to have any money to follow.

Kevin Sands was a career petty criminal. I hadn't expected straightforward honesty from him. George Doggy
was a man of authority and high esteem and I wasn't allowed
to question his honesty. So I was going to have to follow the
money that people were either looking for or giving away. I
wasn't looking forward to it, but I needed to speak with the
police.

It was Monday morning at the airport coffee shop, and
sitting behind the restaurant table Officer Pomfret seemed
even bigger and more inert than he did out in the world.

"Cecil, do you have any legal authority in this matter?"
Pomfret asked. He leaned back in his chair so he could
bring his coffee cup to his lips without clattering the gear
on his utility belt against the wooden table.

"Look . . . Officer . . ." Pomfret's first name was Roy, but
for some reason I couldn't bring myself to call him that. I
kept thinking about the Mouseketeers on that old TV show
of my youth, and I just couldn't shake the image of that fat
old guy named Roy who wore the ears.

"You can call me Roy," he said, and I winced.

"Yeah, thanks. Anyway, I have all the legal authority of a concerned citizen. You know that."

"It's Roy," Pomfret said. "Otherwise it's 'Lieutenant Pomfret,' not 'Officer.' " His voice had a chilliness, and I thought this could have been a record for the shortest route to loggerheads I had ever come across.

"Great then, Lieutenant . . ." The waitress brought cream for my coffee. "I want to know how it happened that one of your officers killed Patricia Ewers."

"You think we did that on purpose?" Pomfret smiled as he looked at me across the mouth of his mug.

"You don't care what I think, Lieutenant." I watched a small plane turn off the runway apron and head back to the tie-downs.

Pomfret put down his mug and tapped his fleshy finger on top of my knuckles to get my attention.

"What does your good friend George Doggy think about her being dead? Now that's something I'd be interested in. He's the guy with the hard-on for Ewers."

Pomfret was staring at me with dead-fish eyes and I looked back out the window to avoid them.

"The *Mygirl* case has been open a long time. When are you guys going to solve it?" There was more sarcasm in my voice than I had intended.

"That case is not open." Pomfret let out a disgusted grunt. He jabbed my hand this time and there was a dark sparkle to his eyes as if he were willing me to catch fire. "Cecil, I don't care a hoot what those defense lawyers tell the papers, the *Mygirl* is a solved case. Richard Ewers was guilty as sin and he skated away because of some bullshit lawyer and some stupid bad luck." Pomfret scowled out the window and the waitress brought him his cinnamon roll.

"Come on, Cecil. Tell me the truth. You've been hired by that goddamn Teller again, haven't you?"

"Now you know I can't tell you about that."

Pomfret had one hand on his cinnamon roll. With the other, he reached across and thumped my chest with the tip of his index finger. "You can tell those bastards I'm not going to do their jobs for them. I'll find Richard Ewers. I'll find Ewers because it's my job, not because of some crap about him being innocent."

His finger felt like the end of a lead pipe. He took a big bite of his roll and pulled his hand back across the table.

I looked squarely into Pomfret's beefy face to see if it would tell what he was holding. "So you know about Ewers being missing. Does Doggy know where he is?" I asked.

"Yeah, right. I guess we can always call the great George Doggy," Pomfret grumbled. "George was a good cop. Hell, probably a *great* cop in his day, but he's not God," Pomfret said, averting his eyes from mine, as if he were nervous about this sacrilegious statement.

"Something for which I've always been grateful."

"Yeah." Pomfret tried to chuckle. "He's not, you know. He's not God. We just keep him in the loop out of professional courtesy. And I get a little tired of everybody throwing him back at me all the time. Everyone makes mistakes, Cecil. Even the great George Doggy." Pomfret spoke to me with his mouth full. He kept staring out the window, keeping an eye on the building wind.

"Richard Ewers was in Ketchikan last week," he said. "Ewers checked into a hotel and checked right back out again. There's not a frigging thing those lawyers are going to do about this. We're going to find Ewers or what's left of him. I'm sure of that, Cecil. Now go peddle your damn papers somewhere else. I know what you're up to."

"I wish I did," I told the storm building outside.

Pomfret shrugged. "Everybody makes mistakes. Stay clear of this, Cecil. You'll be all by yourself. No one's going to pull you out of the shit you're going to land in."

Of course I hate to admit it, but he was right.

There were a couple of volunteer firemen in the restaurant; they looked like they were carpenters by profession but they all wore their fire department beepers. The waitress was standing next to one of them with her forearm draped over his shoulder holding the coffeepot in a sexy, careless way when the volunteers began fumbling for their beepers and Pomfret's radio started squealing. Everyone in the restaurant tensed. One of the volunteers was having his coffee topped off when he brushed the coffeepot aside. The waitress began to say something until she saw his look of concern. Pomfret ran out of the restaurant. He left his unfinished roll.

I could hear the transmission from the fire hall coming through the firemen's beepers: *"All available EMS personnel . . . all available EMS personnel, respond to Verstovia Elementary School. Possible multiple patients. Possible GSW. P.D. responding. Again, possible multiple GSW. All personnel must stand by perimeter of school under direction of Sitka P.D."*

One carpenter looked up at the waitress, the blood drained from his face.

"GSW?" the waitress asked, as the men headed toward the door without paying their checks.

"Gunshot wounds," one threw over his shoulder. "Somebody's shooting up at the elementary school."

I followed after the firemen and begged a ride from one. He asked me if I was a volunteer and I told him, "No. I just have a kid up there," which wasn't strictly a lie but would prove to be inaccurate anyway. As the carpenter's truck sped across the bridge with the blue light flashing on the dash, I knew with a certainty the body tells the brain that Sean Sands would be dead by the time we arrived.

Everywhere were flashing lights and people running. A roundish woman in a denim smock was running from the building. She had her arms sheltered over a child's shoulders. The woman had a handkerchief to her mouth and the little girl was crying so that her face was a silent grimace. All the running men in blue coats were headed in the same direction: across the playground. Three small boys cantered along the edges of a fence where a male teacher kept trying to corral them back into the building. The wind blustered through the swings, and a few raindrops pattered down on the rubber pads beneath the monkey bars. The empty swings squealed back and forth on their chains. I stepped forward and picked up a piece of garbage that was tumbling across the pavement. It was packaging for gauze dressing. The blue lettering on each side was wet with blood.

The police had not yet established control of the scene. Some had their weapons drawn. Others were standing behind pillars and speaking into their radios. The three wild boys ran through the school doors and the teacher chased after them and slammed the door behind. Past the fence line near the trees, a tight knot of EMTs was squatting on the ground. A man in plainclothes and two women in police uniforms stood staring at the muddy ground at the edge of the playground. One of the EMTs squatted on one knee; another bent over something, pumping his shoulders up and down.

I walked toward the group as the school principal pushed his way through a group of kids standing near the glass door of the school. The principal scanned around, making certain he covered every foot of the play area. His face was pale and his mouth was turned down at the corners. He was looking for children. The front of his shirt had a bright spatter of blood running parallel to the buttons. His blue tie was pulled loose. He stood at the doorway, blocking the view of the children inside.

I nodded toward him and he barely let his eyes pause on me. "I'm locking this," he muttered as he reached into his pocket. He dug and dug in his slacks; apparently he couldn't find the key. "I'll lock this now," he said again, then he looked down at the blood on his shirt. "Oh," he said. "One of the children fell while running inside. She cut her lip . . . ," and his voice sagged on the last syllable. He fumbled in his empty pocket and started to cry.

I put my hand on his heaving shoulder. He reached up and took my hand as if to pull it off his shoulder, but he held it instead. "They shouldn't see me . . . like . . ."

"Just wait a second," I said.

"Oh Jesus . . . ," he moaned and wiped his eyes with the back of his wrist. "It's awful to say, but it could have been much, much worse. That officer just happened to be here. . . ."

I dropped my hand and he said, "I had a note from him. That boy. He said he was bringing a gun to school. He said he was going to give it to the cops. He said he was going to give it to our school personal safety officer. Why would he want to kill a policeman, for gosh sakes?" He looked at me as if I had just appeared. "I'm sorry, are you a parent?" he asked, trying to ease back into his official position.

"No. I'm with them." I nodded toward the growing crowd of people in uniforms.

"Ah" was all he said. Then, "We're trying to get them settled into their seats to do the final count."

"Do you know how many were injured?" I asked.

"As far as I know . . . just the one," the principal said, and he wiped his hands absently against his stained shirt and tie before he turned and shut the glass door without locking it.

Under the trees, two candy wrappers blew across the body of the child laid out on the blanket. Blood smeared his white skin where they had cut his shirt off. The top of his blue jeans was unbuttoned and his soft belly spilled out over his belt buckle. The men squatting around him were all in agreement that he had been dead before they had even arrived, and the police officers were now insisting that the scene not be any more disturbed. Sean Sands could have been a sleeping baby, but there was no peace in his expression. An alder leaf blew up against Sean's face, and one of the EMTs absently brushed it away.

"Nothing left now but to write it up." George Doggy was standing behind the EMTs. He was holding an AK-47 and had an empty leather holster clipped to his belt. The AK-47 had a skateboard sticker on the stock. I could read the words *No Doubt* from where I stood.

"You did this?" I asked him, not looking at Sean.

"I went to the trailer. I wanted to go through it once more. I found materials in the trailer which led me to think Sean might be meaning to do someone at the school some harm. Then I got information Sean was taking a weapon to the school. I came here. I saw him with this weapon." Doggy held up the AK-47. "He was walking toward the playground. He brought the weapon up and was taking aim. I told him to stop. He ignored me. I fired one warning shot. He turned toward me and I warned him again. He would not put the weapon down. I fired. I don't like it, Cecil. I never wanted to be in a position where I'd have to shoot that boy. I had no choice."

A wet gust of wind blew down hard. The men held on to their caps. The bloody gauze on Sean's wound flopped down on the blanket, and the EMTs snapped their cases shut. Police officers were spooling out crime scene tape and pushing back any of the people who had come to gawk. Parents pleaded to know if their children were all right, and volunteers were leading men and women toward the principal's office.

"The suspect was the only casualty," I heard one of the policemen say to a worried parent who had heard the rumor of a schoolyard shooting. "Lucky, really," the cop finished.

I grabbed George Doggy by the elbow, pulling him away from Sean's body.

"Who called you, George? Who tipped you that he was bringing the gun up here, and what in the hell was in that photo book Sean wanted so badly?"

"That's part of the investigation, Cecil. It's evidence and closed to the public right now. I'm telling you this because I like you, son. Just stay out of this for your own sake, for the sake of that little girl of yours. Stay out of this."

His eyes were tired and for the first time I thought I heard pleading in his voice. I knew he was telling at least part of the truth. I knew he didn't like killing that boy. Maybe it was a certain meanness in me. Maybe it was the fact that he had invoked my own baby girl. "You don't have the authority to kill a child, George," I said softly with my fists clenched.

"I know what I've done, Cecil." He looked down at me and now his sad expression was starting to make me tired. "He was going to open fire on those children. You want me to *talk* to him while he's dropping his playmates? You want me to *reason* with him then?"

George pointed down to the schoolyard where parents were gathering around the door of the school. Some were banging on the door, and the ones in the back of the crowd were standing on their tiptoes.

"I want to see that photo album, George," I yelled through another gust of wind.

"Go home, son," and the wind sucked away his voice.

"What did you do with Richard Ewers?" I asked. The gust was still pushing through and Doggy's hat blew off his head. He watched it tumble toward the swings but he made no move after·it. He locked his eyes on mine.

"I'm not talking about Ewers. I'm telling you to go home, son. You don't know what you're into here. Talk to me next week when you calm down about . . ."—he waved his hand in the direction of the dead boy—"about all this mess. Call me then, and we'll talk more about splitting wood."

I started to walk away. Then I went back to Sean. One of the officers tried to push me away and I pushed him aside. Somebody yelled my name. The green ammo pouch was lying next to Sean. An EMT's syringe lay on the dirt, and one dry end of the bloody gauze flapped wildly in the cold wind. I touched the boy's cheek. Then I buttoned up his shirt, and covered him with the blanket. A young cop jerked me by the shoulder and laid me flat on the ground. Another one kicked me once. I heard George yell at them to stop. I got back up on my knees. I understood why they had kicked me. I was destroying their crime scene, but I didn't care. I folded my coat and put it under Sean's head anyway. Then I walked out of the schoolyard against the flow of the concerned parents and headed downtown with the rain soaking through my shirt.

"Kevin Sands is not here, I'm telling you, Cecil. He made bail just today," the jailer said.

"Christ, that can't be true," I almost shouted at him. "Who put up the money for him?"

"Dunno." The jailer shrugged. "The detectives were in with him most of yesterday morning. All the time after you left here. Then, all I know is that he had the money. I had to cut him loose."

"Who brought him the money?" I demanded.

"I dunno, Cecil. Criminy, relax a little, will ya? You want to talk to some of the officers, you're going to have to wait. They're all up at the school."

"Did Kevin know about Sean being killed?"

The jailer was backing away from the protective glass between us. "He left before that call came in. I don't know where he went, if that's what you're going to ask me next."

I left the jail and started walking as fast as I could up over the hill and down through the woods. The trees in the old graveyard were sizzling and flailing their limbs. Twigs fell randomly onto overturned gravestones. Black birds darted through the middle story of the forest, where the whole environment seemed to have stepped on some kind of third rail. Everything was sparking with the energy of the coming storm. As I neared the harbor, I could hear halyards slapping against aluminum masts. The flags left on small fishing boats snapped a counterpoint to the hollow rattling. Gusts moaned through the rigging and through the electrical wires. Some fishermen were double-tying their boats, and some were bailing their skiffs. I ran hard down the ramp and turned right toward the last slip on the closest finger.

The *Naked Horse* was gone. Her mooring lines had been left on the dock. One of her bumpers floated just under the lip of the stall.

"He's one crazy character. I tried to talk him out of it," a voice called to me over the din of the gusts.

"Huh?" I asked the man I didn't recognize and hardly looked at anyway.

"Crazy sonofabitch came and cut away. Said he was headed out into the weather."

"How long?"

"Half an hour anyway," the man said, and hunched his shoulders against the wind and sucked on the cigarette pinched between his lips. "Could be a wild old ride." The rain came in spatters, but the drops hit hard. I was only a couple hundred yards from my house.

I ran out to the end of the pier.

By the northern entrance to the channel, the *Naked Horse* was pumping into the swell rolling just inside the breakwater. She was laboring into the storm, but from the dock I could see the *Naked Horse* lunging ahead as if she were a hobbled mare cantering onto a billowing plain.

Chapter Seven

Jane Marie was up on a tall aluminum ladder reinforcing the gutters. She saw me walking down the street in my wet shirt, and although I hadn't noticed it before, my hands had smears of Sean's blood across them. She waved her hammer at me, then she replaced the hammer in the loop on her tool belt and carefully made her way down the ladder.

"Hey, big guy." She hugged me and her old canvas chore coat smelled like the rain. I kissed her cheek and then pulled her close so I could smell the whole storm in her hair.

I hate telling Jane Marie bad news. As a child she'd lost her brother, and she has forbidden anyone to start a sentence with either the phrase, "You'd better sit down," or "I have something to tell you." But she can read my body language from halfway down the street.

"Sean is dead. George Doggy shot him up at the school. Looks like Sean was going to open fire on his classmates and George stopped him. He's dead though. Sean, I mean," I said, as if from my sleep.

Her arms tensed around me and she pushed her mouth down into the cleft between my neck and collarbone. She rubbed her hands up and down my shoulder blades and she murmured into my ear, "What in the world is going on in this town, Cecil? Has everyone gone crazy?"

She looked up over my shoulder to the eerie gray sky.

"That boy lived with every kind of bad luck, didn't he? Some of his own, and some of everyone else's," she said in wonder.

Todd stood at the top of the stairs looking down at us. He had an old movie camera in his hand. "I'm sorry for eavesdropping on you, but did I overhear that someone was deceased?" he said in his usual tone of open inquiry.

"Yes," I said, stepping back from Jane Marie. My nose was running. Janie kept her arm around my waist.

"Sean Sands . . . I was trying to help him. But . . ." I pinched my mouth shut, shaking my head. I wanted to say something more, but I couldn't think of anything.

"I see," Todd said. "Well, I was thinking about going over to Martin's house and showing him this new camera and seeking some advice on the final repair aspects. Will it still fit into the agreed-upon plans for the evening if I do that?"

"Yes, of course it will," I said.

Jane Marie and I went up the stairs. Jane Marie's nephew, Young Bob, was putting together a puzzle while he listened to the radio. Neil Young was singing through the cracked speakers of our old boom box on the kitchen counter. Wendell the terrier was chewing on the tip of Young Bob's shoe as the boy tapped his toe to the music. Blossom was asleep in the back bedroom.

Young Bob was ten and he was using the tip of his prosthetic hand to slide puzzle pieces into place. He had known Sean as an older kid and a distant kind of boy who evoked more fear than revulsion. Young Bob had never particularly liked Sean. Young Bob was being home-schooled by his mother this year, and for that reason hadn't been in school today.

Young Bob didn't look up at us when we came up the stairs. He stared intently at the puzzle and tapped his hook nervously on the tabletop. His expression was grim. We walked past him into our small kitchen.

"I'll have to talk to Bob about it, don't you think?" Jane Marie looked over my shoulder to where the boy sat tap-tap-tapping his steel hand.

"We can do it in a bit," I said. "Did you see anything of

Jonathan Chevalier today? His boat is sailing out of the harbor."

"In this weather? That's crazy. It's going to blow up tonight. Big storm. Seventy, eighty knots, they say. Are you sure he's headed out in it?"

"I saw him pulling out past the breakwater. Storm sails up. He was under way."

"Cecil, who's the doctor who plays in the band with Gary?"

"His first name is Clem . . . I don't remember but it's Clem . . . something. I forget. Why?"

"He knows Jonathan. They were friends when they both first came to town. Jonathan used to take this Clem exploring. They went all over in that boat. You could ask him maybe. The band is playing down the street tonight. I think they should be doing their sound check pretty soon."

I sat down on a step stool. Our old house swayed slightly on the tall pilings as each gust blasted the walls. I looked around the corner and saw the boy tapping his prosthetic hand against the table, while the strange terrier dog gnawed on his shoe. "It was just two days ago, all she wanted was my help. I was supposed to find her husband." I felt a sickness bubbling up from my stomach. "Maybe it's time to go to work for George, huh? What's so wrong with being a chore boy for charter fishermen?"

I couldn't say anything more. I kept hearing the tap-tapping of Young Bob's metal hand on the table.

"People dying, and I'm always too late," I said.

Jane Marie cupped her hands around my face. "Take a deep breath," I heard her say. I felt my lover's hands on my face and could hear her say my name over and over again but from a long way off.

When I was young we had a well in the back of our house. It was a deep shaft, down to where gravel gave way to a cleft in the rock and an artesian spring welled up. Once when I was ten I cut the rope that was laced through the rusty pulley above the well hole. I remember the silent drop, then the splash of the bucket that sent the darkness echoing. I also clearly remember my father tying the sawn-off end of that rope to my beaded belt and lowering me down into the well to retrieve the bucket. This is how I felt as I lay in Jane Marie's arms that day. I could taste the mud and sour ooze on my tongue as I looked up toward our ceiling. Jane Marie wove her fingers through my hair and kissed me. I half expected to see the profile of my knobby-eared father leaning over the edge of the well. He would be telling me that I had to learn from my mistakes, and his voice would set the black water echoing all over again.

I heard the baby crying far off, then a crashing sound, and puzzle pieces scattered across our wooden floor. Jane Marie left me for a moment. Finally I was able to breathe, and the world began to soak through with color again.

"Young Bob took off." Jane Marie stood over me holding Blossom in her arms. "And the little girl woke up. Why don't you hold your daughter while I go after Young Bob? You'll be okay, yes?"

I nodded and reached up. Jane Marie kissed Blossom's cheek and held her out to me, and then turned out the door toward where her nephew had disappeared.

This little girl could fit in a bucket. I usually had a strange feeling of exhilaration and dread when I held her, but today her body still had that sleepy warmth as if she had been lying out in the sun. Her strange dark eyes scanned around the room, and when I held my finger out to her, she grabbed on and put it in her mouth. Then I saw the blood on the back of my hand. My stomach churned and bile pushed up my throat. I jerked my finger back, and she began to squawk, her face turning a radish red. I balanced her in my arms awkwardly while I washed my hands three times with the hottest water I could stand. Blossom squawked and cooed when I sat in the chair and gave her my finger again. She held it, looked straight into my eyes, and for a moment I almost felt known. Her lips formed a tiny O as she yawned. She put the tip of my finger in her mouth and then closed her eyes. I leaned back in the chair. Neil Young stopped singing and I closed my eyes.

* * *

That evening we all ate dinner together. As Jane Marie dished out the halibut and rice, we felt the storm push in all around the house. Jane Marie had brought Young Bob back to the house and she led a discussion about Sean's death. I answered all Young Bob's questions about guns and what they really do to people. He wanted to know about Sean's injuries and I told him. We talked about self-defense and about the police. I didn't really know what to tell him but I tried to tell the truth. By the end of the conversation I think Young Bob felt more at ease somehow, or at least more able to look up from whatever puzzle he was working on after dessert. I felt sick and couldn't eat my halibut. Todd took my portion without complaint.

Todd had fixed the camera and was filming us around the room. It was an old camera with a huge floodlight on some kind of antler-type rack. He panned the room with light so bright it felt as if he were purifying the space of toxins. I lay on the couch reading *Out of Africa* and after he focused on me for thirty seconds I felt as if he were trying to cook me. I suggested that he film something else, and he was able to get some good footage of Jane Marie nursing the ravenous Blossom.

He filmed Wendell chewing on an old phone book Todd had rolled up and wrapped in duct tape. He had about ten minutes of the terrier rolling and barking when finally he turned off the camera and the room dimmed. He looked carefully at his old camera and said, in his well-paced voice which always sounded as if he practiced everything two or three times before saying it, "Cecil, I just wanted to extend my condolences to you on the occasion of the unfortunate death of that young boy."

"Thank you, Todd," I said, and closed the book lightly. I looked at Jane Marie and Blossom, then at Young Bob, sitting at his puzzle, and finally back at Todd, who was rocking gently back and forth. I realized that, like it or not, this odd group of people constituted my family, and I had things I should be doing so I could feel more worthy of them.

"I might take a stroll down to the bar," I said, as all eyes in the room, including Wendell's, came to rest on me. "You think that doctor Clem-something will be setting up down there?"

Jane Marie smiled and nodded sleepily.

I caught the Screaming Love Bunnies between sets. The crowd was small this early in the evening and the Bunnies are known for long breaks, so I was able to coax the drummer into a fairly quiet booth. Clem had already sweated through his shirt, and he was replacing the tape around the blisters on his fingers. This had only been their dinner set, but then the Love Bunnies are not known for their moderate-tempo material.

"Have you seen Jonathan Chevalier?" I asked him.

"Cecil, are you working? I mean, am I going to be subpoenaed or anything? I just want to know now, okay?"

"I just need to find Jonathan. I won't tape our conversation. I won't even write your name on a piece of paper. Just help me find him."

Clem smiled at me and nodded. "I don't really know Jonathan all that well, Cecil. I went out on his boat with him a few times. Something spooky about him. I don't know, something intense," he said, as he stripped off a narrow piece of white tape and then wrapped it around one of his knuckles.

"What can you tell me about him?"

Clem shook his head and rubbed his palm across his bristly hair, which appeared to have been freshly cut.

"I can tell you he doesn't like you much. Other than that, I'm his doctor, Cecil. I don't have permission to talk about certain things. You understand that."

I sat silently for a moment. "He's been giving money away on the street and besides that, I think someone may want to hurt him," I told Clem, trying not to make it sound any weirder or more dramatic than it was.

Clem walked away from the table. He moved a cymbal stand and adjusted his drummer's throne. I was about to get up and leave when he abruptly walked back to the table.

"Let's just talk theoretically, all right, Cecil? Just theoretically, you understand me?"

I nodded that I did.

"Let me tell you about people who are manic-depressive."

"All right," I said, as the barmaid brought Clem's soda and my ice water. He watched her walk away before he started speaking again.

"Okay. Manic depression is properly called bipolar disorder. It is treated almost exclusively with lithium. A patient with this condition has uncontrollable variations in their moods. Let's say we're dealing with a male patient. . . ."

The doctor/drummer paused and stared at me to confirm that our understanding was intact. I returned the doctor's stare and said nothing as he continued with his hypothetical diagnosis.

"A patient like this can be debilitated by despair and then swing the other way and live in an almost frenetic elation. Both states make it hard to function."

"Is the patient aware of this erratic behavior while it's happening to him?"

"Think of it this way, Cecil. Psychosis is a condition of disordered thinking; mania is disordered moods. He sees what we do and hears what we do, but he feels differently than we do about these things. So when he is swinging into a high, he knows it, but it *feels* so good to him that often he convinces himself to stay off his meds. At the upper reaches of the manic highs there is often ideation which becomes disjointed or unconnected. But he's not crazy really, he's just happier than it is normally possible to be."

"What happens if he goes untreated?"

"Well, judgment is often bad. There are feelings of invulnerability, of increased prowess in almost all areas. Some people hurt themselves this way—diving off cliffs and such. But some are artistic adventurers—painters, sculptors or musicians."

Here the doctor smiled and tapped his drumsticks on the tabletop.

"I've seen some interesting paintings recently," I offered.

"I bet you have!" Clem exclaimed. "They can be wild. In

an agitated state, a patient might not sleep for forty-eight or seventy-two hours. His painting will seem an ecstatic expression of genius. Sometimes the work will bear the mark of the genius's ecstasy; think of Van Gogh. But often, with others, their paintings remain only—what?—artifacts of their elevated mood. He feels like a genius. But that's not really enough, is it?" The doctor cracked his knuckles, then grabbed the sticks he had thrust down in the booth cushions, twirled them once and tapped a rhythm on the tabletop.

"Will he hurt himself? Will he hurt anyone else?"

"There is nothing in this disorder which marks a person as more or less violent. That's a function of other things. Like I said, Jonathan doesn't much care for you or the police. But again, who can say?"

Clem played a complex rhythm with his fingers and looked down at the bouncing tips of the sticks.

"In a severe upswing he could be a danger to himself if he takes risks he is not prepared for," Clem said down to the tabletop.

"I think Jonathan has taken his sailboat out into the storm."

Clem didn't say anything for a moment. He stared down at his taped hands. "Okay," he finally offered. "I mean, Jonathan is supposed to be a good sailor. But this storm is a whopper, isn't it? It could be a good example of the kind of bad judgment we were just talking about. We should get him back."

"How long will he be on the upswing?"

"Theoretically?" Clem smiled a moment and then he pushed on, tired of the pretense. "Look, if Jonathan is sick, find him and bring him to me. It's hard to tell what kind of danger he is in or how long this will last. Weeks maybe. The body usually can't sustain the rigors—lack of sleep and the exertion that extreme elation demands—for long. He'll exhaust himself and then he'll crash. If he is untreated then, that is the time to be concerned about self-destructive behavior. The lows are proportionally low, and often the circumstances—the disarray, the alienation in the wake of the high—conspire to make it harder for a person to recover."

Jay, the guitar player, walked past the table and signaled that they had better start playing. Doug and Vern both walked in with their guitar cases. Gary waved from the corner of the tiny dance floor where he had just finished tweaking the sound system. Mary thumped a short riff on the bass. Sitka's own Screaming Love Bunnies were chomping at the bit.

Clem stood up from the table and took a step toward the band, then came back, putting a hand on my shoulder. "Do you think you can bring him back in?"

"I'll try," I said without looking up into his face. But then I added, "Do you know anything about the money Jonathan has come into?"

Clem smiled. "I saw him a couple of days ago—socially, you know—at the coffee shop. I could tell something was going on with him. He was 'up' and I asked if he was taking his lithium and he said he was fine. I should have known he was headed for trouble." Jay played a G chord and stared at Clem. Gary started honking his A harp into the green bullet mike.

"Anyway . . ." Clem waved at his bandmates and then turned back to me. "Jonathan said he had to clean up his boat. Get ready for a trip. That's all."

"Did he say anything about Richard Ewers?"

The band was tuning and the noise in the bar was building. Clem cupped one hand to his ear and said, "Ewers?"

I nodded and the doctor shook his head. "That name is familiar to me somehow but I can't really remember why. Wasn't he a politician or some rich fisherman?"

"Close. He was an accused murderer. He was a crewman on the *Mygirl*. He was found not guilty for the killing of Chevalier's little brother. I worked for Ewers. I helped walk him out of jail."

"Well, that would explain Jonathan's attitude toward you." He watched me as if he thought I was probably making that last part up. "Anyway, Jonathan gave me a hundred-dollar bill and thanked me for everything." The other band members were starting to chant Clem's name into their mikes.

"Why'd he give you the hundred?" I asked as he walked away and sat squarely behind his drum kit. *"Why'd he give you the hundred?"* I yelled across the bar.

Clem clicked his sticks together, giving the Screaming Love Bunnies the time. "He said that I probably needed money and that he didn't have any use for it," Clem said into his vocal mike, and then began the backbeat. The Bunnies ripped into a cover of a song by Southern Culture on the Skids, and people streamed onto the floor in front of the band.

The Pioneer Bar is a classic waterfront bar, but it's not set up for dancing. The Screaming Love Bunnies were set up right on the linoleum floor where the pool table usually sits. There's no riser and certainly not a stage. The musicians stand on the floor with their backs against the two walls of the far corner. Even so, there is only about a ten-by-ten area to dance. As a result, just a few people make a crowd, which I've noticed is pretty true all over Alaska. I had to dance my way through the tight mass of athletic young women dancing with their eyes closed and their hands raised above their heads, and around the young men with ball caps, laughing and clutching their beer bottles as they careened around the floor bumping into the band equipment. I fought through the dancers toward the cool air in the back alley. Gary was blowing a solo on his A harp and trying to steady his music stand with his feet while a young woman spun around and around in front of him, bumping the music stand with each rotation. I waved at him, but he was busy so I headed home.

The wind was blowing much harder now and more steadily. A garbage can rolled down the middle of Katlian Street and a plastic fish box from the fish plant cartwheeled end over end down the sidewalk. Streetlamps trembled in the wind. The whole street seemed in motion. A fat dachshund named Hogan barked at the skipping shadows near his doghouse and pulled incessantly at his chain. A panel truck rolled slowly down the street rocking from side to side. The wind was howling in from the southwest now, and after it hammered against the houses and the panel truck, the gusts seemed to rise straight up through the thin light and disappear into the dark.

In *Out of Africa*, the Baroness wonders if Africa would know a song of her, and if the full moon would throw a shadow that was like her over the gravel of her drive. I had always been struck by the sadness of that question, but what if Katlian Street tonight, this crazy dog, and the wind blowing garbage cans down the middle of the street, what if this was like me? What if this was the song that Alaska was singing of me?

I locked the door to my house against the wind. The storm was supposed to last until late tomorrow night. I listened to the sounds around the house. Todd's radio was on in his room. The refrigerator hummed. The old house creaked on its pilings and I could hear the waves slapping against the rocks beneath the floorboards. I unlocked the door and checked our skiff, which was hauled out on a ramp under the house.

The tide was high, so the storm was pushing the waves farther up the ramp than usual. Some small waves were dumping into the stern of the skiff. I made sure the drain plugs were out and used the old plastic bleach bottle with the bottom cut out to bail water from the outboard well.

Jane Marie had ordered the yellow skiff from a researcher in Mexico. It was a twenty-three-foot Panga open boat with a short canopy for storing gear. The Panga was made of fiberglass with a self-bailing deck so water would run out the aft drainholes while the skiff was running or at anchor. Jane Marie had named the skiff *Amelia*, and she was a stout runner: her high bow and narrow beam made her good for launching through the surf down in Mexico. Her design also made her stable running into the weather. As long as you didn't overload her and kept good headway with the engine running, *Amelia* would stay upright and keep you off the beach.

She was taking a little bit of a beating in the storm, so I cranked the windlass attached to the front piling and pulled her higher up the ramp. I secured the stern with a line on each side and doubled up the bow line. I patted her hull and murmured "goodnight" before I turned to go inside.

Jane Marie met me on the upstairs landing. Her flannel robe was belted loosely around her waist. Her black hair was mussed around her face. "How's the skiff?" she asked sleepily.

"Good. I just pulled her up a little and put a couple more lines on."

She put both arms around my neck and pulled me close as if we were dancing to the faint sound of the Love Bunnies down the street. They were playing "Got My Mojo Working," and I could make out the guitar and harmonica but not the vocals. Clem's drumbeat hit the house like rain.

"What are you going to do tomorrow?" Jane Marie whispered in my ear and pushed against me. I reached inside her robe. Her skin during the pregnancy was as soft as anything I had ever felt and it remained so.

"I've got to get hold of Harrison Teller. I've got to get access to the Ewers file. I also need to try and track down some people in Ketchikan." She was kissing my ear now, and I ran my hands over the small of her back and down her hips, cupping my palm on the outside of her leg. She raised her other leg up into me and backed me against the wall.

"Do you think Teller will know anything about where Richard went?" she said between kisses.

"He must. Teller saved Richard from a life sentence. He would confide in Teller if he would anyone," I said. Then I kissed her back for a long moment.

"Ewers is probably fine," I said, not believing it.

Jane Marie is a particularly good kisser, in almost any weather: slick, shivery kisses out in the snow, or those rare, sun-warmed kisses on a beach towel. Honestly, she excels at both.

Soon I was thinking about what I could do to improve my own kissing ability and not about Richard Ewers or what I was going to do in the morning. I kissed down her neck to the soft cleft of her shoulder.

"I do love you, Cecil," she said.

"Thank you," I told her skin.

She leaned my head back and cupped my face in her hands. Her breath was warm. Her hair was a wild spray around the sparkle of her eyes.

"Are you getting in trouble?" she asked.

"Can you help me get through this?"

"Get through what, baby?" she responded.

I kissed her and could taste the ocean on her lips. "I just don't want to dream tonight," I said.

"I'll try," she answered, pulling me toward our bedroom.

"I love you too, you know," I said, as she undid my shirt.

"Of course you do" was all she said as she shucked off her robe.

What do the gods see when they are looking down at a man and woman making love? Two creatures without fur or feathers facing one another, paddling around in their own shallow reflections, odd white elbows flapping around? I don't know. But that night our bed was a warm pool easing over every centimeter of our skin. We licked and stroked each other, saying each other's name in the dark, filling each other up as if we could pour ourselves back and forth, spilling and refilling our bodies over and over again.

The baby started to cry from her bassinet moments after we came to rest. I got up and brought her into our damp bed and put her between our slick bodies so she could suck at her mother's breast. We sheltered her there in that warm bubble defined by our bed. This bubble could have been our universe as I slept, except for the storm blustering around our house and pulling at the rusty nails in the roof, and if those capricious gods were watching us there in our drowsy bed, I hoped they were disconsolate with envy.

That night I dreamed I was walking through the hull of a boat. I was holding a gun and children were screaming. The shots rang so loud they made my nose bleed and the deck was slick with blood. I heard a young boy whimpering until a banging like nails being driven into metal stilled the boy's voice. The darkness was silent for a moment, then came the rumble of flames.

I heard a sharp knocking. I was still sleeping and thought it was more gunshots on board the *Mygirl*. Or it could have been gunshots from the playground over the hill. The swings were empty and creaking back and forth in the wind. The banging kept on but finally it popped the bubble of our warm bed, and I could tell it was someone at our front door. The knocking would not stop. Just as I lifted myself on one elbow I heard Todd's padded footfall as he walked down the stairs and opened the door.

I cupped Blossom's head in my right hand, feeling her breath on my palm, touching her ear and curling my knuckle against her cheek. I heard a man's voice turn into a thudding commotion on the stairs.

Then I felt the crack of a gunshot shake our bed. Someone fell on the stairwell, and Blossom wrinkled her tiny face like a walnut and started to wail.

Chapter Eight

Kevin Sands was standing over Todd with what looked to be a forty-four-caliber handgun pointed at Todd's head. There was a hole in the stairs inches from Todd's hip. He lay propped up on his elbows with splinters of wood on his pants. His eyes were wide with a distant kind of concern.

"I am not fooling around here," Kevin said evenly.

"It would appear not," Todd said in a soft voice.

I stood at the top of the stairs in my underwear and T-shirt. Jane Marie locked herself in the bathroom with the baby, or so I assumed after I heard her footsteps and the rattle of the lock. There was a window in the bathroom that led to the shed roof from which she could reach a fire ladder if necessary.

"Jesus Christ, Kevin. Why are you shooting up my house?" I said, in what I hoped was a jocular tone.

"You and that cop shot my brother." The gun in Kevin's hand wavered in the air. A forty-four is heavy, and Kevin was trying to hold it in one hand at arm's length. His left hand was on the doorknob, in case he had to run out the door, I suppose.

"I liked your brother, Kevin. I had nothing to do with shooting him." I took one step down the stairs.

"Everyone is saying he was going to shoot some kids.

That's crazy. Sean would never shoot those kids. He's not that kind of boy. He's disciplined."

Kevin's voice was less angry than mournful, the words choppy and blunt. His pale face was blotchy from crying. His chest heaved. "I need the money. I took the risks; I deserve my share and I'm not going to take the fall for all of it. No fucking way. I need to get that money, and I need George-fucking-Doggy off my back." Kevin coughed, blowing air out of his lungs as if he were a weight lifter willing himself to work through the pain.

"We can talk to Doggy. We can work this out with Ewers, Kevin." I was fishing, and Kevin looked at me as if I were a phantom floating above him.

"Nobody's working nothing out with Ewers. I fucked up big time, I mean big time. The only chance I have of working something out with Ewers is if I find Jonathan. I've got to find him. I've got to find him today." The gun seemed to be pulling Kevin's arm down toward the steps. Todd watched the end of the barrel as it traced down past his knee toward his foot. Todd started to sit upright and Kevin pulled the pistol's hammer back.

"Listen, Kevin," I said, sitting down on one of the stair treads, "can you put the gun away? I'm with you on this. I want to find Jonathan just as much as you do."

"Why?" he spat out, and he raised the gun up toward me.

"His doctor asked me to. Jonathan is sick. He needs to come in for his medication. He might be in big trouble if we don't find him."

"He's in big trouble all right," Kevin snorted and then uncocked the gun. Todd sat up and started pushing himself backwards up the stairs.

"We were counting the money. That's all I'm telling you. We were supposed to be alone. Ewers's wife came in. Fuck, man, I told you this. She was screaming. She wasn't supposed to be there. She didn't know the story. Shit! I got that money straight up. It was mine. Sean didn't know a thing. I was supposed to protect him. Then the cops came breaking through the door and things got way crazy. I didn't know it was the cops. At first I thought it was someone else. I didn't even see her get shot. I was pushing Sean out of the way. That fucking Chevalier just grabs the money and dives out the back window."

Kevin was leaning against the doorjamb, breathing hard, and I walked slowly down the stairs toward him, stopping when I reached Todd sprawled out on the stairs. Todd was listening intently to Kevin, but I could feel him shaking as I eased past him on the narrow stairwell, placing my right hand on his shoulder.

Kevin took a long breath and raised the gun back up, pointing directly at Todd's head, about four feet away from the end of the muzzle.

"Everything was working fine until you came on the scene, Cecil. You and George Doggy show up and people start dying. I don't get it. But you are out now . . . you understand me? You are off this case." His eyes narrowed and he pulled back the hammer on the gun once more. "I'm going to find Jonathan, and I'm going to take this retard with me. You follow me, or I get wind of you doing anything about me, the money, or Richard Ewers, and I'll kill your roommate here. Nod your head so I know you understand."

Todd's expression didn't change appreciably. I don't think he was offended by the term "retard." I'm not even certain he knew to whom it referred.

I lifted up my hands to Kevin. "Listen, please. Todd is innocent in this, Kevin. We . . ."

Kevin lunged forward, jutting the barrel of the gun up under my chin. He pushed it so hard it forced my tongue back into my throat. His voice was a tight vent of steam. "Don't even say the word 'innocent.' Sean is dead. You were snooping around our trailer the day before he got shot. My neighbors saw you. You got their dog barking when you crawled out from under my trailer. I know you know about that gun, Cecil."

The barrel of Kevin's pistol was long enough that I could clearly focus on his hands around the grip as he pressed the gun into my throat. His knuckles were white, his index finger tight around the trigger. I thought I saw the hammer lift from its position. A forty-four slug would push a large chunk of my head onto the back wall of the stairwell, leaving my face a flabby Halloween mask. I cleared my throat.

"That was Sean's gun, Kevin. You know that," I whispered.

Kevin's eyes narrowed to black beads. I could smell the stale tobacco on his breath. "That wasn't Sean's gun and you know it. You fucking well know it. Sean was taking that gun to the police. That's why he was killed. All I need is for you to keep out of it. I just have to get to Jonathan and get back the money and the rest of it."

"I have no idea why you think I'm in on this." I was stammering now, trying to get my mind on some soothing subject, something that would relax the mechanism on the forty-four.

"I'll help you, Kevin. Don't take Todd anywhere. I'll help you." I was having a hard time breathing.

"Like you helped Ewers?" Kevin spat out.

I could hear every movement in the house, the fan in the heater, the ticking of rain on the tin roof. Jane Marie stepped out of the bathroom and I heard her voice just around the corner. "Cecil . . . ? What the hell is going on?"

"We're just working some things out," I called up to her. "Just wait there, okay? Don't come down just yet." I heard the bathroom door shut and the flimsy door lock click again.

"I don't need any help from you. I need the money and I need that old cop off my back. It's just between us, the old cop and me. You have to stay out of this, don't you see? You have to stay out. You are off the case." Kevin grabbed Todd by the elbow. "You can come with me. You'll be fine. We're going on a boat ride." He was speaking to Todd, but was looking at the gun.

Todd took several steps forward. Our rubber boots were piled on the floor and Todd dutifully put on his red rubber boots and then his parka with the attached hood. Then he stood flat-footed and ready to go. He was staring straight into my eyes, looking for reassurance that he was following the rules. Kevin lowered the gun to waist level.

The bore of a forty-four is so huge that when it's pointed at you it seems like a weird flashlight that only casts a shadow. I tried to will my body to lunge at Kevin as he opened the door, but I felt the shadow of a gaping hole in my chest.

Todd stood out in the street. It would not have occurred to him to break and run. He put his hood up to the wind. I could see a piece of newspaper blow past. Kevin waved the gun in my direction before he forced it into an inner pocket of his fisherman's coat. "You call the cops, I'll kill him. You follow me, I'll kill him. I'm serious. I've got no family left. I've got nothing to lose. I'm going to get all of it back. If I don't, I'll just have to kill George Doggy. But you stay out of it. Don't choose this time to make believe you're a real detective. People die when you play detective, Cecil."

Kevin shut the door and I was left standing alone. Upstairs I heard the bathroom door open tentatively. "Are you all right, Cecil?" Jane Marie's voice was reed thin.

"Kevin Sands has taken Todd. He says he's going to kill him if I follow," I said, as I slumped down on the stairs.

"You're joking." She stood with Blossom in her arms at the top of the stairs.

"No. I'm not." I rested my face on my knees.

She came charging down the stairs and stepped past me. "If *I* catch that little shit, he'll be dead."

She was halfway out the door in her robe, still holding Blossom in her arms. I grabbed the hem of her robe.

"Cecil, we can't let him take Todd out of here! I have plenty of sympathy for Kevin. But I'm going to rip his heart out for this."

The woman I love does not mince words.

I walked with Jane Marie back upstairs and called Lieutenant Pomfret. The storm was reaching its full peak now. I saw some lightning to the west and powerful gusts of wind pounded against our poor wooden house, rattling the plates in the cabinet and twisting the house's frame on the pilings, causing ancient dust to sift down from the upstairs floorboards into the living room. No boats were in the channel, which was lathered with whitecaps.

Pomfret was hard to reach, and I kept getting jockeyed back and forth to the desk officer. I was told Pomfret was in a "task force" meeting, but no one would offer any explanation of what that meant or why he couldn't take my call. By the time Pomfret did answer, he sounded tired, and he was more polite to me than I was expecting.

He took all the information about Todd's kidnapping, from the events of the morning down to the caliber of Kevin's gun, the threat against Doggy and the direction I thought they might have been headed. Pomfret was alert and his voice showed concern. He also started recording our conversation, which I knew because of his clumsy pause and the plastic rattle of his fumbling for a tape in the background. He interrupted himself several times and spoke to the dispatch sergeant, playing this like the hostage situation it was, but still I had a hard time knowing if he was taking my call seriously or not. He came back to me and took down more background information about Todd. He needed an exact physical description: age, height, hair color, clothes and such. Then Pomfret asked me if Kevin was alone, which he had been. But the next question stuck in my mind for many hours. A gust was rattling the town and interference blew through the phone's connection.

"When was the last time you saw George Doggy?" Pomfret asked. His voice had a forced casualness to it. I told him I couldn't remember.

"Do you know where he might be right now?" Tension started to bubble up in the lieutenant's professional tone.

"Home, I expect" was all I could offer.

I heard Pomfret speaking to someone in the background about sending a unit out to Doggy's address. He was on the radio and was about to come back to me when Jane Marie turned pale and raised her arm toward the window. She looked stricken, and I followed the trajectory of her slender arm out into the channel, then hung up the phone.

Kevin Sands's fishing boat was churning through the channel. It was a Bristol Bay–style bowpicker. He had bought it for long-lining. It was aluminum with a low stern house and two massive engines. It could make twenty-five knots in good weather. I could see Kevin in the wheelhouse with the sliding hatch open to the foredeck. In the bow, pulling in the bag buoys, stood Todd. He was wearing an old-fashioned life preserver bunched around his neck. Back in the wheelhouse, Kevin was gesturing with something shiny in his hand. He was still holding the forty-four-caliber and probably telling Todd exactly how he wanted the buoys secured.

Jane Marie immediately called the Coast Guard. After several heated exchanges and transferring of her call, she was told that the Coast Guard would not intercept Kevin's vessel. She would need to talk to the Sitka Police or the Alaska State Troopers. There was a container ship and a commercial fishing boat foundering off the coast, and all their helicopters were en route to evacuate the crews. If the boat in question was in danger, they would have been able to get some resources to her, but they were not responding to any law enforcement matters when they had to deal with loss-of-life situations.

Jane Marie slammed the phone down. In three minutes Kevin would be beyond the breakwater; in ten minutes he would be moving past the sheltering islands; and in fifteen minutes Todd and Kevin Sands would be in the mouth of the biggest storm in recent history.

The stern of our skiff was swamped and partially shifted off the ramp. Jane Marie laid Blossom in bed and came down to drain the carburetors on the engine. She tied safety lines from the stern on both sides of the steering station toward the bow. There is no house or dodger on this skiff, which makes for a wet ride, but the lack of shelter gave the wind less to push around. She took the canvas tarp down and secured waterproof bags with survival gear in the bow. She drilled wood screws into the hatch where our anchor was stored, secured it with three screws, and then lashed a lanyard to a cleat. This lanyard secured a crowbar and some bolt cutters in case I needed to gain access to the anchor in a hurry. Jane Marie brought two survival suits and an exposure suit and threw them down to me as I mixed the gas and secured straps around the battery.

I put on the exposure suit, which is a thick pair of coveralls made of flotation material with an inflatable collar to keep my head up if I went in the water. I would wear this while driving the skiff. The exposure suit would keep me warm for a few minutes in the water, but if I was going to be in for long I would have to crawl into the survival suit, a Gumby-style, loose-fitting wet suit with attached mittenlike hands and a tight hood. Water trapped in the roomy survival suit would warm with my body temperature, and I could survive for hours in the forty-five-degree water. Without the suit, I could be dead within thirty minutes.

Jane Marie secured the survival suit bags on either side of the steering station, so I could pull the suits out of the bags by ripping out the tabs without untying the bags themselves. There was one suit for me and another for Todd if it became necessary. There was no mention of the possibility of a suit for Kevin Sands.

The preparations took more than half an hour. Our skiff could travel at about the same speed as Kevin's boat, but hopefully because of its narrower beam and smaller area exposed to the wind, our yellow Mexican skiff would be able to overtake him.

That is, if I could find Kevin's boat. He was after Jonathan and the *Naked Horse*, and there was no telling where the *Naked Horse* could have gone. If Jonathan was staying in his manic high but maintaining at least a semblance of good judgment, I was betting he would have gone straight out past the outer rocks off the coast and then set a course to the west-northwest that would take him out into the Gulf of Alaska. Here, his solid old boat could battle the storm on its own terms, far from the rocky shorelines that would splinter her hull like an antique chest of drawers in the surf. Once outside the bay, he could ride out the storm as long as the *Naked Horse* remained upright and watertight. The *Naked Horse* could probably even weather a knock-down or rollover and maintain her hull integrity. That is, she would stay afloat with an area for the skipper to keep dry. Even in the worst of it, it was possible for the *Naked Horse* to float like a coconut. The chances of survival for my skiff were much worse. If the engine kept running, I could stay upright in most of the worst winds. But I could not turn off the engine without risking being tumbled down the face of a wave, and once upside down, my open boat would float but would not right itself. Once our *Amelia* turned turtle in the waves, she would be prey to every breaking wave that rolled on top of her. At least I would have some hours to think about it. This was preferable to what Kevin's aluminum bowpicker could expect. His vessel was powerful and the engines were reliable, but if compromised by taking on water, she would float upside down for a matter of seconds, then go down like a brick.

All of these things kept running through my mind as I worked on tightening the engine bolts and taping down the latches on the engine cowling. The wind in the channel was strong and there was a short chop streaked white by the wind blowing off the tops of the little waves. The sea just behind our house looked like a dirty cement floor being cleaned with a high-pressure hose.

I wasn't feeling particularly optimistic about going to sea when Jane Marie brought down the last of our cold-water survival gear.

"Here is the emergency locator beacon." She held up the fist-sized packet with strobe light attached to the top. "I'm going to attach this to the top of your survival suit. If you go in the water, pull this tab and flip the switch. It will send the radio signal out. It will be secured to your suit. Stay with your suit."

She paused and studied me carefully. Her eyes were strained with worry. She didn't want me to go, but that not wanting was at the end of a long line of things she didn't want to happen. She knew I was going.

"If you are not back by dark, Cecil, I will get someone looking for you. If you are not back by morning, I will look for you myself."

She kissed me. Then she gripped the scarf around my neck in both of her fists and held me there for a moment.

She released me quickly and turned to attach the emergency beacon to my survival suit.

I loosened the bowline and we shouldered the bow of the boat down the slick log ramp. As the weight of the boat shifted down the ramp, Jane Marie began playing line out on the winch. I held a thermos of honey-sweetened tea in one hand as I teetered down the ramp in the exposure suit. I waded into the water as a gust started to swing the stern back toward the beach. I hopped onto the bow, rowed three short strokes to clear the skiff from the rocks, and started the engine on the first turn of the starter switch.

"I know you can do this, Cecil. I know you will find him," Jane Marie called out over a gust rattling down the waterfront. She waved three times, then walked away.

I listened intently to the outboard motor as I headed out toward the gap in the breakwater. The engine sounded strong and even, no missing or sputtering. I took the rubber plugs out of the stern so the motion of the boat could drain the water out. I also secured a bucket on a line from the stern cleat. The yellow boat twisted and bucked a little in the wind as if she were a young horse who didn't want to work. I increased the RPMs and she lined out a bit and settled on her course.

I increased speed and brought the boat on plane just inside the breakwater so we were skimming the surface of the water. As I turned to the west beyond the harbor, the bow was immediately buried in a six-foot wave. Water filled the stern and I gave her more gas, allowing the drainholes to work.

The wind traced white lines that looked like claw marks across the gray surface of the sea. I found a safe speed and a slightly quartering course. This made it a little easier to take the pounding as the skiff blasted over the top of each wave. I stood at the wheel trying to absorb the shock of each drop with my knees. Water began running down the inside front of my suit, puddling at my crotch before running on down to my boots. Both my watchcap and gloves were soaked.

Beyond the airport, the sea appeared to be an endless gray prairie with rolling hummocks of thatched white waves. A lone merganser jetted past me headed downwind, her short wings pumping furiously to keep altitude. The rocks of both capes to the north and the south broke with acres of white foam. At the crest of each wave the bow of the boat would lift slightly with a brief feeling of weightlessness before crashing down the other side. I could feel the shadow of each wave ease up my back as I sank into the smothering trough.

From the top of a swell I thought I saw the light of a workboat off to the west. Just a flicker of some sort of structure beyond the rocks was all I could make out before the bow shuddered into the wind and crashed down the other side of the wave. I noted the compass bearing and set my course. The boat felt smaller and smaller the farther I went into the storm.

The waves were two stories high. The sky was a distant ceiling overhead; milky clouds smeared toward the mountains of Baranof Island. At the top of the next swell I saw a flash of light off to the left of my heading. When I tried to correct my course at the top of the wave, I felt the freight train rumble of a gust, and *Amelia* turned sideways to the wave. I gave her more power and sledded down to the bottom where I buried her again as she clawed her way back on top. *Amelia* seemed as small as a toboggan, but it was the hills that were moving, sliding over and under me.

A black curtain of clouds billowed in from the southwestern horizon. Rain hit like pebbles falling from the sky. Now every gray surface was frothing white. The gust knocked hard against the hull of the boat so she groaned over, her rail almost buried. I eased forward on the gas, and broke over the crest of the next wave. She slammed down hard on the wave and slid to the bottom, and her bow was buried again. The deck where I was standing was suddenly awash with water. The skiff didn't rise as quickly to the next swell. I bailed furiously with my free hand. The rain stung my face like tacks. On the next roll *Amelia* groaned over to the lee and for an eternity hung on the rail. I pushed myself to the weather rail and reached across to bail where the icy water was gathering in the stern. Just three inches of hull cleared the sea where there should have been fifteen. More gas to the motor lifted her bow and water spilled over the stern.

Todd would not be liking this storm. I thought of him inside the wheelhouse of the plunging aluminum fishing boat. Todd's mind could not process this kind of circumstance. He was not particularly coordinated, and in his everyday life he was extremely cautious. He processed everything in his physical surroundings slowly and deliberately. He walked down the street flat-footed with his gaze directly forward and down, as if he were stalking a small animal in the path ahead of him. He would not register this storm with the kind of fear I was experiencing. The unfamiliarity of it all would cause his brain to short-circuit. He would be entering a state of pure physical seizure. If Kevin's boat sank, Todd would be found gripping whatever he had been holding on to when he first got in the boat.

I tried to pull into the lee of the outermost island near the final cape before I launched out to the open sea. I was hoping to find other boats crowded next to this basalt upwelling, but the island was a lathered chaos of white water. I battled the wind at my quarter to get behind the island, and just as I turned near the beach a gust slammed in, nearly rolling the boat over. As it righted, I felt sharp needles of pain all over my body and a clattering filled the boat. The gust was flinging rocks and sticks off the island.

I crouched down in the skiff until the squall passed. As I stood up, I spotted a small patch of water some fifty yards off the black rocks where the wind seemed to oil the water down and I could hold the boat for a few moments to bail and collect myself.

Out to the west the sea changed into bright peaks of motion. The wind was a constant rumble in my ears. It picked up elegant spumes of water, twisting them into arcs.

A swell curled in behind the island. Before I dropped down it I caught the glint of metal somewhere out on the gray sea, just a glint, and then I was down in the trough. On the next motion I looked in the same direction, holding my hands near my eyes to shelter them from the wind. The glint came from the sharp edge of an aluminum boat. It was impossible to tell how far away it was, for the waves built so tall it seemed as if space was collapsing in on itself. I thought of avalanches and the wetted manes of wild horses stampeding over cliffs. I was fighting a strange vertigo but I thought I saw the upturned hull of Kevin's boat wallowing at the base of a wave.

I gunned the engine and rode out past the next wave and the next. My only hope was to go upwind of Kevin's boat and then gradually ease back on its location while bailing hard enough to keep my own boat upright.

I don't know exactly how big the wave was that took me down. I just know it made the sun set, and the dark shadow of its trough filled me with a giddy apprehension. I asked more of the engine, and as we went up the front of the wave it felt like I was driving up a long steep hill. *Amelia*'s engine lugged down as the angle became steeper and we approached vertical. I was locked in fear and indecision, but then the storm relieved me of all my responsibility: the wave pitched out into a massive curl just above me.

It had the strange feeling of a carnival ride. As I passed vertical, I heard the roar of water churning toward me. I saw the windscreen break off and felt it hit my face. I could feel the boat falling more than seventy feet to the bottom of the wave. I thought of Todd, underwater, gripping the sinking rail of Kevin's aluminum boat. I thought of Jane Marie's misplaced faith in me, and I thought of our tiny daughter, as my fear gave way to a sickening regret.

Chapter Nine

When I came to, I was floating near the skiff, and there were athletic shoes floating in a calm sea. The sun was shining weakly through a high overcast. I was in a survival suit. I had no memory of putting it on, and my vision seemed intensely sharp, as if my whole life up to that point had been a dream and I was just then waking up.

I dimly remembered the fall and the sharp teeth of the cold water chewing into my body. I remembered thinking that there was something I should be doing as I tumbled over and over through the crush of the foaming wave, and I knew I would get to this important thing just as soon as I stopped falling. I remembered the salt water in my mouth. I remembered the burn of cold water pushing through my nose. I remembered reaching out my hands to grab on to something solid in the world gone to burning water.

But I didn't remember anything about the athletic shoes that were now bobbing around me on the easy swells. There were hundreds of them, maybe thousands, with knobby rubber treads and fat tongues flopped out like open mouths. The horizon was an etched line of blue, and I was inexplicably hot. I pulled the hood off my head. I looked around and saw gulls circling the tangled mess my life had become.

The *Amelia* floated upside down just three feet from me. A

loop of the safety line had tangled around my legs, tethering me to the skiff. I found all of this interesting but I kept staring at the athletic shoes. These were brand-new shoes; some were floating on their soles like little boats. Most were tipped on their sides floating half-full as if they were greedily sucking down sea water. They were black-and-white shoes with a red wedge up the tongue continuing back through the heel. Expensive shoes, I thought, for so many of them to be floating out in the middle of the ocean.

A gull flew close and dove at one of the shoes. I saw a small scoter beating the air with her stubby wings just above the water. As she passed me I could hear a slight squeak with each of her quick wingbeats. Then she was gone over the lip of the next swell.

"Strange," I said out loud, for no discernible reason other than the strangeness I felt at being alive and being able to see everything so clearly for the first time.

I heard the faint buzz of an engine. I splashed the surface around me, turning and leaning back in the water, but I could see only the angry gulls.

The overturned yellow hull floated stern-down, so I could slide up until most of my torso was out of the water. My suit bulged with water at the feet and the heaviness of my body pressed in on my bones. I felt bruising pain everywhere I had feeling. I unzipped the neck of my suit. I stretched my neck and looked around. The air was cool on my clammy skin and I noticed that I was shivering.

Far off, away from the direction of the sun, I saw a helicopter on a straight-line course running parallel to my position. It was so far away it could have been a dragonfly. With my hood down, I could hear the buzz and flutter of its rotors drifting away.

"Hey," I whispered in a voice that didn't sound like mine, "hey, come back."

I found the shoes comforting. They were all the same kind, all the same style. Floating there, they were just as lost and improbable as I was.

I couldn't untangle the line wrapped around my feet but

was finally able to rig myself under the armpits so I could lie against the overturned hull. Most of my chest was above the water and I was able to rest my head back on the bunched-up hood and close my eyes.

When I opened my eyes, the light on the sea was more intense and the shoes had fanned out around the skiff like a widening puddle. Everything—athletic shoes, seabirds, even the rippled surface of the gentle sea—sparkled as if lit by stage lights.

I heard a blast of breath somewhere around me, the explosive wheeze of a large animal. My body was stiff with pain and I could not stand up or crane my neck to see, but a huge mammal was swimming close. I heard the breath again, then again. Fifteen feet toward the sun, a massive head broke through a wave and a gray blocky form dabbled the surface. As it sank away I could hear water rushing in on its wake. There was another breath and another. Pure white gulls with black feet wheeled above me and the massive backs of the whales pushed toward me like islands magically being pulled along.

Four sperm whales tipped to the surface with great forward jets of vapor from their bulbous heads. They circled the skiff once, then dove. I looked down into the milky gray-green water. I saw animals the size of tractor trailers passing twenty feet below. It seemed to take minutes for them to pass: great long backs, furrowed and blunt. The water was alive with a snapping sound, and then the push of car-sized flukes. Water pushed up all around me, oiling over the surface. Then they were gone, and I closed my eyes again.

I awoke in the dusky light of a red sky. I didn't know if it was a sunset or sunrise. Black clouds flared crimson at their edges and the clouds on the horizon were streaked through with color. Something bumped into my leg and I was able to lean over to see what it was.

A blue heron floated in the water, her yellow eyes open and alive. She was twisted unnaturally on the surface of the water, unable to lift her wings, unable to fold them against her body. Splayed out on the water, she looked like a broken chandelier. Birds can be caught unaware by the intensity of a storm. The heron had probably been knocked down into the water by a gust and then flailed against the wind, unable to make her wet wings work. Her eyes flamed. The plumage on the back of her head fanned out in the water as she tried to kick away from me. I thought that if she could get on top of the boat at least she would dry out and perhaps be able to fly. I lifted her gently with my clumsy gloved hand and could see one of her long legs was broken like a twig. She hadn't the strength to lift her head as I held her body, but in one jerking motion I felt her rise up and then go slack.

Even through the thick rubber mitts I knew she was dead. "It's all right . . . ," I said lamely. I tried to wipe the tears out of my eyes but the rubber mitts made it ridiculous. Then, as a slight gust broke on the top of a swell, I let the heron go downwind.

A helicopter buzzed a long way off over my right shoulder. I lifted a mittened hand and waved halfheartedly as if to a passing acquaintance in the hall.

"Hey," I said to myself, "I'm over here." My throat burned as if my vocal cords were scabbed over. I rested my head back down on the deck and listened to the sound of the rotors thinning out into the hiss of the wind.

I turned and looked opposite the sun and saw the even horizon of the sea in a hazy gray light. Just beyond the tip of my foot I saw a distant hump on the horizon. The hump had a light emitting from it. The light was a strong beam as thick as a tunnel sweeping across the waves. The light seemed very near.

Without warning or flicker the light went off. I could see nothing on top of the waves except a few tiny dots I assumed were athletic shoes. I knew I was going to die. Surprisingly, I wasn't panicked, just a little disappointed. Then disappointment sank into a kind of relaxing melancholy as the cold clamped down harder on my bones. I decided to close my eyes again.

But before I could, as if from the very interior of my head, I heard the faint tangled rhythm of Latin dance music.

I closed my eyes to listen. There were conga drums rattling, and the churning of guitars, then the urgent pleading of a trumpet. I could feel light burrowing into my body, and I felt a lifting in my chest as if I were being pulled out of a deep, deep hole in the ground.

Chapter Ten

I could hear water slapping a hull just under the blare of music. I opened my eyes. The hull of the *Naked Horse* was lunging toward me. She had lost her masts, and her rigging was a snarl of loose hardware and wire rope. She had a short piece of broken spar propped up and lashed upright on the foredeck. A small square of sail billowed out from this rig.

In the stern, a figure stood at a tiller. The tiller was a broken piece of oar lashed to the rudder post. The figure held a bright spotlight and the Latin dance music seemed to issue straight from this light. Blinded, I shaded my eyes with my hand. The light clicked out, and I could clearly see Jonathan Chevalier standing in the cockpit, his hair flailing from his shoulders as he danced to the music blasting from the speakers he had propped up on top of the cabin of the crippled wooden sailboat. He was naked except for a belt with a sheath knife hung around his skinny white waist.

Much of the rigging on the *Naked Horse* had been sheared away. Sprung ends of wire rope dangled over the side. The storm rig was lashed with black nylon cord. Sailcloth lay on the deck, torn and bunched into awkward bundles. One corner of sailcloth was held full by a long wooden oar. Heaped on the deck were dozens of athletic shoes.

Jonathan waved to me as his boat eased up and around

into the wind. The forty-foot hull came gently to a stop less than fifteen feet from me.

"You don't look so scary to me now." Jonathan smiled and reached over to turn down the music. "Little windy last night, don't you think?" The music was now turned low, but Jonathan was still rocking back and forth on the balls of his feet.

"Hey," I finally managed to say.

Jonathan moved quickly around the deck, jumping and lashing things together. As the boat rolled in closer, I could see that he wore a pair of fingerless gloves and a scarf around his neck.

Jonathan tied a line to his belt and climbed down a narrow rope ladder in the stern. He dove into the water and swam to me. I thought he was going to beach himself like a magical seal right on my overturned skiff, but instead, he swam under and attached a line to a cleat, tethering *Amelia* to the *Naked Horse*. Then he pulled himself up on the skiff. He was shivering, but he seemed to be pulsing with energy.

"Cecil, I'll get you up on board. It's a mess down below, but we're pretty warm. You didn't come out here looking for me, did you?"

I gaped up at my savior. His hair dripped in the sun; his forehead was bruised, and I could see dark spots of purple on his shins and forearms. His skin was fishbelly white and rough with goose bumps, but he seemed strong as any wild creature.

"You looking for me?" Jonathan asked again.

"Yes," I croaked. Jonathan hooted with a wild bubbling laughter.

"Well, you're a little late, I suspect." Jonathan kept laughing as he pulled out his knife.

I pulled back from him but he leaned forward and cut the lashing away from my chest so I slipped down toward the water. Eventually he got me out of the suit and pulled the two boats close together. He nimbly passed a line under my armpits and pulled me aboard by using his hand winch and running a sheet through a block on the end of his makeshift boom.

Lying on a piece of sailcloth, I felt my skin begin to warm in the sun. Pain eased up out of my body into the atmosphere.

"Night soon," I said mournfully. I felt I couldn't bear the thought of darkness coming back.

Jonathan jerked around and stared at me as if he were thinking of eating me.

"Night? It's morning, man. Morning of the first day. You know what I'm saying?"

I didn't argue. It was morning. That was fine with me, if Jonathan could change the rhythm of the sun. That was fine with me.

Looking back on it, I realize I had been drifting in and out of consciousness and the entire day I'd experienced was probably just a few minutes of dawn.

"A container ship dropped some vans into the drink; I guess one burst open and spread shoes all over hell and gone. You know how much these shoes are worth, man?" Jonathan was sitting next to me.

My hands were soft and wrinkled from being in the suit; so soft, in fact, that I thought my hair was going to slice my fingers open. There was a lump just above my right ear. When I pressed it I felt a light crunching, as if there were a layer of dry paper under my skin.

"I've been netting up these shoes," Jonathan went on. "This is better than fishing. I mean, these are one-hundred-dollar shoes."

Shoes were scattered like dead birds on the deck: dozens of them of various sizes, but apparently all of the same style. "Do you have any matched pairs?" I was finally able to ask.

I realized I was still shivering even though the sun was a delightful balm on my face. Overhead a large bird with a short neck and long crescent wings drifted on the currents of air.

"Albatross," I muttered, and followed it out of sight.

Jonathan hopped around the deck. He had tied off a tiny triangle of sail by lashing the oar he was using as a boom straight up to the snapped-off piece of spar he was using as a mast. He was rigging to get under way. He prattled at me as he tied off lines and cut some away with the knife he kept on his belt.

"Why don't you have any clothes on?" I asked him dreamily.

"I wanted to feel it. You know what I'm saying, Cecil? I wanted to feel every ounce of that storm's energy. It was a rush. I was in it, you understand. It was a perfect way to go back to the beginning."

"Aren't you getting cold?"

"A bit. But I go below. We're really pretty toasty there. I can't start the engine because I fouled the prop when I lost the rig. I had lanyards and all kinds of shit wound around the wheel. I thought I had it cleared away, but when I started the engine I bent my shaft and sprung the only leak of the night. Right up through the stuffing box. But I had a big can of pine tar and I soaked a blanket and some other stuff and plugged up the holes. I was able to jam the goo down and stop the leak. Then I tacked some lead flashing over. We are tight again, but I can't use the engine. Doesn't matter now anyway.

"Why don't you go down and warm up a bit? Like I said, it's a mess, but we're doing good. We've got lots of fuel for the stove now that the engine's down. Lost the stack, of course, but I was able to rig it a bit."

I could see the open end of a soup can sticking up through the cabin of the boat near where he had his music speakers propped up. A fine diesel smoke came shooting into the air.

"It's pretty hot down there. You'll want to get out of those clothes and get dried off." He opened the hatch leading belowdecks and welcomed me down, but I was unable to stand. In my first attempt, I swung my legs underneath me as if they were newly carved prosthetic devices, and I clattered down on the deck. I pulled myself to my knees. Instead of trying to help me, Jonathan smiled patiently as if I were very drunk and he didn't want to embarrass me by drawing attention to my condition. I crawled over the deck and over more of the bundled sailcloth to the hatchway.

Jonathan was fussing with the sound system mounted on the ceiling of the house near the top of the hatchway. He moved out of the way and let me crawl headfirst down the ladder.

I fell the final two feet and found myself in a heap on the floor. Jonathan turned on the music and closed the hatch. Below, I could hear the hull of the *Naked Horse* lapping into the swells and from above came the blaring sounds of Jonathan Richman's band, The Modern Lovers, launching into a live version of "Roadrunner."

The cabin of the sailboat was a gloomy jumble. Six small ports let in very little light. The engine hatch was thrown open, and there was a strong oily smell. Books, charts, hand tools and bags of cereal were scattered on the floor. The stove was turned on high, and the old cast-iron stove top glowed cherry-red. It was, in fact, as hot as a sauna. I stripped off my wet shirt and crawled toward the forward bunk. I crawled under the table and over several thick art books flopped open on the floor. I banged my knee against a pair of bolt cutters.

In the hot and tarry space, I clawed my way up toward the forward bunk and was able to hang on to the lip of the bunk and pull myself up to the mattress. After three tries, I settled into the dark berth. Clothes were scattered on the bunk and I bunched them into a pillow behind my head. I listened to the waves lapping on the other side of the cedar planking by my head. The Modern Lovers seemed more distant now, but I could still hear Jonathan's bare feet beating a rhythm on the deck.

In the dark I heard a soft groaning. Not an arm's length away, on the opposite bunk, I could see a hump of what looked like duffel bags. At the far end of the bunk I saw a pale face with a pair of glasses peering over the edge of a blanket.

"Hello, Cecil," Todd said.

I have never trusted good news. I always thought that if I didn't see the cloud, there could be no silver lining. So when I heard Todd's voice, my heart sank momentarily because I thought for certain this was evidence that Todd's haunting had entered a new, more explicit stage. The next thing that came to my mind was that my injuries were truly as severe as I was beginning to suspect. This crunching in my skull was going to leave me with some sort of loopy, Oliver Sacks–style neurological deficit, and I was going to be the chapter in his next book about the private eye who sees ghosts of the people he has failed to save. Maybe Todd was dead. Maybe I was dead. It was conceivable that this boat was being run by a naked angel, and we were all being conveyed to heaven. It seemed a little less likely that the angel would be playing Jonathan Richman and The Modern Lovers, but who was I to judge?

The Todd figure spoke again. "We flipped over after a big wave filled up the bow of the boat. We rolled over pretty easily. We had caught up to the sailboat. Jonathan picked me up out of the water. I wasn't in the water a long time really. But I got cold. I'm just staying here in the bed. Do you think staying here in bed is the right thing to do, Cecil?"

I was able to reach over and touch Todd's toe. "Yes, Todd, I think that is a good thing to do."

"I had to urinate, Cecil. This boat has a bathroom but I don't think it's operational because I opened the door and there was stuff, you know, smelly stuff, all over. I didn't go in."

"That's okay, buddy. You can go up on deck and pee over the side." I was lying back down with my eyes closed. There was warmth and lightness easing around my chest and moving up toward my eyes.

"Well, I didn't really think that would be appropriate because I didn't want to interfere with the operation of the boat, and I didn't know the protocol for doing such a thing."

"What did you do?" I asked.

"Well, I don't know if this was the right thing, Cecil, because I know it's not appropriate, but, given this seems to be an extraordinary situation . . . I urinated in a pot I found and then left it in the sink. You think that will be all right, don't you, Cecil? I mean, no one will be . . . upset by that, do you think? I promise I will wash the pan when we get settled again," he said, with real anxiety building in his voice.

"Don't worry, Todd. I'll take care of the pan. I'll wash it out for you too. You did the right thing."

I hadn't let go of Todd's toe. It was warm, and I felt that warmth running up from my hand and through my arm. My chest was heaving.

"Are you crying because of what I did in that pan, Cecil?"

"No, Todd, it doesn't have anything to do with that pan. You've done a great job. I'm proud of you."

I let go of his toe and wiped the tears away from my eyes. When I looked at my hands, they were tinged red by the tears running through the blood scabbing over my face.

"What happened to Kevin?" I asked Todd.

"I don't really know, Cecil." Todd began to sit up slightly. "He got into one of those rubber suit things—"

"I don't suppose he helped you into one," I interrupted stiffly.

"Oh no, Cecil, he did. He gave me a suit, but I was . . . rather confused. I wasn't able to put it on. He tried to make me put the suit on, but I was afraid he was mad at me. He kept screaming about getting to the sailboat. He said he wasn't going to jail. I didn't know what to do. I didn't know the protocol. I just held on. So Kevin got extremely angry, and he was pulling something on the side of a white plastic barrel that was on top of the boat when the wave dumped on us. I never saw him after that. The boat filled up with water and then it rolled. We were close to this sailboat. Kevin had been yelling at Jonathan, but I doubt they could hear each other. The boat filled up with water and then . . . capsized. I didn't see him after that."

Todd reported the facts as if he were in a booth watching a soundless movie on the other side of the glass. I closed my eyes.

"Cecil?" I heard him say a few seconds later.

"What is it, buddy?"

"Are you sure it will be okay about the pan in the sink?" he said.

"I'm sure of it. You did the right thing," I said with my eyes closed. As the *Naked Horse* pushed through the swells, I could feel the rise and fall of her hull. I could hear the water pushing past me and the warm air licked me all over. I dreamed of Jane Marie, and I dreamed that there was a thread rising up out of my throat, floating around and around the cabin of the boat until it rose up out of the stovepipe and into the air above the boat. There were miles and miles of this thread tangled in the air. It twisted and knotted throughout the northern Pacific sky. My thread had packaged the clouds and was entangling seabirds in flight. Finally I could feel a tugging, and I knew that somehow Jane Marie had hold of the other end of that thread. I could feel her tugging on it, pulling her way toward me, slowly and patiently.

The hatch bumped open and Jonathan bounded down into the cabin. I could see him in the gloom, which had brightened a little now that the hatch was open.

He was shaking and trembling but smiling nonetheless. He was still naked except for the scarf and belt. His eyes found mine and locked down on them, and when he did, everything seemed so still we could have become detached from time, just frozen in the moment when he saw me and held me in his gaze.

"You know, Cecil, I am in love with the modern world!" Then he hooted and danced near the stove. I could see now that he was wearing a pair of the athletic shoes he had netted out of the sea. He was incorporating his shivering into his strange spasmodic dance. He stood so near the stove his bare legs brushed against the red-hot top. He jerked away and added that into his dance. The cabin was stifling hot now. I was stripped down to my damp underwear and T-shirt, but sweat beaded off me. I wiggled my toes and was able to pick up my legs and swing them over the edge of the bunk. I could just barely support my own weight. I found a small plastic bottle of apple juice rolling on the floor. I undid the lid and drank it down in several long gulps.

I threw the empty bottle on the bunk. I could see that Jonathan was exhausted. He had been keeping himself cold in order to stay awake, but even his clouded mind knew he was starting to wear down. He clutched at his face and pinched his cheeks. His hair was matted down and twisted in damp tendrils. His legs were beginning to give out, and I saw him slump down on the floor by the stove. The cabin began to fill with the sour odor of singed hair.

I walked unsteadily toward him and pushed him away from the stove and he jerked awake.

"I'm on watch!" he blurted. "I'm on watch!" His eyes were barely open. The heat seemed to be melting his resolution to stay wide awake and in love with the modern world.

"I think I can handle the boat, Jonathan. Get some rest."

"No!" His arms frantically waved around him as if birds were caught in his hair. "Can't sleep," he croaked. He slumped naked on the floor, the knife still in place on his belt. His body was giving out, and the expression "cracking up" came to my mind; for the first time it seemed strangely accurate to me, for it appeared as if his exhaustion was squeezing the consciousness out of his body.

Jonathan pinched at his face with dirty trembling hands. His hands scraped open the scabs so blood began to mark his face like some kind of tribal paint.

"No sleep. Must not sleep." His voice was quavering. His eyes were closed.

"Where is your lithium, Jonathan? I'll get it for you."

He opened his eyes and looked at me as if I were about to attack him. His hand went to the handle of his sheath knife and his eyes flared at me as if he were the lion in Rousseau's painting *The Dream*.

He wanted to kill me. I could feel it like the rage of the storm. I suppose he wanted to kill me because I wanted to wake him out of the ecstasy of his nakedness. He knew I wanted to make him reality's prisoner, all bundled up and anesthetized.

I held my hands apart and stood helpless in front of him. "I'm telling you the truth," I said apologetically. "You need your medicine. You will still love this world. I'm telling you the truth."

Tears tracked down his face and mingled with blood in the stubble of beard. He stared at me, then slumped over and pointed to a zippered bag laced onto a cord above the sink. He pointed to it in defeat as if I had beat it out of him.

"Oh, Cecil," he said, "don't you know that honesty is the last costume we wear?"

I found yellow pills and white pills. I even found little blue ones which I thought I recognized as tranquilizers I used to abuse. The pills were lying around loose in his zippered shaving kit. Seeing them there like ripe little berries and breath mints, I was tempted to take them all myself. But I didn't. The teakettle was off the stove. I poured some of the tepid water into a cup with a broken handle and gave him a handful of assorted colors. There had to be some lithium in there.

He looked down at the pills, looked around the boat as if saying good-bye, then popped the pills into his mouth and swallowed. I got him some clothes, washed his cuts, and then helped him into a bunk. As I headed up the ladder to the cockpit, Todd reminded me to dump out the pot in the sink and clean it. I turned around, gave him a thumbs-up, and as I looked back I saw Jonathan curled like a child on the bunk next to Todd, whose emotional vacancy seemed a blessing to me now. I waved and went on deck, and the first thing I did was dump Todd's pot over the side.

There were flat-bottomed cumulus clouds to the west. The sun lit the tops of them so they appeared like gigantic battleships floating in the sky. The sea was a flinty blue, rolling like a billowing sheet in all directions. Jonathan had lashed the tiller in place. There was a lot of leeway in this rig because the winds were relatively light and we were carrying a tiny bit of sail. We were headed slowly on a quartering downwind course to the southeastward, 180 degrees from the direction the storm had blown us out to sea.

I had found pants and a dry coat down in my bunk and I zipped the coat up to my chin. I searched through the dozens of shoes lying on the deck and found a left and a right that would fit on my feet even though they were different sizes. None of the electronics on the *Naked Horse* were in working order. The antenna for the radio had been lost, but worse, it must have come unbolted from its station because I had tripped over the broken casing while moving toward the ladder. The running lights and most of the bowsprit had been stripped away.

To the south of us I had seen helicopters transiting back and forth. I supposed they were dealing with the container ship. The helicopters were flashing their lights and flying straight, purposeful routes. They weren't looking for us. The *Naked Horse* limped along on the gentle wind.

I held the tiller for what seemed like several hours, but after discovering that the sunset was in fact dawn, my internal clock was broken. I tried to triangulate our location by lining up three distant mountain peaks and trying to spot a rough position, but it was promising to be a long trip because by my calculations the *Naked Horse* was standing absolutely still.

Soon Todd came on deck wrapped up in his warm, damp clothes. He didn't say anything to me but sat slump-shouldered in the cockpit and stared out to the mountains. He sat as if praying for almost an hour before he asked, "When do you estimate we will be home?"

"I have no idea, buddy," I said truthfully. "But we are safe for now."

The gulls seemed to have gone back about their business after the storm and a group of them were feeding to the west of us. A few gulls wheeled behind us, taking long angular dives back and forth across our tiny wake. Some sat on the water and by paddling hard were almost able to keep up.

Jonathan came back on deck. I estimated he had been below some five hours.

He said nothing to me as he lifted himself out of the house and into the cramped cockpit. "How are you, Todd?" he said, as he stepped over Todd's legs so he could flop down opposite him. Todd just nodded hi, not knowing how to answer the question politely.

"Well, I ruined my boat, didn't I?" Jonathan said.

"She's battered, but we're floating and under way. I'd say you did a hell of a job," I said, sounding a little Pollyanna-ish. Jonathan didn't respond. He kept rubbing his face with the flat of his hands. When he took his hands away I could see his eyes were deeply bloodshot and his hands were shaking badly. He was wearing a baggy fisherman's sweater and an old pair of woolen hunting pants. He had no shoes on, but judging by the condition of his feet, that was probably normal for him on board.

"I used to fish with my uncle," he said. "That old man was a righteous drunk. But he could catch salmon, I'm telling you. . . ." Jonathan let his voice trail off. We both watched the luffing sail.

Finally Jonathan got up to trim the rig but he kept on with his story. "We trolled all around southeastern, my uncle and me. We spent a lot of time up on the Fairweather grounds, but hell, we'd go all over. He was a good fisherman. Once he passed out in the tubs in Tenakee and I thought he was going to melt away or drown. I lugged him out of the bathhouse and loaded him into one of those garden cart things they used to have to get stuff to the ferry. I just slung him in there and took him back to the boat. My uncle loved the dream of his life, man. He loved the funky smell of his clothes, and I don't begrudge him that, you know? I don't begrudge him, but I never drank a drop of alcohol, you know why?"

Jonathan wasn't really asking, so he tore right on. "I never drank because I thought I might end up like him. On a wreck of a boat, you know, making believe that my life was an adventure instead of a smelly old mess."

I gestured around at the wreckage on the deck, then said to Jonathan, "Quite an adventure, isn't it?"

The sun was starting to send brilliant shafts of light through the clouds, which pooled silver on the glittering sea to the west. Jonathan's smile was a sad grimace as he looked out over the water.

"I hate taking these drugs," Jonathan said, and we sailed on.

After another hour or so, Jonathan brought up cups of soup and crackers. He also found a jug of cold water. Todd, who would usually drink only out of his own clean cup, swilled directly out of the jug, the excess sluicing down the sides of his mouth and onto his shirt.

Jonathan stayed silent. He would occasionally pick up a

broken piece of equipment, a cup or the radio casing, and he'd hold the broken pieces together and forlornly shake his head, then put them down carefully on some clear space on the deck and move on.

Finally, as we were eating soup, he spoke up again.

"You know, my uncle was drunk the night the *Mygirl* caught fire. Albert didn't like staying on the boat with him. Albert was a . . . good boy, Cecil."

Jonathan's voice drifted off, then he shook himself as if he were waking up. "We were in Kalinin Bay and had sold to the *Mygirl* just that night. We had been trolling on the outside and down into Salisbury Sound. We were catching lots of fish that year and the price was fine, you know. My uncle bought a gallon of whiskey and he sang 'Boy Named Sue' or some darn thing he always used to sing, and then he went to bed. Albert went to the scow. He hung out there because there were other kids. I took him over to the *Mygirl* in my uncle's little skiff. He was going to spend the night.

"It was later, you know, lots later, that I saw the flames come up through the windows. I was on my uncle's boat. I think I even heard popping sounds before the flames but I could never really be sure. I was asked about it so many times I couldn't ever really be sure. I got into the skiff and went over to see if there was anything I could do to help, but by the time I was within twenty yards of the *Mygirl*, that barge was burning so hot I couldn't get any nearer. Glass was melting down into the inside of her steel hull. But I saw that skiff pull away from the stern. His face was lit by the fire. He yelled over at me that he was going for help, and he took off out the mouth of the bay."

Again Jonathan stopped and he stared out at the sea as if he half expected to see the skiff operator come into view.

"You never fingered Richard Ewers as the skiff operator," I said. "You knew Ewers. Even in the dark you would have recognized him. Was it Richard or not, Jonathan?"

He didn't speak for a moment, and once again he rubbed his eyes with his shaking hands. "I wanted to help. I wanted to stop what was happening. Really, I did."

He coughed. "I sat down with a book of photographs

those cops put together. There were thirty photographs, maybe forty. I'd say more than half of them were of Ewers. A couple of the pictures were taken of Ewers when he was in the police station. It was a joke. I knew what the cops wanted from me. They wanted me to finger Ewers. The officer gave me the photo book and told me, 'We've got our prime suspect in here. You would really be helping us if you could pick out the man you saw driving the skiff that night.' I wasn't going to finger Ewers. All I could do was point to one and say, 'This one is most like the guy I saw.' Then they would let me alone. I had to give them something."

"But tell me now, Jonathan. Was it Ewers? You know. I know you do. I don't care anymore about the trial. Did Ewers kill your brother or not?" I asked him.

His glittering eyes scanned the sea. He did not look at me. "I testified at trial and they grilled me on both sides. The prosecutor only asked a few questions, but the defense attorney took me over and over every little detail. How many times had I been shown the photo book? How many times had I been interviewed? Had they mentioned anyone else's name other than Ewers's? Had they encouraged me to be more certain than I had been? None of that shit matters, Cecil. My story is my story. Nothing they might put in a fucking magazine was going to change that."

I sat without speaking. The mewing of the gulls seemed to crawl up my neck.

"So who killed the Sands family and your brother, Jonathan?" I asked him.

"Ewers wasn't convicted of it. That should have been enough for him."

Gulls worked the air just above Jonathan's head. Their broken singing seemed to set him on edge. Out to the south I saw a boat on the horizon, black smoke coming from her stacks. I raised my arm and pointed, but Jonathan started to talk.

"My story is my story, Cecil. Nothing new will help Albert now. Nothing new will help Richard Ewers either. I don't have anything else to say." Then his voice wore out and Jonathan sat staring down at the cuts on his shins.

"There!" I blurted. The binoculars were broken in half, but in the blurred circle of the monocular, I saw the wavering image of the *Winning Hand* steaming toward us. I saw someone at the helm on the flying bridge, and by the way the figure was standing and steering with one hand while she scanned the sea with her own binoculars, I knew it was Jane Marie.

I refocused: the image became clearer. A figure stood at the front of the bow wearing a bomber jacket–style float coat and a blue ball cap. This figure had bandy legs and walked the foredeck like a cowboy.

"I think George Doggy is with her," I said, and heard Jonathan go below. The *Winning Hand* was bearing down on our position and I watched as she grew larger in my vision.

I heard a clatter on the stairs. Then Todd cleared his throat and said, "Uh . . . Cecil." When I looked toward the hatch, I saw Jonathan standing there. He had a 30.06 hunting rifle in his hands. The rifle had a large scope and a leather sling. I watched him jack a cartridge into the chamber and level the scope at the bow of the *Winning Hand*.

Chapter Eleven

Y ou might wait for them to rescue us before you start
killing people," I offered, just as a place to start.
Jonathan's right hand trembled on the rifle bolt, and
I tensed to jerk it out of his hands, but instead he mumbled
something, took the rifle butt from his shoulder, then stared
at me with a cockeyed look that reminded me of his cat
chasing phantoms.

The *Winning Hand* steamed closer, wobbling on the
horizon like a toy boat. I waved and the figure standing on
the flying bridge waved back with a wide-arced, country-
style hello. Jonathan propped the rifle in the cockpit and
went below, still mumbling. With every passing moment, I
could sense him sinking deeper into the fog of his medi-
cated life.

"I wonder if they'll have a camera with them?" Todd
mused, easily gliding over the incident with Jonathan and
the rifle. "Seeing this boat in its somewhat dilapidated condition would certainly be worth documenting."

I took the cartridge out of the rifle's chamber. I considered putting the gun back down below, but I kept it right
beside me.

The *Winning Hand* seemed to glow white as she rolled
through the swells. Gulls cast their shadows on the water
as they dipped into her wake. Every moment of terror and

violence the sea had visited on me in the last two days seemed to be somewhere over the horizon.

I headed the *Naked Horse* up into the wind and lashed her jerry-rigged sail hard back to the stern so the sail acted only to position and steady the crippled boat. This would allow Jane Marie to bring the *Winning Hand* alongside more easily. I heard Jonathan clattering around belowdecks, and I slid the rifle a bit closer and wondered how long it would take me to jack the round back into the chamber if he came charging out of the cabin with another weapon. Jonathan was a long way from stable, and I couldn't quite predict his next move, but because of his fatigue and the lithium I didn't expect the next move to be either sudden or violent. Still, I didn't have much of a track record in predicting anyone's behavior in the past few days.

George Doggy was indeed on the bow of the *Winning Hand*. He nodded to me as the boat circled around our bow so she could head up into the wind and come alongside. Jane Marie, on the other hand, was jumping up and down at her steering station, waving and blowing kisses as she steered the large old fishing boat she had re-outfitted for her marine research. The *Winning Hand* heeled over as she made the turn, and then Jane Marie cut the power dramatically as she eased up alongside. Doggy put out large inflatable bumpers, tying them off to the handrails along the deck so the two hulls would not bang together.

As she came alongside, I could see that Jane Marie's eyes were red, and the crookedness of her smile betrayed a storm of emotions beneath it.

"There are my boys!" she called out over the idling engine. "There are my boys." Her smile turned down and broke as she started crying. Doggy threw a line, and I wrapped it once around a cleat amidships and absorbed the shock of the larger boat's momentum. Jane Marie dove down the ladder. She poked her head in the main cabin of her boat and slammed the door shut. Then she pushed past Doggy, jumped into our cockpit, and started kissing my face.

"Hello, you," she whispered, between slippery snotted-up kisses. "Hello, you."

It was when I felt her breath on my eyes that I started crying too. My face hurt from the bruises. My head hurt from her hands brushing against the swollen lump. She kissed me, and I was overwhelmed.

She turned from me quickly and sat next to Todd and started smothering him with kisses. He wiggled and laughed much like a puppy or a ten-year-old boy might, delighted, but still wanting to squirm away.

"Oh, you boys, oh, you boys, I'm never letting you out of my sight ever, ever, ever again," she cried.

Todd sat back away from her and looked at her with curiosity. That someone would be happy, loving, and crying all at once was something he could only comprehend in an abstract way.

"The harbormaster wouldn't let us leave the slip during the storm. He refused to let me leave the harbor. I'm not kidding. I'm sure he didn't have any authority to do that, but still. Refused. I left just as soon as I could. I can't believe how the wind laid down so fast. We've got swell but not much wind today." Her voice was prattling away almost more quickly than her mind could make sentences. She jumped over to me and touched the cuts on my head with her thumbs and when I winced she touched my face lightly with her fingertips.

"Why weren't you in the other suit? The other suit with the beacon? Everyone was wasting half the day trying to locate that beacon. It deployed when it pulled out of the pouch. We were chasing it around to the west of here, and then we just happened to see you a little while ago."

"The skiff . . . The *Amelia* is gone," I was finally able to croak out. "I'm sorry, but it's gone."

She kissed me on the lips and I thrilled to the taste of her: coffee, lip balm, and the hint of lemon drops. "We'll get another skiff. The Coast Guard said that you couldn't have made it offshore and that you were either dead already or would wash up on the shore of one of the close islands. They had no distress call from you. They had spoken with

Jonathan on the radio earlier in the storm, and he insisted everything was fine. That's why they wouldn't let us look for you. They had their hands full with the cargo ship. Did you see all the shoes? Isn't that amazing?" She started kissing me before I could answer.

I held her, with my chin resting on her shoulder, as we both took long deep breaths. "Where's the baby?" I asked. "Where's Blossom?"

"She's up in the galley in her bunk. She's sleeping. You know how she sleeps on the boat."

I wanted to move up onto the deck of the *Winning Hand* and go to sleep next to my baby girl. I started to climb up off the battered sailboat when I heard George Doggy's gravelly voice above us.

"Well, how are ya, fella?" I looked up, and the sight of Doggy was almost obscured by the sun directly behind him so that his voice emanated out of the halo of light. "We almost started worrying about you," the voice said. Then I heard a clattering behind me, and Jonathan Chevalier bounded up onto the cockpit seats, his red-rimmed eyes scanning the higher deck of the *Winning Hand* where George Doggy stood looking down on us.

"Hello, George," Jonathan said coldly. I saw the sun glint off the blade of the fillet knife he held in his right hand as he jumped between the boats.

"You planning on gutting some fish?" George asked the bedraggled man coming on board.

"No," Jonathan replied. Then he walked by the old policeman and straight into the cabin of the old seine boat.

"Now what was that all about?" Jane Marie asked Doggy.

"I feel sorry for that boy," Doggy said, in a less than sympathetic tone, as he pulled a leather sap out of his back pocket. He slapped the narrow finger of iron shot onto his palm. "But not that sorry," Doggy added as he looked past Jane Marie into the cabin of the boat where Jonathan was looking around for a place to set his knife.

Doggy looked at the deck of the *Winning Hand* as if he were weighing a question. "Just the two of you on board then?" Doggy asked.

I looked him squarely in the eyes. "Just the two of us, plus the skipper, George. Have a look for yourself if you want."

"No, I believe you," George said.

I lashed the towing lines from the *Winning Hand* through what was left of the bowsprit and secured them to the anchor post. I lashed the tiller in place so she would track straight in the wake of the old seine boat, then I pulled myself up onto the back deck. I was working slowly, trying to ease the stiffness and pain out of my limbs. I played the tow lines out as Jane Marie eased the throttle forward. Soon the *Naked Horse* moved easily astern, and Jane Marie increased the power and steered her course for the breakwater in Sitka. It would be a slow ride home, but we would get there in one piece. I watched the sailboat for a moment then turned, stumbling on an orange bundle lashed to the deck. I bent over to examine it and saw that it was a deflated raft. Jane Marie, who had given the helm over to George, put her hand on my shoulder.

"I found him early this morning. He was drifting to the west of here. The life raft must have tumbled like a barrel over the falls all night long. He was almost dead."

"Who?" I asked.

"Kevin Sands. I picked him up this morning. What could I do, Cecil? I couldn't leave him out there."

"Kevin's here? On board with us right now?" I asked, not really believing it. Jane Marie nodded, her expression a strange mixture of worry and wonder, as if she had won a prize she never really wanted: a bag of snakes or a primed bear trap.

We stepped into the deckhouse. George set the autopilot on the flying bridge and came down the ladder, following right behind us. The deckhouse contained the steering station and the navigation center. Jane Marie had a laptop computer set up on the chart table to the left of the small steering wheel, which was jogging back and forth under the pull of the chain-driven autopilot that steered our course. The depth sounder and radar screen were bolted to the ceiling. A bench along the aft wall served as the skipper's bunk.

There was also a table with one captain's chair bolted to the deck. This chair could swivel to face in any direction. Here Todd sat, piled up in his old clothes, awkward as a bag of laundry perched there. Jonathan was stretched out on the bench. Jane Marie glanced at him and shrugged. She looked at George Doggy, who was conspicuously silent, scanning the sea directly ahead of us.

"George, I don't understand. You wanted to find Jonathan. Don't you want to talk to him?"

"There's plenty of time for that," the old man replied.

Jonathan put his forearm over his eyes and smiled silently.

I moved past George Doggy without saying a word and stepped down into the steamy warmth of the galley. There was a compact cooking area within arm's length of a table. Here Jane Marie had built a small bassinet hung on two sets of gimbals, which allowed the weighted bassinet to stay fairly even with the horizon line. The little bunk was bolted to a pedestal at one corner of the table, out of the way, but still within reach of anyone passing by.

Blossom was asleep on her back, her arms pulled up on her chest so the weird little nubbins of her fingers touched her mouth. Her lips made a slight pulsing motion as if she were kissing the air or dreaming of feeding at her mother's breast. Her dark hair frizzed up from her skull like a tiny bird's plumage, and under her eyelids I could see the motion of dreams. The expression on her face changed every second. I imagined concern, then delight, surprise, relief. I watched her for a full minute until I realized that all of these were things I was feeling, and that I had no clue, really, about how to interpret her expressions. I spread my hand across her chest. My hand was weathered and scarred, and it looked wooden. I rubbed my index finger across the softness of her cheek.

Jane Marie handed me a towel and her traveling first-aid kit. "You better clean up those cuts and scrapes. Take a quick shower if you want to. We'll have enough hot water. I don't think anyone else wants to. I already asked Todd, and Jonathan is not responding to questions yet."

At the far end of the galley I took one more step down and looked into the forward berths just on the other side of the door to the head. There, lying in a pile of sleeping bags, was Kevin Sands. His eyes were open and he lay perfectly still.

His face was swollen and deeply bruised. His hair was a matted tangle. His lips were dried and cracked. He looked like a snake lying on a warm rock.

"It seems we both had some luck making it through that storm, huh?" I offered as neutrally as I could manage.

Kevin Sands closed his eyes slowly and then opened them again without moving any other muscle on his face. The *Winning Hand* rolled through the sea, and I balanced on my feet, swaying like my daughter's bassinet in order to keep my balance, yet Kevin seemed to be eerily inert, as if something burning inside of him could find the horizon without regard for sight or gravity. He seemed like some strange pivot point.

"Are you all right?" I asked him, but he didn't move, other than to slowly turn his eyes toward me. He did not speak.

I walked into the head to clean myself and dress my wounds. The water was hot, and I wedged myself into the tiny space, gently scrubbing the salt out of my eyebrows and ears. I sponged off and dabbed at my cuts with a clean towel and then peroxide. Water sloshed in the helmet-sized sink as I shaved quickly once and then more carefully a second time. My father's old shaving brush sat in the drawer to the right of the sink and the warm bristles were a comforting memory.

Jane Marie knocked and told me she had hung a clean shirt for me on the hook outside the door. I combed my hair, and when I looked in the mirror I almost laughed. I was feeling like Montgomery Clift, but in the mirror I saw a battered Wallace Beery. I put on my clean white shirt, drained the sink, walked out and touched my freshly scraped cheek against Blossom's face. I closed my eyes and felt her breath on my skin.

When I came up on the deck level Jonathan was sitting

on the bench glaring at George Doggy as if he believed he could turn the old policeman to stone.

Jane Marie stood by the wheel. She could make adjustments to the course heading with the autopilot's toggle switch mounted near her right hand. She scanned the sea ahead of her and pretended not to be paying attention, but next to her left leg, wedged down near a sliding door to the narrow deck, I saw she had placed a gaff hook, well within reach.

"I said, what do you know, George?" Jonathan uttered through his clenched jaws.

George Doggy stood on the other side of the pilothouse from Jane Marie. He kept his eyes on the course ahead.

"Not much. You?" Doggy grinned. Todd sat in the chair, rocking back and forth, lacing and unlacing his fingers. I crossed to him and suggested he wash up. Jane Marie told him she even had put one of his movie cameras on his bunk. When he heard the words "movie camera," Todd bolted down the galley steps.

"By the way," George Doggy said to Jonathan, "you don't happen to know where Richard Ewers is, do you?" Doggy rubbed a hand across his mouth. He had a day's growth of beard that was a sandy white on his chin and his eyes drooped.

Jonathan didn't take his burning eyes off the old man's. "You know, George, there's a lot I don't know in this life. I don't know what would have happened to Albert if he'd gotten the chance to grow up. I don't know what my life would have been like if Albert and me hadn't ever set foot near the *Mygirl*." Jonathan looked down on the deck as if he were looking back into the past. "I don't know where Richard Ewers is and I don't care anymore."

Jonathan stood up and his hands trembled by his sides. Jane Marie reached down and laid the gaff hook in plain view just next to the wheel. Jonathan glanced at the hook and then brought his eyes to bear on George Doggy once again.

"I don't know why you should be so worried about him, George," Jonathan said.

Doggy glared at the skinny wild man by the bench, then spoke to me with his old voice of authority. "These boys always think they are smarter than they are, Cecil."

"Uh, Cecil . . ." I heard Todd's voice come up from the galley. "Cecil . . . I . . . I . . ." Todd's voice was agitated.

I turned to look down the passageway, and as I did I nearly bumped noses with Kevin Sands coming up the stairs.

"Jonathan, what the fuck are you doing?" he asked. Kevin's face was a mess. The raccoon bruises around his eyes had flared into a bright purple. His dirty hair spiked. He shouldered by me and stood in front of George Doggy. Kevin was holding Blossom tightly in his arms.

"Listen to me," Kevin said in a voice that was clear and urgent, "I do not want to hurt this baby. I just want the money from this crazy fuck." He gestured toward Jonathan. Jonathan grinned and leaned back against the bulkhead, perfectly relaxed.

"I dumped it, dude. It's all gone," he said, smiling.

"All of it?" Kevin said, as if he were going to break into tears.

"Every penny."

"George, listen." Kevin gripped Blossom all the tighter and turned to Doggy. "This is not my fault. This is not my deal. He gave me the money, you know it's true. Hell, I've lost my entire family. I've lost everybody. It makes sense that I should keep the money. I didn't have a thing to do with your deal here."

George Doggy held up his hands to calm the young man down. He clearly wanted him to stop talking.

Kevin swung around to talk to the rest of us. His eyes were wild and I could see the muscles tensing in his arms, clutching the baby as she began to squirm. "I need to talk to George here, in private. I promise you I will not hurt this child." Then he backed toward the stern door to the back deck. Here he could see everyone on the boat. No one was at his back. Jane Marie walked steadily toward her child.

Kevin looked straight at Jonathan. "I don't believe you got rid of it all."

Jonathan spread his hands and smiled at Kevin. "It wasn't mine. Never was, and it's gone now. Don't sweat it, dude. It's for the best. Trust me."

"We'll just see about the money. I don't know what the fuck is keeping me from blowing you away, man."

Kevin looked at me. "I would never kill a child," he said. "But George would, wouldn't he?" He looked at Jane Marie and his expression was pleading. "George shot Sean. He killed him." Kevin was breathing hard, and the baby twisted in his arms. Her eyes lolled around the room.

"He killed Sean. I raised him, you know. Ever since our parents died." Kevin was breathing deeply from his chest. "I liked my brother. That sounds weird. But I liked Sean. He saw shit that would twist most people up into knots. He sucked it up. He never talked about it." Kevin sagged as if he might drop the baby, then snapped back to attention. "He never talked about it . . . and still you shot him."

Kevin was staring at George Doggy. Blossom started to cry softly. Reflexively Kevin started rocking her back and forth in his arms, and the harder he rocked the more she quieted. "That money was for me and Sean. Richard Ewers gave it to us. I was going to take my little brother to California. I was going to let him go to Disneyland every single day if he wanted to. Now you fuckers are going to kill me. This is not fucking fair. I didn't take the money. Neither of us did. But still you're going to kill me, aren't you?" Kevin seemed to be addressing all of us.

George Doggy leaned against the bulkhead, listening as he slowly put his leg high up on the captain's chair. Jane Marie was looking at nothing but her child.

Todd spoke. "Cecil, was I supposed to . . . detain him?"

"No, that's all right, buddy. Don't worry now."

Todd turned and sat back down in the galley with his eyes staring straight ahead, his hands folded tidily in his lap.

Jonathan spoke slowly and calmly to Kevin, in a tone wholly different from the way he had spoken to me or to George. His eyes stayed locked on Kevin's. "You're not alone, dude. Just keep it together and remember you are not alone."

"Okay . . . okay . . ." I said. "Let's just calm down a little and figure a few things out. Kevin, where is Richard Ewers?"

A muscle in Kevin's cheek twitched. He looked at me as if I were a great distance away. "I have no idea, Cecil. I had nothing to do with that. I wanted that money, I admit it, but I didn't have any part in that." He was speaking so fast I had a hard time believing he could be making it up.

Blossom was starting to fight harder and harder against Kevin's grip. She wiggled her shoulders and her face reddened. Jane Marie walked toward Kevin with her arms wide, offering to hold the baby. Kevin held the child tightly to his chin, his forearms cradling her bottom and around the back of her neck. He turned away from Jane Marie, and she stopped moving toward them.

"Okay . . . okay . . ." A thin siren of panic blared in my ears; all I wanted to do was change the mood in the cabin. "Okay, Kevin, I believe you," I lied. "What is it that George wants from you? If we come up with some money and work a deal, would you put the baby down?"

Jonathan stepped between us. "Kevin, keep your fucking mouth *shut*."

George was scratching his leg and acting suspiciously casual. He spoke to me, but never took his eyes off Kevin, who stood sobbing with my daughter squirming in his arms.

"They have the proof of what happened to Ewers," George said softly, and he kept scratching his leg.

"What was in Sean's photo album, George?" I asked him.

George waited before answering. "It was sick stuff, Cecil," he said. "You don't want to know." George looked down at the deck and away from my eyes.

Kevin gripped the baby so tightly it appeared he was closing off her airway. He was sobbing and rocking back and forth, snot and tears dripping down his face.

"That's a lie," he sobbed. "He was a good sweet boy. I'm not going to listen to any more of this." He was looking directly at Jonathan.

George's hand went to his leg, and he pulled the snub-nosed pistol from the holster strapped there. He pushed me away and in two steps had the gun to Kevin's skull, straight in the center of his forehead. Kevin held Blossom up near enough to the gun so that she would have been burned and no doubt deafened by the muzzle blast.

Jane Marie called out in a shaky voice, "For God's sake, just give me my baby."

Blossom's face was turning blue. Kevin was holding her so tightly up against his neck that she could not move. Without loosening his grip, Kevin said only, "George, can we step outside and have a talk?" He motioned toward the back deck.

Jane Marie checked the autopilot, then motioned for Jonathan to stand closer to her. All of us in the cramped pilothouse moved awkwardly around the man with the gun. Kevin moved toward the door. George Doggy never let the gun drop and his arm swung in Kevin's direction. As he did so Jane Marie stepped toward the door, her arms out for Blossom.

"Jonathan, you stay here!" Jane Marie barked, her eyes still on her child. I could hear Todd rustling around down in the galley, but I didn't turn to look, falling in behind George Doggy and beside Jane Marie as we awkwardly squeezed through the narrow door to the back deck.

Kevin Sands stood on the deck closest to the stern. Cold wind off the water whipped through Jane Marie's hair. Engine noise blared out on deck. Behind Kevin, the wake of the *Winning Hand* frothed in a widening V. The *Naked Horse* tracked along behind. Blossom was crying helplessly now, her tiny arms twitching and jabbing the air near Kevin's chin. Kevin appeared to be pleading with George Doggy. We could not make out his words over the engine noise and the sizzle of the wake.

Jane Marie and I moved to either side of Kevin. I heard Kevin say: "I'm not a fucking snitch. . . ." His face was slick with tears. He was not arguing but pleading. George Doggy's firearm was a large-caliber wheel gun with a three-inch barrel. It would be very loud and very messy at short range. The hammer was pulled back. George had his finger through the trigger guard and his knuckle was white on the outside of the trigger itself.

"So, we have a deal, right?" Kevin asked Doggy.

"Give the baby back." George Doggy said it slowly and clearly.

"George, when you didn't give a fuck about my brother, why do you care about her?" Kevin whimpered.

George Doggy pushed the barrel of the gun hard against Kevin's temple. Kevin was leaning back over the bulwarks of the *Winning Hand*. He held Blossom higher to his chest. His shoulders were out over the prop wash. Jane Marie put her hands on Kevin's shoulders.

"You don't have to do this," Jane Marie said softly. "You are not a monster."

"Hand the baby over and we will have an agreement, Kevin." George's voice was husky with tension now. "Hand the little girl over."

Kevin smiled at me. "He's going to kill me anyway, Cecil. Either him or Jonathan. They're going to kill me, don't you see? Don't listen to them. I'm alone in this now."

In my memory, the next seconds break down to a jerky silent movie. Kevin tries to slide down the bulwarks onto the deck, but George lunges forward with the gun and Jane Marie lunges forward to grab Blossom. I try to reach around behind Kevin's back to keep him and Blossom on board, but gravity and momentum were doing their slippery work. Kevin began to fall backwards.

The weight in Kevin's face lifted, his eyes were wide open and he held Blossom out to Jane Marie. "Take her. Take her," he mouthed as he went over the side.

His legs flipped up and he bounced once against the sloping stern and then disappeared in the foaming wake. I watched his head come to the surface just as the hull of the *Naked Horse* overtook him. I threw a buoy out onto the water to mark the location, but I didn't see his head come up again.

The baby was screaming and squirming, like a tiny piglet. Jane Marie was shushing and kissing her, wiping her own tears away while stroking the baby's cheek with her free hand.

"We have to go back and look for him," I said.

She looked at Blossom, stroking the down of her hair. I put my hand on Jane Marie's elbow and cupped my daughter's snail-sized foot in my hand. Neither of us said a word nor did we make a move to turn the boat around.

Chapter Twelve

Fifteen seconds passed. George Doggy put his revolver back into his ankle holster. "I wouldn't worry. I doubt that I could have pulled him back on board, even if I had been able to keep my grip on him."

Jane Marie looked away from Blossom for the first time since she'd had her back in her arms. Blossom had stopped crying; her hands were tucked under her chin. Jane Marie's voice was stiff with anger as she looked at Doggy but spoke to me.

"Cecil, we have to go back and find him. Take her."

She shifted Blossom into my arms and ran to the stern, taking a sharp knife from her belt. She sawed through the two lines of the towing yoke. The second line popped free, and the *Naked Horse* fell away from the wake of the *Winning Hand*. Then Jane Marie ran to the pilothouse, pushing past Todd, who was standing in the doorway with his old super–8mm camera. As Jane Marie moved past him, Todd turned and went back into the cabin. I started to follow Jane Marie, but she came back quickly, handed me a pair of binoculars and pointed to the stern.

"Here. Don't take your eyes off the buoy you threw. Find it and don't take your eyes off of it. Come up to the flying bridge. Stand next to me. I'll swing her around. We've *got* to find him, Cecil."

I walked into the pilothouse with Doggy behind me. Jane Marie stopped him. "*You* stay off my bridge." She jabbed her finger into Doggy's chest. "You look for the buoy and you look for Kevin in the water but never lose sight of the buoy." Her voice accused. She stood on the ladder one rung above George Doggy, holding his stare. This old man was not used to taking orders from a nursing mother. Jane Marie was about to say one more thing, but turned up the ladder instead. Doggy retreated to the stern.

The flying bridge sits exposed to the air, without a roof or windows. From this steering station we had a much better view of the sea. I climbed the ladder with one hand and carried the baby with the other. Jane Marie had made a cradle out of a five-gallon plastic bucket cut in half the long way. She took Blossom and laid her down under the cover of a little plastic screen near her legs. Then she powered up both engines and put the *Winning Hand* into a sharp turn.

"We can come back for the *Naked Horse*," she yelled over the engine noise. "I hated cutting those lines but we've wasted too much time as it is."

Perhaps ninety seconds had passed since Kevin had gone over the stern. The buoy was now about three hundred yards to our stern. The wind would have blown the buoy to the west of the probable location of a person down in the water. I found the buoy easily and began to scan the sea around it. I saw nothing. No water-soaked head of hair, no waving arm. I saw a few floating shoes.

"Don't take your eyes off the buoy, Cecil." Then she added, "I don't mean to bark at you. Just keep your eyes on the buoy. That's our only reference point. You'd be amazed how fast you can lose it. I can watch you and understand our position, and I can keep looking around for Kevin. Just don't lose that buoy."

The bag buoy was a salmon-egg red. It rose and fell on the seas as if it were waving to us. Nothing swam near it. Nothing moved into the tunnel of the binoculars' vision: nothing but the wind pushing ripples upon the surface of each lunging swell.

When we were fifty yards directly to the east of the buoy, Jane Marie shut down the engines. She flipped switches to shut down pumps and electronics.

"Listen . . . ," she whispered. "We should listen. You can look around now. Scan and listen. I'm going up."

She climbed the mast that ran just to the stern of the flying bridge. From the crow's nest, every angle of the view would be unobstructed.

The absence of engine noise eased over the ship like snowfall. Gulls flew past, uninterested in our presence, and the *Winning Hand* wallowed on the water. In all directions I could see nothing but the scalloped edges of the waves: miles and miles of uninterrupted plain, as if all the prairies of the Midwest were laid end to end. The wind buffeted my ears and it sang in the wire rigging. Waves slapped the hull with a predictable hushing sound, but there were no sharp human cries, no flailing arms against the water. The quiet began to feel like a burden.

"I don't see anything," Jane Marie called down. "Wait. Wait. Wait." Her voice grew urgent. "Down there, right next to the boat. To the right of the bow. Do you see it?" She was pointing with both hands.

George Doggy walked down the outer deck. He unlashed a pike pole from the rail and fished down into the water. He came up with something and held it up as if it were a trophy fish.

"A shoe," he called up to the crow's nest.

We gathered in the pilothouse to decide what to do next. Todd had tried to engage Jonathan in conversation, but according to Todd, Jonathan Chevalier kept his wild-eyed grin, staring out over the compass to the horizon. Then without a word, Jonathan motioned to Todd that he was headed below.

In the wheelhouse, Jane Marie took the helm from Todd. I was holding the shoe. This was not one of the new shoes spilled from the container ship. The laces were in all the eyelets and the tread was worn. It was not waterlogged. This shoe had not been floating long.

"What was he wearing?" I asked the room.

"I didn't notice. I never thought to look," Jane Marie said softly, as she rocked Blossom against her breast.

Todd cleared his throat. "That is unquestionably Mr. Sands's shoe," he said without emotion, as if the conversation were really only about the shoe. "I had noticed earlier that he was wearing a conventional walking shoe intended not merely for court activity or athletic events but for walking. I had noticed this because of the presence of all the shoes in the ocean. I had been thinking how little use the floating shoes would be to a person who preferred another style."

"That's it," George said in a voice that intimated he was taking command. "We'll just have to make a report back in town."

Jane Marie would have none of it. Kevin had been in forty-eight-degree water twenty minutes, without a survival suit; the chances of his survival were narrowing with each second, but I could tell she was not going to stop until his clock had long run out. She marked the location in her navigation gear and started the engines again so the *Winning Hand* could hold her position. Then Jane Marie called the Coast Guard and filed a report demanding an aerial search of the area.

The next three hours were spent scanning the sea and listening to the crackling voices of the helicopter pilots on the radio as they beat the air around us with their rotors.

We filed the report as a Passenger Overboard. We gave all the sketchy details we could come up with of what he was wearing and of his physical condition. We agreed to save the shoe in case the match could be used to identify a corpse if it washed up somewhere on the coast.

Darkness came on, and the Coast Guard released us to return to town. We went back to the *Naked Horse* and got her under tow again. Jonathan continued to sleep; Todd sat quietly in the galley staring out the back port because looking through the range finder of his old movie camera was making him seasick. Jane Marie steered from the flying bridge, and George Doggy came into the pilothouse and touched my elbow.

"Don't worry about it, son. It couldn't be helped. You were defending the child. No one could say you were to blame."

I looked at him a long time without speaking. I was starting to feel what countless suspects had felt at the beginning of a conversation with Doggy: I wanted to explain myself.

But I resisted: Nothing I could say would have helped me. Already my memory was being revised and edited by my fear and guilt. I remember Kevin was falling and I was standing back because I didn't want Blossom to go into the water with Kevin. But all I could reconstruct was Blossom, and Kevin's expression as he thrust her toward her mother. Then there was churning wake and Blossom in Jane Marie's arms. I felt sick and scared and was willing to give up the truth of the situation to the old man in authority.

"Accidental drowning. I'm with you all the way on this, son."

I hated the sound of his voice. It was both cloying and accusatory. I thought of Kevin Sands disappearing under the water, falling three thousand feet in a slow descent to the ocean floor. His body would be there on the bottom for fish and invertebrates to feed on; he would not be made buoyant by the rotting of his own flesh. Without some buoyancy to keep him out of the intense cold and pressure of the deep ocean, Kevin Sands would not rise. George Doggy knew that the only substantial things left of him were words—our words about what had happened—and George Doggy was now ordering these words into a script as the *Winning Hand* churned through the outgoing tide.

I heated some canned tomato soup on the oil stove as we crossed Sitka Sound, heading to harbor. All of us ate silently except Todd, who slurped and rattled his spoon against the plastic mug. Jane Marie stood at the helm taking occasional sips from her mug. We tied up to the *Winning Hand*'s slip in the harbor in the pitch dark. As soon as the bumpers nudged the dock, George Doggy jumped off the boat and walked directly over to the *Naked Horse*. As he started to step onto Jonathan's sailboat, I yelled over to him, "I've got a call in to Pomfret. I figure the Sitka P.D. is going to want to go over Jonathan's boat." I said this even though I had no intention of calling Pomfret.

George Doggy looked up at me and he seemed indecisive. He balanced his weight back and forth until finally he stepped back down onto the dock. He walked away quickly up the ramp.

Jonathan was still sound asleep on board Jane Marie's boat and he couldn't be roused. I called Clem at his house from the harbor pay phone. I told him that his patient Jonathan was here on board the *Winning Hand*. The doctor had just gotten in from moving band gear back to the practice room. He was happy to hear Jonathan had survived the storm and told me he would come down to the harbor later that night and check on him.

Jane Marie set to work cleaning up the boat and storing the running gear. She had called the harbormaster and was given permission to move the *Naked Horse* into an empty slip near the *Winning Hand*. Jonathan would have to move her to her own slip or out to the shipyard in the next few days, but the harbormaster didn't make us deal with her during the night.

I crawled into the *Naked Horse* to make sure she was secure for the night. Some of the wiring was dangling so only one of the cabin lights worked off the weak battery. Scattered around the cabin were gloves and rain gear, needlenose pliers, a couple of toothbrushes, boxes of noodles and freeze-dried soup. There were equipment manuals and boxes of clips and hardware, broken mugs and saucepans. There was a copy of *The Odyssey* and the complete works of Shakespeare. There were two Hornblower novels by Forester and a novel by Jean Genet, but I didn't see any of the money that Jonathan had insisted would not be there.

Finally I walked toward the stern and looked to the side of the engine compartment. I had seen a flashlight in the sink and after shaking it a while was able to turn it on. With the flashlight I could see the lead flashing Jonathan had tacked over the leak. I pried my way into the space by pulling with my hands. Holding the flashlight in my teeth, I came to the flashing. When I ripped it back, a thick smell washed over my face. I picked up the flashlight again. There, in the narrow compartment surrounding the shaft, was a tarry mass of currency stuffed down into the hull to plug the leak: hundreds of twenties, fifties and hundred-dollar bills, black as rotted leaves.

This had been an expensive repair.

I reached down into the sticky mess. The bills were a composted goo. I pulled my hand out of the mess and scraped what was probably a thousand dollars off onto the edge of the engine compartment. I wedged myself around looking for something to clean my hands on and I was almost overwhelmed by a smell so strong it pushed me back against the hull of the old sailboat.

In the far corner of the engine compartment was a green waterproof pack, the kind that's commonly used by river guides or skiff outfitters. The heavy rubberized fabric is waterproof, and the bag itself has a large volume in one main compartment. With one hand covering my nose and mouth against the stink, I extended the other to pull the bag closer and by using my foot I was able to open the folded-over flap and look inside.

The warm smell of sour blood eased out of the bag. I tried to push away from it. I shined the light down into the mouth of the bag and saw blood crusted in thick folds around the sides of the bag. In the very bottom, maggots swam on a shallow puddle of blood.

I pulled myself out from the narrow space in the stern and headed to the bow to see if I could find a towel to wipe my hands. Just under the V berth in the bow was a scattering of 9mm ammunition. This was not for the rifle I had seen. Just above the bunk, attached to the hull by a rubber strap, was a 9mm revolver with heavy rubberized grip. It seemed to be an odd handgun for a painter to keep within reach during his sleep at sea.

I found a towel, wiped off my hands, left the *Naked Horse*, and hobbled back to the *Winning Hand*. Both boats were secure, and Jane Marie sat nursing Blossom at the chart table. We didn't speak. I started to reach out to touch the baby's head but just as I did I caught a whiff of the rotted smell on my sleeve and yanked my hand back.

We walked up the dock and the half block to our house. The familiar smell of home seemed a balm to me now. I suddenly felt the bruises and a heavy tiredness reached up my spine and tried to force my eyes shut.

The answering machine was blinking with ten messages. I didn't want to push the button, so I waited until after I'd given Blossom a bath. She shuddered with what I'll call delight as I sponged her off in the little bath container we set up on the dish drainer. Her lips made her trademark O and her eyes scanned my face as I sang to her.

Once I had toweled her off and handed her to Jane Marie, I pushed the message button. Two calls from the police wanting to speak to someone about the report we had filed. Two from the Coast Guard Search and Rescue center. One from a bankcard solicitor promising to consolidate all my current debts into one reasonable and "customer-friendly" monthly payment.

Then there was a message from Harrison Teller, who said he would be flying to Sitka and needed me to pick him up at the airport. He said he had something to talk to me about, immediately.

I looked quizzically at Jane Marie as she passed the open bedroom door putting on her nightshirt. "That first day you went out, I called Teller. I thought he should know what was going on with Patricia," she said.

The next message was from Patricia's parents, telling me in a very stiff tone that they had hired an investigator in Seattle who wanted to talk to me about the circumstances of Patricia's death. They left the investigator's number and the message clicked off. The next two messages were from people asking about Todd because they were worried that they hadn't seen him in the last couple of days and it wasn't like him to break his routine.

The last message was from a friend of mine at the Department of Social Services saying that Sean Sands's funeral was tomorrow morning at ten o'clock. "I just thought you might want to know, Cecil." My friend's voice sounded

tired and frustrated, for it would not be easy drawing mourners for the funeral of a suspected schoolyard shooter. I called
her right back and thanked her for thinking of me, promising I'd be there.

I made a recording of the two messages having to do
with the Ewers family and was about to clear the rest of the
messages when the phone rang. I looked at Jane Marie and
she signaled to me that I should let it ring. But I shrugged
my shoulders and answered.

"Oh, Cecil, thank God you are there. Are you okay? Is
everything okay? Where is the baby? You didn't take her out
in that flimsy little boat, did you?"

I immediately recognized my mother's voice. She was
calling from our old house in Juneau. I could picture her sitting at the kitchen table with a glass of wine and a cigarette.
Yes, I was fine, I told her, and gave her a highly sanitized version of the events of the last few days. Ever since I started
drinking in junior high school, I have always cleaned up my
adventures for my mother so that nothing very interesting
or life-threatening ever seemed to happen to me. As I was
speaking, it dawned on me that my lying about the specifics
all these years had given her the impression that I was nothing much more than a kind of dimwitted bumbler. I'm not
saying it's necessarily an inaccurate impression, but I wondered what our relationship would have been if she had
known the spectacular depth of all my mistakes.

She wanted to talk to Jane Marie, as always, believing I
was a totally unreliable source of information concerning
her granddaughter. Jane Marie sat cross-legged on the
couch, holding the sleeping baby, with the receiver cradled
against her shoulder as she spoke to my mom for almost half
an hour. I closed my eyes and felt the room roll with the
motion of a wave. I heard my mother's muffled voice float
above me, calling out back and forth to Jane Marie as if they
were two gulls circling my overturned skiff. It frightens me,
the connection women have. I'm not even married to this
woman, but just by the fact that she has given birth, she is
more related to my mother than I'll ever be.

Finally she said my name and listened to my mom say something, and then they were both laughing.

"Here, she wants to talk to you again." Jane Marie held the receiver out to me.

"Now what's all this about you interfering with George?" my mother demanded.

"Has he called you?" I asked.

"No, Cecil," she clicked back as if she were gathering steam. "I've been ringing his phone off the hook all day long. When I couldn't reach you at your house, I called Jane Marie's sister and she told me you were out in that terrible storm."

"Why did you call George?"

"I called George because I've always called George when you were in trouble, Cecil. My goodness, George Doggy has hauled you out of your scrapes ever since you were a teenager. You wouldn't have survived to adulthood, to the extent you have, if it hadn't been for Mr. George Doggy. You haven't forgotten your debt to him, have you? The drinking and driving problems and later that scrape with suborning perjury?"

"Mom, I served time for that," I offered in my own defense.

"Not nearly as much as it would have been without George's help."

"Okay, I understand," I said, as I tried to ricochet to another subject. "Why do you think I'm interfering with him?"

"Because I've spoken with him just tonight, and he's worried you are going to get involved in his murder investigation. He says he cannot protect you forever. What does George mean by that, Cecil? For heaven's sake, what have you done now?"

I didn't speak for several moments.

"Cecil?" she said softly.

Somewhere out to sea, gulls were flying through the dark. Fish passing near the surface would trace phosphorescent lines causing the gulls to dive down on them. The waves pushed and pulled against the sky. I was listening to all this as my mother waited for my reply.

Finally she said softly, "Oh honey, you know George was one of your father's closest friends. He was so much like your father. He knows what he is doing. He's a professional down to his bones. Whatever it is you are involved in, I want you to leave it to George. And . . ."

Now my mother was silent and I could hear her taking several sips from her glass before speaking again.

"And if this has something to do with you still being angry with your father, you should just let it go, honey. Don't fool around in this investigation of George's. Don't mess up other people's lives with all that old business."

I had a lifetime of things I could have said. There was invective and impeccable reasoning, armchair psychology and brutally honest insight. I could have summoned a half-assed sermon on the subject of "old business." But instead I said, "Okay, Mom."

"Good." Her voice lifted. "I'm glad you are all right, Cecil. You always give me such a fright. When are you going to bring that baby to Juneau?"

I handed the phone back over to Jane Marie. They chatted for a few more minutes, and when they hung up I was standing by the window watching a Coast Guard cutter lit up like a birthday cake ease up to the dock on the other side of the channel. Her lights streaked in wavy lines across the water.

Jane Marie came up behind me and wrapped her arms around my waist.

"Do people ever really grow up?" I asked her.

"Some people do, Cecil. Of course, not many men, but some people do." She kissed me on my ear and squeezed me tight.

"Cecil, what really matters to you now?" Her cheek was flat on my shoulder. The wind fluttered the banners on the ship across the way.

I turned her around. "Sleep," I told her.

She looked at me and waited, so I felt the need to continue.

"Sleep, and making sure we're safe. You, Todd, Blossom . . ." My voice trailed off.

"Well, that's a start," the woman who loved me said, and held on tightly enough so I couldn't float away.

"My mom wants me to stop being pesky and leave George Doggy alone."

"And what do you think?" the woman who still loved me asked.

"I think George is involved in a murder. I think I'm going to have to be pesky for a little while longer." I cupped her cheek in my hand.

She kissed me lightly and gripped her arms all the way around me, burying her face in my chest. She started to say something, paused to reconsider, then kissed me again.

That night I dreamed I could see my hand holding the gun. The darkness smelled like gasoline, and blood was spattered up my shirtfront. Schoolchildren were screaming, and the gun in my hand jumped, spitting a flash from the muzzle. Briefly in the flash I could see the frightened face of Tina Sands cowering in her bunk on the *Mygirl*. I left her there and turned the corner to the next bunk where George Doggy was lying dead. Then I heard the rumble of flame.

When I woke I didn't feel any pain. My body felt like a drift log. But each new movement of the day seemed to tear different bunches of muscles. My tongue felt cottony and swollen, my eyes were puffy, and my head felt like a beehive. It reminded me of a full-body hangover after a night of bar fighting.

But we were up in time to shower and put on our nicest clothes for Sean Sands's funeral. I wore a dark blue suit and my slick-soled shoes. We walked across town, where I saw for the first time the snapped tree limbs and lifted roof corners left behind by the storm. I carried the baby and Jane Marie drank a cup of coffee as we walked.

Sean was to be buried in the small cemetery up against the hill, where many of the old people without families from the state home were put. Some of the graves were sunken in with their mossy headstones tilted at odd angles to each other. Plastic flower petals rimmed with fungus blew across the uneven ground. A milky sunlight filtered down at the gravesite, but just ten feet toward the hill the rain forest darkened into a green wall.

Four people were gathered around the hole: a minister, a social worker, the school principal, and a reporter from the paper. Each shifted from foot to foot and spoke softly as Jane Marie and I walked up the hill. I handed the baby to Jane Marie and hugged the social worker. The reporter had her notebook open and scribbled something. As we walked closer, the preacher hiked up his sleeve and checked his watch, then stood on his toes to see farther down the hill, where no more mourners were coming.

"I think we can get started," he suggested in his baritone voice.

I knew the minister from around town. He had a small church with a loyal, rather left-leaning Christian following. He had volunteered to do the funeral when no one else had offered. I was ready to dislike him. I was ready not to argue with whatever he was going to say, but to discount it. Grief didn't need whatever feeble protestations he could offer on this chilly autumn day.

He opened his Bible and started to read from the Book of Luke: " 'Blessed are you poor, for yours is the kingdom of God. Blessed are you that hunger now for you shall be satisfied. Blessed are you that weep now for you shall laugh. Blessed are you when men hate you and when they exclude you and revile you and cast out your name as evil, on account of the Son of Man. Woe to you that are rich, for you have received your consolation. Woe to you that are full now, for you shall hunger. Woe to you that laugh now, for you shall mourn and weep. Woe to you when all men speak well of you, for so their fathers did to the false prophets.' " The preacher lifted his eyes. He looked not at me or the gathered, but straight up toward the dark tree line and up beyond to the hillside dusted with a fine new snow.

" 'But I say to you that hear, love your enemies, do good

to those who hate you, bless those who curse you, pray for those who abuse you.' " He cleared his throat, staring down at the coffin laid out on two timbers on the wet, turned-up earth. He closed his Bible.

"Sean Sands didn't leave us many memories of him, and those he did are sometimes painful. All of his worldly keepsakes are now like a foreign currency neither he, nor we, will ever be able to spend. It is only through love that we can make sense of this world, and in this too, young Sean was among the poor. To those who knew him I can only offer this: where we feel deficient, God is full; where we may have failed, God will succeed. Where we may have turned away from justice, God's eyes are unmoving. This is our faith, our answer to grief." He stopped speaking. Back in the trees a raven made a hollow kind of knocking sound in its throat. The minister asked if anyone wanted to offer any testimonials for Sean and our small group was silent.

The reporter held her notebook to her side and her head was turned toward the coffin. The social worker took off her glasses and wiped her eyes. She tried to speak but gave up and the raven called out from the shadows.

The principal finally straightened his shoulders and, wiping his eyes, said only that Sean was a quiet boy and he hadn't known him well. He said that Sean had suffered a great deal in his life and he certainly didn't deserve it. He said he hoped that Sean was at peace now.

I started to walk away. The gravediggers were sitting on the backhoe as Jane Marie, Blossom and I walked the path to the road. In a couple of seconds I heard the chomp of a spade. I saw my friend from Social Services standing a few feet away looking at another grave. I walked to where she was, my slick dress shoes slipping on the damp grass.

She was wiping her nose with a balled-up tissue as I came up and touched her elbow. She glanced at me, then stared back down to the grave.

"It's so sad, Cecil. So many disturbed young boys with guns."

I read the name on the grave. It was Albert Chevalier's resting place. The tombstone lay flat in the ground. Grass had almost completely overgrown its edges so that only the name could be made out in the center.

"Albert was a disturbed boy?" I asked.

"Whoa!" she said, rolling her eyes toward the sky. "Scary. I don't think I ever met a more twisted little guy." She looked up at me, her bloodshot eyes incredulous. "I suppose it's okay for me to say this now, but he was really a bent kid. We almost stepped in to take him out of the home and away from his parents. Albert was really frustrated, very withdrawn. I think he must have cleaned out all of the pets in his trailer park."

"Cleaned out the pets?" I echoed.

She rolled her eyes again. "Whoa, big time," and she leaned closer to me. "Albert used to kill small animals. Sometimes he took his own sweet time, if you know what I mean." Her voice was low and confidential as if she were sharing some particularly juicy gossip.

"Frankly, I was surprised he was the victim of a crime. I always saw him the other way around. You know, I was expecting him to be where that Richard Ewers should have been. In jail the rest of his life."

We didn't say anything for a while. The trees above us gave out a long sigh.

"Of course, he's dead now . . . Albert, that is, and poor Sean too. So many sad little boys."

Somewhere the raven tittered and clacked.

"Cecil, do you think we'll be judged for the things we failed to do?" my friend said, watching the men shoveling wet dirt onto Sean's coffin.

I didn't answer her but excused myself and walked down the hill.

Jane Marie went back later that day and put flowers and some comic books on Sean's grave, but I had nothing to leave him. All I could think about were Sean Sands's keepsakes and what the minister had said about justice.

Chapter Thirteen

At the bottom of the gravel lane leading back to town I saw a bearded man in a wheelchair. He was wearing blue jeans and a Burberry coat that tucked into the armrests of his chair. As I came closer his blue eyes locked on to mine.

"Younger, shit, man, I'm glad I caught up with you."

Jane Marie was carrying Blossom, and they scooted around past me. Jane Marie squeezed my hand good-bye as she passed.

Teller nodded up the hillside with his chin so that his foot-long beard swayed away from his chest. "You just bury the Sands kid?" he asked matter-of-factly.

I nodded but he went right on. I had been Teller's investigator. He didn't really want to chat with me.

"George shot him. These cops! Don't they give them some lessons when they hand out the weapons? Maybe George got mixed up when they told him 'women and children first.' What do you think?"

A sly raven flew from under the canopy of trees and landed on the gravel not twenty feet from where we were standing. He was a large bird with a crown of feathers on his head and almost a lion's mane around his throat. He had what looked like a baloney rind in his beak. I knew Teller wasn't really asking what I thought.

"Listen, Cecil, I know you're in some kind of early re-
tirement thing—"

"What do you mean by that?" I interrupted him.

"Well, you know, I've heard you don't do much criminal
work anymore, and trust me, I don't blame you for that, I
guess. . . ."

I finally started to say something when Teller held up his
hand. "It's just, I know for certain that bastard George
Doggy murdered Richard Ewers."

I let the words sit like the gravel at my feet.

Teller turned so he was pushing his chair slowly away
from the graveyard. "We had offers from movie people and
tabloids. At first, Richard didn't want the money. He said it
would just bring more heat on him. I didn't blame him, you
know. I mean, I wasn't particularly wild about him telling
anybody anything. I figured the families might come back
with a wrongful death suit. They'd use his statements to the
press any way they could. Hell, even the fact of him getting
the money might incite them to file a suit. But then Richard
came up with a plan."

Teller stopped talking and studied me for a moment.
Then he pulled a check out of his pocket. It was made out to
me for a thousand dollars. "Cecil, listen, I hate to dump this
on you all at once. So take this. You know I'd feel better if
we had a business relationship."

I looked at the check and counted the zeros. Teller was
impossibly hard to work for but he was generous with his
clients' money. In this instance he also wanted to make certain that anything he said to me would come under the
umbrella of "work product" and attorney-client privilege.
Once I took his thousand dollars, the privilege of what to do
with the information belonged exclusively to Richard Ewers
or his heirs and representatives. Even if I wanted to talk to
the police, Teller could stop them from using anything I
said in court.

"Thank you," I said, taking the money.

"Richard wanted to give half the money to the Sands
brothers. Mind you, he only had half the money. He was going to get the next fifty grand from the tabloid after he

taped his interview. He said before he went to the papers he wanted to give the troopers information that he thought would get them off his back forever. He wouldn't even tell me what it was. Believe me, I was against it but he insisted I arrange a meeting with Doggy."

"Why did he want to give the money to the Sandses?"

"All he would say was that those boys deserved it. And that he couldn't keep all of the money for himself."

"Was he going to give any money to Jonathan Chevalier?"

"Not that I knew of. Chevalier had jerked him around at trial. All of that 'It could have been him' bullshit. Christ, that guy should have been horsewhipped."

He let his words fade. For a moment we were both lost in our memories of that trial, then Harrison brought us back to the present. "This past spring I offered to set up a meeting in Ketchikan between Richard and George Doggy. That meeting was supposed to happen ten days ago."

The raven hopped three times toward Teller's shoe. The big bird still held the meat rind.

"Richard wanted to go alone. He didn't tell his wife. He didn't tell me much because he said no one could have the information until he got the money to Kevin Sands. I didn't want him to do that. I agreed to it only if Richard wore a wire and taped everything that went on in the meeting."

"Did he take the money to the meeting?" I asked the raven.

"He made it to Ketchikan. Richard said he was going to mail the cash to Sands as soon as he got to Alaska. He said he was going to settle all accounts only after he knew the meeting was solid and he was back in Alaska."

"Those are the words? 'Settle all accounts'?"

"Yep, those were his words. He got off the plane. He rode the ferry across the channel, he took a cab into town and rented a room in a hotel downtown. And that's the last we know of him."

I was about to ask an obvious question, but I didn't. The raven dropped the rind on the ground, walked two stubby steps away and came rushing back. In that time I answered my own question.

"You didn't raise an alarm because you didn't want the tabloid reporters on it," I told Teller. "You didn't want them trying to uncover the story before you had possession of it."

"We were acting in Richard's best interests. I negotiated the next fifty grand and I'll give them the interview. It's a better story for those fuckers anyway. 'CRAZY COP KILLS INNOCENT MAN.' "

I shook my head and looked down at Teller.

"Hey! It's not for me, Cecil. The money goes to Patricia and Richard's folks."

"Why do you think George killed Richard?" I asked the bird again.

Teller reached into the pocket of his Burberry coat again and pulled out a piece of paper.

"On the day the meeting was to take place, George Doggy flew down to Ketchikan. When he landed there he reported that his handgun had been lost or stolen by the airlines. He reported that he forgot he was carrying a weapon until he got to the airport, and he was forced to check the gun through baggage in a special container the airlines keep for such things. When he showed up in Ketchikan, he claims the gun wasn't there. And the interesting thing is that this lost luggage claim was made four hours after the flight arrived."

The raven made a terrible clatter. He shook himself as if he had just been doused with water. Then the black bird hopped twice on the gravel and flew down the lane toward the corner of the road with the baloney skin in his beak. Just as he was about to disappear, he dropped the prize in the road and flew up into the trees.

"And you think George Doggy did this to cover himself?"

"Younger, you know him, he's kind of like your old uncle or something. We've talked about this. I don't hold it against you. But now it's serious. You can't let some sort of family loyalty stop you on this."

Teller looked up at me as if he were commanding himself to walk . . . or me to crawl. "George Doggy killed Richard in what he thought was retribution for the deaths on the *Mygirl*. Doggy shot Richard, disposed of the gun and the body, then called in the phony theft of his handgun in case the body should be discovered later."

I thought about George Doggy, and then I thought of where the raven had gone. The woods are a tangle of limbs and fallen trees, all but impenetrable. The bird could navigate by instinct and uncanny awareness of his surroundings. Despite my growing suspicions, I had always thought George Doggy would be lost trying to lead a life of crime. His instinct was not made for it. Or so I thought.

"The report of his missing gun would be too easy to tear apart. If it were phony, it would collapse. The timing stinks; there would be too many witnesses. It's sloppy," I said, piling up as many objections as I could come up with.

"Cecil, listen, you are working on *making* a case now. I need some belief, not your trademark skepticism." Teller stopped the pumping motion of his arms and shoulders as he pushed the chair. He looked up at me with the headlights of his eyes.

"I'm sorry, Cecil." His voice was softer now. "I'm angry. I'm not at my best. That's why I need you."

We traveled on in silence for a moment. A rock pinched out from under his chair's tire. He stopped again.

"Christ, I'm tired. I haven't slept. You drive this thing a while," and he gestured vaguely down the road.

I stepped in behind him, took the grips of his chair and pushed him down the gravel road.

"And as far as its being sloppy," the old lawyer went right on, "murder's almost always sloppy, don't you think?"

I had carried water for Teller during some of the worst months of my life. I had chased down foolish leads and organized mountains of paper. But he had never asked me to push his chair before. He knew that too and it was another example of how he used the chair to manipulate his audience. I felt strange tenderness for this old warhorse even while I knew he was conning me into working for him.

"Harrison, help me with one thing. I'm not sure I

remember, but did Richard ever mention seeing Jonathan Chevalier the night of the killings? I mean did he ever talk about Chevalier *before* Chevalier's testimony at trial?"

"No, Richard never mentioned Chevalier. He was sure pissed off after Chevalier testified on direct, though. Come on, you remember, Cecil. My cross of Chevalier was the coup of the case. I chopped Chevalier up, and then he nearly wet himself trying to help us. Why the hell are you bringing that up now?"

As we rounded the corner, the raven landed on the ground right in front of us. The bird's hackles were distended and he seemed to have grown to twice his normal size. This raven roared at us as if he were trying to wake us.

"Sorry," I said, "I was just thinking." We moved in a wide arc around the angry bird. "One other thing: In all the other suspect materials, the drug enforcers and the mafia killers, we never really considered the possibility of murder/suicide on the *Mygirl*?"

"Oh, I thought about it, Cecil. But that leaves the fire. Who started the fire? Maybe Richard, but I couldn't defend him that way. Nobody's going to buy that he burned the evidence but didn't commit the murders. Why?"

"I've been thinking about the *Mygirl* a lot, is all," I said.

"You said it yourself, Cecil. The *Mygirl* is done with. We'll never know. I'm quoting a great investigator when I say, 'What would the guilty party say, but that somebody else has done it?' Besides, the sides have switched now and we are hunting the hunters. I want you to talk to Doggy. I want you to memorialize your conversation as thoroughly as possible."

This was the code Teller used to let me know he was expecting me to surreptitiously tape my conversation. The Board of Ethics made it impossible for him to ask me to do so directly, but it was not illegal in Alaska for me to secretly tape on my own. We had played this game before.

I left Teller on the street in front of the hotel downtown, where he had a van waiting to take him back to the airport. Then I walked across the parking lot to the state building and through the back door to the police station. I asked to see Lieutenant Pomfret. Surprisingly, the desk clerk buzzed me straight in and pointed me back toward Pomfret's office where the large man sat behind a tiny desk.

"Younger, people keep dropping around you like flies. What's up with you? It's like the plague around you."

"I dunno, Lieutenant," I said rather smartly.

"Cecil, I'm going to want to get a full statement from you about the incident with Kevin Sands."

"It was an accident."

"So I've been told. Your buddy George Doggy has been in here already."

I didn't much care for the way Lieutenant Pomfret said the words "your buddy."

Pomfret leaned forward. "What did Kevin Sands say before he died? Just informally. You know, what did he talk about while he was on the boat?"

"He was angry with George Doggy."

"Did he say why?"

"I think it had something to do with the fact that George had just killed his brother." I tried my best to keep a damper on my sarcasm.

"Anything else? What else went on between Doggy and Kevin?" Pomfret was still leaning forward, which had to be an uncomfortable position for him, sitting down with his gun around his waist and all.

"Who are the suspects here, Lieutenant? Can I ask that?"

"Cecil, the witnesses keep dying, and you and your buddy George are still alive. That's getting to be a problem for me. Now, you can tell me about Kevin's conversation or I can think about whether you are obstructing justice."

I cleared my throat. "Kevin Sands was angry about the death of his brother. He also said something about deserving to keep the money."

"The money Chevalier had been giving away?" Pomfret leaned back, picked up a pencil and made a show of taking a note. Now I was certain Pomfret was tape-recording our conversation.

"I suppose that was the money he was referring to. He seemed exasperated that Doggy hadn't really cared about finding the money in the first place. Then he asked to speak to Doggy in private on the back deck. Kevin was holding my daughter in his arms. When I got to the back deck, all I heard him tell George was 'I won't tell,' or words to that effect."

Pomfret looked sad now, as if he were turning a corner he didn't want to see around. "Sands said he wouldn't tell? Do you know what he was referring to?"

"I do not," I said and waited. The lights hummed, casting a sickly light down on Pomfret's jowls.

"Why did he want to talk to Doggy in private?"

"Don't know," I said, conscious that my answers were getting shorter.

"Now, Cecil, I have to ask you flat out. You know you are not in custody. You can walk out of here anytime you want. That door to my office is not locked, and you can walk out anytime you want. You realize that, don't you?"

My stomach tightened as I heard Pomfret clear himself of his Miranda obligations.

"Yes," I said.

Roy Pomfret laid his pencil down in a practiced, offhanded gesture as if he wasn't really worried whether I was a murderer. "Did either you or George Doggy push Kevin Sands overboard? You can tell me the truth, Cecil, and I'll do my best to help you through this."

I have listened to hundreds of hours of confession tapes. The officer always lets the subject know they can walk out anytime they want. This makes the interview "non-custodial," and hence there is no need for the standard warnings that your rights are about to be tested for their usefulness. I have also listened to dozens of well-heeled corporate lawyers facing the same situation, and I chose to answer in their style rather than babbling about my rather ambiguous innocence with regard to Kevin Sands's death.

"I appreciate your concern for me, Roy, and I look forward to cooperating fully with you and your investigation. I look forward to clearing this up, right after I speak with my attorney."

Roy Pomfret's face sagged as if I had just turned into a

large pile of excrement on his carpet. "I want my lawyer" are still the magic words in Alaska. Non-custodial or not, the interview is supposed to end.

"Eat me, Younger," Roy Pomfret muttered.

"Not now, thanks," I said, smiling, and started to reach for the door. "You know, Roy, I really enjoyed this little chat. But the truth is, I didn't come by to talk to you about Kevin Sands."

Pomfret reached around and took the microcassette recorder off the shelf where it was sitting behind a stack of paper. He snapped the record button off.

"You can get up and go talk to your damn lawyer, Younger, but I'm telling you, if you do that, I'm going to try and hook you up for obstruction of justice at the very least. Do you know what I'm saying? Obstruction of justice . . . if not full complicity in the death of Kevin Sands . . . and maybe others." Pomfret just couldn't help himself with that last jab. He stared at me hard, as if trying to decide on the best way to throttle me.

"Listen, Lieutenant, I might help you if you help me a little bit. What I came by to talk to you about is this: Have you recently collected a sample of Richard Ewers's DNA?"

Pomfret stared at the top of his tiny desk, as if he were trying to levitate the entire thing. His jaw was tight and his hand moved down toward his belt next to his leather holster.

"What we've done with Richard Ewers's DNA is none of your concern, Younger," he spat out toward the floor. Now his hand rested on the outside of his holster.

"But you have some, don't you? You have a known sample of Richard's DNA?"

"Listen, this interview is over. You want to talk to your lawyer? You are free to do that. Now . . . if you want to sit back down and talk to me, to answer my questions, let's do that, okay?" He picked up his little tape recorder again.

"You have a known sample, don't you?"

"You and your buddy George Doggy are going down on this, Younger. Doggy wanted Ewers dead. Sands didn't mind having Ewers dead but he wanted money to keep quiet. Chevalier didn't want any part of it. He tried to get rid of the money. Kevin was pissed and was going to snitch George off. So Kevin ends up dead. Don't think George can protect you, Cecil. Not on murder. Not on this kind of murder." Pomfret threw the empty tape machine across the desk. "But we weren't talking about that, were we? Let's just sit down and chat." He said the word "chat" as if it were a death threat.

I didn't say anything more. I have used the two–tape recorder method, making a show of turning one machine off and letting the other run. This was a very bad time to try to explain myself. Particularly when I didn't really know what I knew.

I walked out of Roy Pomfret's office telling him only that I was looking forward to cooperating with him in the future. Which was almost true. I knew I would have to cooperate with him eventually. I just wasn't looking forward to it.

I also knew two things for certain and had one pretty good guess. One, Richard Ewers was dead. Two, the police had a sample of his DNA. And my pretty good guess was that they had collected the DNA sample from Ketchikan, Alaska a little less than a week ago.

Admittedly, I have a high tolerance for ambiguity. Some have claimed that I prefer uncertainty to knowledge, equating uncertainty with a kind of passive wisdom. This may or may not be true, but almost against my will I was beginning to come to a kind of knowledge I thought could possibly flower into a type of certainty. I felt an exhilarating freshness in my brain as if I had just woken up from a long and dreamless sleep. There was just one more piece of evidence I needed to see.

I walked to Gary's house in my uncomfortable shoes and asked him if he could give me a ride out the road. Gary was working in his machine shop. He was adjusting the settings on his large lathe with his left hand as the machine spun an eight-foot shaft on its spindles. Gary was blowing on an E harmonica in his right hand. He yelled at me that it would take a couple of minutes to shut down the lathe, but then he'd run me out. He needed a break anyway, and maybe we could go for coffee on the way.

"Nice suit!" he yelled over the machine noise.

I telephoned Jane Marie and told her that if George Doggy came by to meet me at home to hold him there until I got back. Not to let him leave. If he did leave before I got home, she was to call me at George's house and tell me. Jane Marie listened to these directions carefully and didn't ask me the obvious questions. She recognized the tone of my voice. She would ask questions later.

I then called Doggy at home and told him to meet me at my house right away. I told him I knew about what had happened to Richard Ewers and that we needed to talk. Doggy tried to pull me into a conversation, but I cut him off by suggesting his line might be bugged. I told him again to meet me in town at my house. George said he would be there right away and that it would take maybe twenty minutes to drive from his house to mine. I hung up just as Gary was ready to go.

Gary didn't ask questions but kept playing a lick he was learning off of a new Paul deLay album. "I think it's really set, Cecil. Paul deLay is coming to play in Sitka. Do you believe it?" I told him I didn't, and the truth was, I didn't. We don't get many top blues harmonica players passing through Sitka, Alaska. But I didn't doubt Gary's enthusiasm. We went downtown and bought coffee for our five-mile drive out the road. George would be close to town now, and I doubted he would recognize me heading toward his house sitting in Gary's truck.

This was the second residence I had broken into in a week, which is strange because I'm not particularly good at breaking into houses. The whole procedure gives me the creeps, even if I don't really have to break anything to gain entry. George Doggy didn't lock his doors, and I walked into the too-quiet house, carrying my shoes in my hands as I walked across the thick white carpet. George Doggy's house was always warmer than I cared for. He kept the woodstove in his basement going all the time. The furniture upstairs was a rugged overstuffed fifties style. I had the impression

Doggy didn't spend any time in the living room. There was a dining room table near the big windows that looked over the bay. Uncomfortable formal chairs ringed the table as if waiting for a meeting to begin. There were paintings on the wall that no one would look at twice: northern mountainscapes with the pinkish glow landscape painters are always using to try to capture the last light on the hills. This was the museum George maintained for his wife, but he didn't live in this part of the house.

Doggy's office was in the basement off the shop. Here were his desk and his gun case with six hunting rifles lined up like toy soldiers. Here was a safe. On his desk were scattered papers, catalogs, letters from insurance companies, old checkbooks. The gun case was locked, both the glass doors to the rifles and the drawers that would hold his handguns. I looked through the drawers in the desk. Nothing. I stood in front of the safe. I almost despaired of trying it, but then I remembered that I had a safe at home too. But I kept forgetting the combination, so I wrote it on the door of the safe. Finally, I completely stopped locking it. I was hoping Doggy's memory for numbers was worse than mine.

The handle of the safe clicked straight down, and my heart rose and fell in almost equal proportions. I was lucky to have it open, so that must mean what I was looking for wasn't there. I opened the door, and there, in fact, was exactly what I was looking for.

Sean Sands's photo album had been his treasure. Doggy had implied that the album contained proof that the boy had been planning a schoolyard shooting. I could believe this from the things I had seen in Sean's room: the AK-47 and the photos of his schoolmates with some of them ominously X'd out. George had thought of the photo album as crucial evidence, but he had never turned it in, and he was keeping the police from looking at it.

The album cover was red plastic made to feel like leather. The evidence tape had been ripped away from the edges of the covers. The inside of the safe had a chilled and musty smell, like bad memories. I took the album and laid it carefully on the desk. I have reviewed ugly evidence in the past: postmortem photographs of children beaten to death, the wild diaries of men twisted toward murder. I always have a sick feeling just before opening up those files. There is always a push-pull of dread and fascination, the voyeurism of crime and the fear of what might resonate in oneself when faced with brutality. I always open the files.

The first page of Sean's photo album was a portrait of a man and a woman: black-and-white with a hazy studio background. The woman was seated. She appeared lovely and young, her hair curled under at the shoulders. She wore a pale sweater and a string of pearls. The man stood behind her with his hand spread awkwardly on her shoulder. He could have been a young Robert Mitchum, soulful eyes and a hard, worn face. He wore a wool sportsman's style jacket and on his left hand he wore a thick wedding ring. Underneath the photo in very deliberate handwritten print were the words: "Mom and Dad."

There were baby pictures of Sean, birthday parties; toddler Sean dressed as a pumpkin, crying up toward the camera; young Sean in a Superman suit, with the lettering underneath describing "Super Sean!!!"

There were two young boys dancing in and out of a wading pool in the drenching sunlight of some backyard patio. The inscription read, "Me and you at the Douglases' house in Juneau." The next shot was a color Polaroid of Sean in a suit, awkwardly holding a flower, standing next to a TV set in what must have been their old trailer. The inscription said, "Handsome Dan, waiting to go to a dance."

Kevin must have started putting this album together for his brother. Both boys were dead now. Pressure built up behind my eyes, and a cavernous, sick feeling settled in my stomach.

In the back of the book Sean had started putting pictures in the album. He had cut out school pictures and pasted them in. Sean's handwriting was an awkward combination of printing and cursive, an uneven scrawl. Underneath the picture of a boy in a torn T-shirt was written, "Rodney James, most best friend forth grade. Moved to Anchorage in fifth." There was a picture of a pretty girl with dark hair and a wide smile. There was a heart drawn around the picture and only the name "Chandler" written underneath it. There were other pictures of friends with nicknames or simple exclamation marks. One page had "Girls I Like" written on the top, and the facing page simply said "SNOBS." The majority of the pictures were on the "Girls I Like" page.

Sean Sands never had a chance to be cool. He never had a chance to grow strong and thin and say a self-assured word to pretty, smiling Chandler. I hated thinking of that. I recognized, too, that the photos I had found in his bedroom were only scraps he had rejected from placement in this book. The discarded photos weren't a hit list.

This was the evidence I always look for and rarely find. This was evidence of innocence. On one of the final pages of the book was a large picture of Kevin Sands sitting on a couch, smiling and looking happily at the camera. The inscription read: "My Bro."

That was where the pictures should have ended. But the Sands boys had added a postscript to the book. On the last pages there was a series of pictures of two young boys standing in bright sunshine. They were in the glen just off the beach in Kalinin Bay. One of the boys in the photos was Sean and the other was Albert Chevalier. In one, Albert was wrapped up in a blanket in front of a campfire. His eyes looked dulled and exhausted. Sean sat beside him smiling into the camera lens. In another photo, Albert was kneeling beside a fallen log. On top of the log were lined up dozens of dead squirrels. Albert was not leaning like a hunter but was standing over the dead animals with his gun propped on the log and the barrel pointing straight at his own head. The rifle was an AK-47. Albert's face was half in shadow and he looked lost in thought as if he couldn't quite take his eyes off the creatures he had killed. Underneath this picture someone had written, "No rest."

Then I saw the sticker on the stock of Albert's rifle. There in the photograph was the sticker of the cartoon boy sailing his skateboard right into a brick wall. There were the words on the logo: *No Doubt.*

I didn't hear the phone ring. Finally I recognized Jane

Marie's voice coming over the answering machine: "Uh, hello. I'm calling for Cecil. I forgot to call earlier. Are you there? Uh, Cecil, George left here about fifteen minutes ago. I guess you guys got your wires crossed. I told him you might have thought the meeting was out at his house. I didn't really understand what you wanted and George was, well . . . in a hurry, and I had to take care of the baby and I remembered you wanted me to call when he left. So . . . I am. Uh . . . I guess that's it then, bye-bye."

I felt cold metal nudge the back of my head, and with Sean's photo album in my hands I turned around to see the muzzle of a large-caliber handgun at my nose.

"I knew I should have locked the safe," George Doggy said. "But you know, I keep forgetting the damn combination."

He pulled back the hammer of his revolver and I closed my eyes.

"I don't want to do this, Cecil," Doggy said, with what sounded like genuine remorse in his voice.

Chapter Fourteen

Why did you take this album, George?" I asked.

The old man let out a long sigh, stepped back and flicked a switch near the door.

"I kept it because I thought it contained evidence that I had killed Richard Ewers in Ketchikan."

George Doggy was now standing near the basement door, which was opposite the safe and the desk. I stood up and walked toward the center of the room. George's gun followed me. I stared at him and tried to imagine what Sean Sands had been thinking before George's bullet murdered him.

"I saw that picture of Albert holding the rifle. I knew it was the missing gun from the *Mygirl*. It was the gun Chevalier saw Ewers carrying in the skiff that night. But I didn't know what to do with it. I just wanted to find what it was the brothers had that tied me to Ewers's death, but I swear, Cecil, I never intended to kill that boy on the playground. I got a call: a voice I didn't recognize said that Sean Sands was taking an automatic rifle up to the school. I went there, and sure enough he had. I asked Sean to put the gun down on the ground and he didn't. I argued with him, and he would not move. I watched him. I wanted every other option. He raised his rifle to fire at me, and I had no other choice. If he had shot me, that would only have been the beginning. You know that, Cecil. That boy would have shot those children." George Doggy's hand was shaking, and he ran it through his gray hair. His voice shimmered with uncertainty.

"George, I have no reason to believe Sean Sands was a killer. It seems more likely to me that he knew something about your involvement with Richard Ewers's death. Sean knew something about Richard's disappearance. Kevin surely did. Is that why you killed them both?"

Doggy sat down and set the shiny stainless revolver on the desk. He covered his eyes with his hands.

"I swear to God, Cecil, I didn't plan to shoot that boy. I wanted to know what he knew. I knew the Sands brothers knew about Ewers. I had tracked them down through the money. Patricia Ewers had sounded the alarm. That afternoon we were cutting wood, she'd gone to the police. They knew Ewers was missing. The Sitka police heard that Sands had a lot of cash. I knew nothing about the raid. It was a mistake. A mess. Patricia grabbed a gun and that young cop shot her. A woman dead and no chance of getting either Kevin or Sean to tell me what they knew. It was a mess, a stupid accident.

"I took the album because the boy was obviously protective of it. I thought for sure it had some evidentiary value, something about Ewers. But it mostly . . ."

"Mostly, it was full of innocent schoolboy memorabilia," I said, walking to the edge of the desk, yelling down at my father's most trusted friend. "And the only reason Sean didn't want you to look at it was he didn't want you to know the soft part of his heart. He didn't want you to trample on the only real evidence of a normal life he ever had. He didn't want the men with guns to know that he was just a goofy kid with a crush on one of his classmates and a sick feeling about his past."

"You're enjoying this, aren't you, Cecil?" Doggy looked up at me with tired eyes.

"I liked that kid. I was hoping to help him. Now the cops think I'm helping you in your efforts to cover up the murder of Richard Ewers. They think you and I killed Kevin Sands to cover our tracks. That's more felonies than I care to count. No, George, I'm not enjoying this."

George sat at the desk a moment. Then he stood up.

"I'm not going to shoot you, son. I was a little excited when I saw you going through my safe. I got excited. Let me put some more wood on the fire and let's just talk."

He headed out the back door. I walked over to the desk, emptied his revolver and put the gun and shells in the pocket of my suit coat.

Doggy came in with an armload of firewood and opened the stove with a dirty potholder. After he fed the stove, he sat on a stump he used for splitting kindling on winter days. He looked over at his desk and then sadly up at me.

"Do you have my gun? Are you going to shoot me now, Cecil?" He seemed tired and resigned to whatever was going to happen next.

"I've got the gun," I said slowly. "You don't need it if you aren't going to shoot me. Besides, I'm sure you still have another one strapped to your leg."

He smiled and didn't answer. He was wearing stiff, baggy jeans that were cut long in the leg, so I couldn't see for sure if I was right about the ankle gun.

"Harrison Teller called me this spring," Doggy said. "He said he wanted a meeting between me and Ewers. He said Ewers had sold his story to the press and he wanted to give me what I wanted to clear up the *Mygirl* murders."

"Are those the words he used, he wanted to 'give you' something?"

"That's what he said. He said he was going to give me something." Doggy paused a moment as if checking his own memory. "I went to Ketchikan, and when I got to the airport my gun didn't show up. I was in a hurry. Ewers had said if I wasn't in the hotel by a certain time he would leave. You know the airport in Ketchikan, the ferry runs on the half hour. I tried to fill out a report, but there was a long line. Several people had lost their luggage and it was the tail end of tourist season so it was busy. I missed one ferry and I was just about to miss another, so I bolted from line and just made the second ferry and caught a cab to town."

"Did you communicate with the troopers or anyone else from the D.A.'s office? Did you tell anyone at all about this meeting?"

Doggy shook his head. "No . . . I didn't tell a soul. And frankly I didn't know what I was going to do with Mr. Ewers. I knew he was going to lie to me. I considered busting him again. I don't know for what. I just wanted to see him in cuffs."

"You thought about killing him?"

"Goddamn right I thought of killing him!" Doggy said without apology. "This was a world-class killer who had not only gotten away with four murders but was about to be paid off by the press for his troubles. Yes, I thought of killing him."

The new logs on the fire had caught, and Doggy adjusted the flue on the stack and then the vents on the bottom of the old cast-iron stove.

"But I didn't kill him," he said, watching the light flickering through the vents. "When I got to the hotel he was already dead. Someone shot that bastard through the head with my own gun and left the gun there on the carpet."

The stove rumbled now, and George Doggy flicked the vents all the way closed. "This is my biggest mistake and the thing I am most guilty of: I didn't call it in right away. I turned around and walked out. I didn't touch a thing. I never even picked up the gun, which I should have done if I was going to cover the whole thing up. I walked around town for an hour or so. I have to say, Cecil, I wasn't upset much by Ewers's death. Seeing him there, laid out, gave my soul some peace. I thought of those two kids he shot and burned. The mom and those sweet children on the *Mygirl*. I was glad that bastard was dead. And I wanted to enjoy the feeling before I phoned it in and they took me in for questioning."

"Did you ever phone it in?" I asked.

"I went back to the hotel. I went up to his room. The door was still unlocked, and when I went in, Ewers was gone, the gun was gone. There were fresh sheets on the bed and only a faint hint of blood on the mattress. The maids said they knew nothing. The desk clerk had Richard Ewers checking in that day and swore he'd checked out an hour ago. He was gone, and there didn't appear to be a trace of him. No—I never called it in. I know I should have."

"George, not only didn't you call it in, when the police started looking for Richard you dummied up. You offered nothing because you didn't want them looking for Richard, did you? You were obstructing justice," I said, trying hard to keep a scolding tone out of my voice.

"Don't talk to me about justice and Richard Ewers, all right? I know it was stupid," Doggy said in disgust. A flare of sunlight moved through the room as a cloud pushed past. Everything—the gun case, the photo album, the black stove, and George Doggy's tired face—glimmered in the light.

"So, who do you think shot him?" I asked, as the cloud shaded the world once again. For the first time in my life, I was feeling a slight sense of superiority over the great George Doggy, not for what he had done in Ketchikan, but for what he had failed to see before he got there.

George looked at me with mock surprise. "I knew the Sands brothers and Chevalier had the motive to kill him because of what Ewers had done to their families. That's why I was following the money. That's why I wanted to know what those boys knew."

"But you couldn't work closely with the police because you thought Chevalier and the Sands brothers were poised to frame you. They were also afraid of you, knowing that you were the only one who might tie them to Ewers's murder. But I'm wondering, George, if it's harder for you now that the Sands brothers are dead? Or is it easier?"

"I don't know, Cecil. All I can go back to is this: the truth is the truth is the truth. And the truth is, I didn't kill Ewers, and those Sands boys knew it. The Sands boys could have cleared me, but now . . . it looks like I've been killing witnesses."

"The truth is the truth is the truth," I repeated softly, considering the plausibility of the statement.

Doggy opened the door to the stove, and the firelight played on his face. "It's a hell of a way to go out after all these years, isn't it, Cecil? I wanted Ewers myself. I wanted him in jail. I wanted that smile off his face."

"I should be enjoying this, George. I never get to hear you whine. But the truth is I'd like to help you out."

"There is nothing you know that will help me now," Doggy said without looking at me.

"George," I said, "it's not something I know. It's what *you* don't know. You were wrong about Richard and the *Mygirl*. You were always wrong. I feel warmly toward you because, for the first time, I'm right about something and you are wrong, and I'm going to get you out of a jam instead of the other way around." I reached over on the desk and took a piece of notebook paper from Sean's photo album, stuffed it in my pocket.

"I think we should take a ride and go see someone."

George looked up at me with an expression I had never seen on his face before. I appeared to be in charge and this was a new circumstance for both of us. His face was a blank mask, like an old man afraid he is losing his memory.

We walked up to his pickup truck and Doggy slid behind the wheel. I told him we needed to head to town. We could park near my house and walk. The fall afternoon was a battle between the sun and clouds, moments of sparkling clarity browned out by clouds across the sun. We turned onto the main road, and George accelerated the powerful truck. We passed a crew of kids picking up trash on the roadside; they wore orange vests and carried bright yellow bags. A murder of crows hopped the ditches in front of them, nibbling up any scrap of food they could rescue.

"So, professor, what are you so right about?" Doggy said without taking his eyes off the road. Doggy sighed.

"Shoot, Cecil, you and I have both heard hundreds of theories about the *Mygirl*, everything from drug enforcers to alien abductions. They all start with one slightly fuzzy fact and end up in the imagination."

"Okay, George. You never got a conviction on the *Mygirl*, so you are hardly the expert."

Doggy bristled and his eyes narrowed as he kept looking down the road.

"Let me just ask you this: did Richard ever mention seeing anyone else the night of the fire? Did he mention a second skiff? Did he mention seeing anyone else on the water that night?"

Doggy shook his head and spoke as if he were humoring me. "You know all this, Cecil. First Ewers said he hadn't been on the *Mygirl* that night. Then he claimed he had just come into town to drink. Finally he admitted he had taken some of the money but knew nothing about the fire. He claimed he never saw the fire. That's where he stuck. But he was lying all along."

We passed Sandy Beach. I looked out to see if anyone was surfing and sure enough Bob and Nels were getting into their wet suits. The storm had stirred up surfable waves that would last for at least a couple more days. I imagined those guys wading into the water and shuddered, thinking about the *Amelia*, our lost skiff.

"So even at trial, even when it would have saved his ass, Richard never mentioned seeing someone coming over to the *Mygirl*. He never even floats the possibility of another shooter. He never mentions seeing Chevalier coming over on the skiff. But Richard, the arsonist, would have seen Chevalier perfectly because Chevalier's face would have been lit up by the fire he was moving toward. Richard never even tells his lawyers about this other witness until after that witness gets a little pissy and testifies on direct that 'maybe' Richard Ewers was the arsonist skiff operator. Richard never mentions to anyone that he saw Chevalier on the water that night because it never happened."

"Ewers was lying through his teeth, Cecil. He had stolen the money and was headed into town. Maybe he planned to kill everybody, but more than likely he was caught in the act. He shot the first person who came on him and then had to kill everyone else to make his escape."

"How much money was on Ewers when he was interviewed in Sitka just after the fire?"

"He had spent a couple hundred at the bar, and he had a hundred dollars on him."

"He killed four people he worked with, a woman and

children, for three hundred bucks? Where was the rest of the money? There had been thousands on board the *Mygirl*, most of the money was found in the safe. He could have forced someone to open it. Why didn't he take *all* the money?"

"I don't know, Cecil . . . and neither do you. Ewers was a liar." George Doggy's voice was bitter.

We passed the grocery store, which sat on one of the most beautiful pieces of waterfront property in town. Gulls circled the Dumpsters.

"I agree, George. He's a liar. That's the truth. But there are some other liars to consider here too. Look at the whole thing, George. Try to not think of Richard as the killer for a second. Who would have more reason to kill Ewers in Ketchikan than you?"

George was staring intently at the road as if we were driving through a snowstorm and his gaze could part the curtain of white he was riding through. He was thinking hard, I could tell, sorting and re-sorting his facts, but more importantly, I could tell by the tension in his body, the firmness of his grip on the wheel, that he was challenging some very old and entrenched assumptions. Finally he spoke. "Shit" was all he said.

We parked on the waterfront near my house. George knew where we were going. I fell in step beside him. He patted the outside of my coat pocket. "Don't you think you'd better load that gun, son?"

"Here, you take it." I fished the empty revolver and the shells out of my suit coat and held them out to George.

"Ah, criminy," he muttered, flipped the cylinder out, loaded it, snapped the wheel shut, spun it and checked the hammer. Then he handed the gun back to me. "I've already got one. He won't expect you to be carrying."

I took the revolver, although I didn't like the heft of the thing. George pointed to my pocket again. "Hammer's down on a hole, you know, so you have five. Use two hands. Pull back the hammer and squeeze. It's loud as hell, so it scares most people to death, even if you don't hit anything."

We turned the corner to the harbor and walked down the

ramp and out to the last float. The *Naked Horse* was tied up in its own slip. She was ragged and weary-looking, with her rigging hanging off and shards of broken mast on the deck.

George jumped into the cockpit and the old boat rocked easily. I followed. George rapped on the hatch, and we heard a clatter of tools falling into the sink.

Jonathan Chevalier looked up at us and his expression was neither surprised nor concerned.

"You feeling all right, Jonathan?" I asked.

Jonathan took a long breath and looked back at us. He had shaved, and his long hair was combed back neatly over his head. He still had bruises, and his eyes were rimmed with dark circles. When he started speaking, his voice was sleepy and a little cracked.

"I'm feeling more . . . normal, you know what I mean?"

"You know, Jonathan, I got to thinking about how you said you saw Richard coming from the boat that night yet there was firelight on his face."

Jonathan didn't say anything, but took a step up on the ladder and craned his neck around on the deck as if he were out at sea checking on the wind. He was staring toward the bow as he spoke kind of absently. "When I saw Harrison Teller in town I figured something was up. What are you guys—playing detective?"

"I'm just curious," I said, and sat down in the cockpit eye to eye with Jonathan as he stood on the cabin ladder.

Doggy tugged on my sleeve. "Cecil, come on. What is this guy going to tell us now? Everyone else is dead. He knows he doesn't have to talk to us. Come on, let's leave him alone."

George Doggy, the master of confessions, was paying me the single greatest compliment of both his and my career: he was signaling me to take the lead on the questioning. He would be the skeptical good cop; that left only me, the bad cop.

"This guy doesn't have to talk to us," Doggy repeated. "I'm sorry we bothered you, Jonathan." And Doggy made a show of tugging on my sleeve.

Jonathan looked at us as if we were Laurel and Hardy.

"I think Jonathan wants to talk to us," I told Doggy. "I think he's wanted to talk to someone for a long time, and now would be a good time."

Jonathan snorted; he shifted his weight nervously from one foot to the other. "Why is that?"

"Because it's really over now. The others are dead. Before, one of you couldn't break away or the other two would point the finger. When Richard wanted to talk to George and when he gave the money to the Sands boys, you thought it was over. You thought he was going to tell the truth about what happened on the *Mygirl*. But that's not going to happen now, is it, Jonathan?"

I was fidgeting in my suit coat pocket. I didn't like the heft of the gun there.

"So . . . ," Jonathan said, "is any of this supposed to make a difference to me?" His voice quavered enough to let me know he wasn't as calm as he pretended to be.

"I don't know, I just think someone should tell you it's all right. That we know it wasn't your fault."

His eyes narrowed. "What wasn't my fault?"

"It wasn't your fault that you had to kill your brother."

"My brother was a good boy."

"It must have been hard all these years. Living with it. Never being able to tell anybody. You saved the lives of all the others on the *Mygirl*. You saved Richard, and you saved Sean and Kevin. They knew you saved them and that's why they went along with you for all these years."

Jonathan Chevalier's eyes narrowed to slender crescents. He was crying.

"Albert was a good boy," he said softly.

"Albert was a deeply troubled boy. He had an AK-47 he used to blast anything that moved. He would tear squirrels' bodies apart with his bullets. He tortured small animals."

"That doesn't mean anything. You never knew him. You don't know." Jonathan wiped at his nose.

"I was always curious why he had been shot in the arms and legs," I said. "The parents were shot through the chest.

Straight kill shots. The little girl was clubbed maybe to keep her quiet. Maybe to play with her, like he played with the animals he tortured."

"He wasn't a monster," Jonathan snarled.

George was staring at me, his brow furrowed. He was working through the problem. He was not interrupting me.

I went on, letting it spill out as if my dreams were bursting through to my waking life, sick of being cooped up in the dark. "But Albert's first wounds were to his legs and arms. Shots meant to stop him. Then there was one close shot to the head, and that was the last shot, wasn't it?"

Jonathan stared up at me as if he were a wolverine caught in a leghold trap.

"What was it, Jonathan? Did the little girl find him torturing the animals? Did he hit her on the head by mistake? Did he hit her in fun and maybe misjudge his strength? And then her parents found them and they started screaming, so Albert started shooting?"

Jonathan's hand was shaking as he ran it through his hair.

"You don't have anything, Cecil."

"That's not quite true," I said softly.

"We never meant to hurt a soul."

"I believe that. I really do, Jonathan," I said. "You heard the shots and you came over in the skiff and you found your brother Albert in a rage. He had clubbed Tina Sands and shot her parents. He was headed back toward where Richard Ewers and the Sands brothers were sleeping. He was going to kill them too. He had to, by that point. You got the gun from him and tried to stop him but he was wild. You shot him in the arms and legs and the wounds were bad. Worse than you expected. He was bleeding to death, he was suffering, so you put him out of his pain. Then you looked around and you saw all the dead bodies and the gun was in your hands."

George Doggy looked at me closely. "Jonathan had to split up the suspicion, so he gave Ewers some money and told him to leave as fast as he could. Ewers, being a dumb scared kid, split. Then Jonathan swore he was going to kill the Sands boys if they told the truth. Albert had killed their family and Jonathan had killed Albert. There was no more justice that was needed and Jonathan swore if they said anything to the cops about Albert, he would finger Kevin and Sean for the killings. Kevin was just criminal enough to know he could be made-to-order for the killings."

"Kevin took the rifle back to his uncle's boat and later gave it to Sean as a keepsake," I added sarcastically.

"Like I said," Jonathan muttered, "you don't have anything."

"Well now, son, we have the AK-47," George offered.

"And there's a picture in Sean's album of Albert with the gun," I said, "and if we need it, we can find some old slugs in that stump where they did target practice in Kalinin Bay. That puts the gun on the *Mygirl*. We've got you lying about the gun to the police. We've got you lying about how you saw Ewers coming from the burning boat with the light shining on his face, which would be impossible from the angle you claimed to be coming from."

Jonathan said nothing, but shook his head from side to side.

"Okay," I said, and I laced my hands behind my head. "Let's go back to the night of the fire. Two men pass each other in skiffs. The *Mygirl* is on fire. It is fully involved in flame. The gas has sent it up like a firebomb. One man is coming toward the boat to see if there is anything he can do to help. The other has just set the fire and is leaving quickly. It's a dark night and as they pass each other, the fire is at the back of the arsonist's skiff. The arsonist can get a good view of the man who is coming to help. The man coming to help can only get a dim view of the arsonist's face because the figure is lit up in profile with his face to the darkness, his back to the flames. Only the arsonist can see the other clearly. But it doesn't matter because you never saw a skiff operator leaving the burning scow."

Jonathan was shaking his head back and forth as if trying to keep a bug from flying into his ear. "You think you are so smart but you are stupid. You don't know. You don't know a thing about what it feels like to try and protect a brother or what it feels like to see him suffer like that."

"It must have been hard for you, Jonathan. It must have been harder still when you learned Richard was going to talk to the press, when you realized that he was giving the money to the Sands boys for the murder of their family. Kevin wanted the money. Why not? He had lost his family and he had kept quiet, but he didn't understand the dynamics, did he? He didn't understand that his shelter was going to fall down after Richard pulled out and took the Sands boys with him. Richard was tired of keeping quiet for you, Jonathan. Particularly after you hedged on your description of him at trial. Richard pulled out and took the Sandses with him. You were left out. No one was going to believe you hadn't done all of the killings, were they, Jonathan?"

Now the master of the *Naked Horse* was slumped on the top of the companionway. He was shaking as if freezing to death. Doggy reached his left hand out and placed it on Jonathan's shoulder. The other hand Doggy slid near his ankle.

I continued, "Richard was going to give you over to George. You found out from Kevin. You flew to Ketchikan on the same jet George was on, didn't you? Somehow you got George's gun from the baggage handlers and you made that first ferry to town. You killed Richard with George's gun. Then when George just walked away from it you got scared. You waited around but you didn't know what was up, so you cleaned up the room and stuffed Richard into your green river bag, then waited to dump him over the side during the storm. There was no chance anyone would follow you out into the storm. Once Ewers was dead, Kevin finally got the picture. He was going to get fingered not only for the *Mygirl* but for killing Richard as well. Everything was really broken now. All the agreements you made the night the *Mygirl* burned. The whole dynamic that held your silence together had collapsed. When Kevin realized it was over he wanted to cut a deal with George. That's what he wanted to do on the back deck. Kevin didn't really know if George had killed Ewers or not, but it didn't matter. He felt better confiding in George at that point. Maybe in his own reptilian brain he wanted to re-create the shelter of your original agreement."

"You still have nothing. Richard Ewers did the whole thing. Who's going to argue with me now? I'll say I didn't testify against him at trial because I was afraid he was going to kill me. No one's going to believe you, Cecil. You've got nothing and there's no one left to give you anything." Jonathan was smiling weakly now, staring down into the darkness of his sailboat.

I felt almost light-headed from happiness and vindication. "What would the real killer say?" I mumbled to myself. Then I pressed on, because I needed just a bit more from the master of the *Naked Horse*.

"You're right about that, Jonathan. There is no one left. Sean was going to turn the AK-47 in to the police. He was going to take the gun to school and give it to the officer there. So you called George to report the schoolyard shooter. Whatever happened, you made sure you were down one witness."

"You're fishing, Cecil."

"Then, of course, I have this." I held up the scrap of paper from Sean's photo album. "Sean was worried about his brother. He couldn't let Kevin go down for you. When Kevin was in jail and you were dancing around on the street giving away all the evidence, Sean wrote me a note so he could protect his brother. Brothers are like that, aren't they?" I studied the haggard man in front of me. Jonathan reached down and pulled on a heavy wool pea coat. He stood in the sun and wrapped his arms around his shoulders. He looked from me to George and back again.

"I'm tired" was all he said.

Then he reached into his coat and pulled a heavy revolver from his pocket. Doggy's hand slid up his shin. I pushed myself back in the cockpit, fumbling in my pockets.

Jonathan smiled at both of us, placed the gun squarely in his mouth, and squeezed his eyes shut tight.

"Wait!" I shouted. Jonathan opened his eyes.

He looked at me. His tired eyes were both sorry and

hateful, if that is possible. The barrel of the gun rattled against his teeth. He squeezed his eyes tightly shut once more.

Across the harbor I heard a woman laugh. A car horn sounded in the distance.

Jonathan took the gun out of his mouth and shot George Doggy in the forehead.

I heard people yelling and footsteps on the ramp. I remember my hand feeling sore and the smell of burning fabric, but I don't remember pulling the trigger on the revolver in my pocket. I don't remember seeing the slug from the gun I fired hitting Jonathan in the throat or reeling him backwards down into the darkness of the *Naked Horse*'s cabin. I do remember kneeling over George Doggy's body, reaching out with hands that seemed to be someone else's. I remember that he seemed very, very far away, and I wondered if he could even see me from where he lay.

The shots echoed up and bounced around the harbor. Gulls rose up into the air. People ran down the dock; someone screamed at them to stay back and call 911. Jonathan lay sprawled on the deck of the cabin. The back of his neck was a mass of torn flesh and bone fragments. He must have looked much the same as Richard Ewers looked when Doggy found him in the hotel room in Ketchikan.

I cradled Doggy in my arms; I laid his limp body on the top of the cockpit hatch and jumped down to the cabin's floor. There, in the dark with the smell of powder, I felt as if I were standing at the bottom of a well. When I looked up to the sky, I saw the misshapen outline of George Doggy's head. I took a pencil stub from my pocket and picked up Jonathan's revolver through the trigger guard and held it up to George's body.

"Does this gun look familiar to you?" I asked him, holding up the gun that had been stolen from him back in Ketchikan, the gun that Jonathan had used to kill Richard Ewers and, now, my father's oldest friend.

Chapter Fifteen

I remember George Doggy's funeral. It was a community event along the lines of some sort of medieval festival of grief, with speeches and fund-raisers for law enforcement and midnight vigils to "Stop the Violence."

The funeral itself was held in the Harrigan Centennial Hall, the largest room in town, most often used for concerts and important public meetings. The Governor came and made remarks concerning a legacy of decency and respect for civilization. The entire trooper detachment from the training academy was there wearing sidearms on their dress uniforms. When the Governor called upon all of the assembled to live their lives in accordance with George Doggy's example, I felt all the cops in the place glaring at me.

After the speeches there was food, crying, backslapping and more food, or so I was told. I went home early. As I walked out the door past a group of glaring law enforcement cadets, it struck me that there were so many flowers at his funeral you would have thought George had won the Kentucky Derby rather than getting gunned down by the man who had tried to frame him.

The town was generally split on whether I was to blame for George Doggy's murder. On the side of my being guilty sat almost the entire law enforcement community of the State of Alaska and my mother. On the side of my being innocent were Jane Marie, Toddy, most of the bar crowd who thought I didn't have enough balls to have pulled it off, and strangely enough, Sitka Police Lieutenant Roy Pomfret.

Pomfret had responded to the scene down on the *Naked Horse*. He found me on the cabin floor holding George's gun with a pencil. I was sitting flat on the deck at the bottom of the companionway steps. Pomfret crawled down, took the gun away and stood me up gently. He patted me down and found the other revolver still in my pocket, the fabric of my coat singed by the muzzle blast. I had, apparently, not taken the gun out of my pocket when I fired. Pomfret took the gun and placed it carefully on the chart table and said, "Come on, Cecil, let me get you out of here."

Pomfret turned the scene over to the troopers from the crime lab who happened to be at the academy in a forensics training session. This had been a busy week for gunshot wounds in Sitka, and the cops were benefiting by getting unprecedented practice in processing crime scenes. State purchasing agents had to lay in two new cases of latex gloves.

Pomfret took me to the police station. He didn't read me my rights, but that was fine, since I wasn't saying anything anyway. I sat in a room wearing my best suit, singed and smeared with blood. I stayed there until they must have gotten a search warrant, because after an hour sitting silently on the folding chair in the interview room, they came back, took all my clothes, and gave me a hospital robe to wear.

After about two hours, Pomfret came in and held up a microcassette recorder, which appeared to be covered in dried blood. He had taken it off of George's body. They had also gone to Doggy's home and taken the tape from the tape recorder that had been running in the basement. George had been recording our entire conversation, from the moment he came in while I was going through his safe, to the confrontation with Jonathan when I had showed him Sean's note, and right up to the time Jonathan shot him in the head. The recorder had whirred silently away in his coat pocket while George lay dead in my arms.

Pomfret had listened to the tapes. He had gotten the first draft of the story from the lab techs at the scene. He only had one critical question that wasn't cleared up by the tapes. "What was in that kid's note?" he asked me.

I handed him the paper from Sean's album, which I was still gripping in my hand. Pomfret spread it out on the metal table in the interview room.

The note was written in Sean's blocky handwriting. All it contained was a girl's name. It read, "Chandler, Chandler, Chandler . . ." down the entire length of the paper. There was a heart drawn at the end of the page.

"Jesus Christ," Pomfret said.

"It was a bluff" was my only statement to the police that day.

George Doggy has become one of the great law enforcement martyrs in the region. In a few years there would be a junior high school named after him. No one questioned his motives in the deaths that autumn that had culminated in his own. No one dispelled the belief that George had saved lives at the school when he shot Sean Sands. No one doubted he was involved in a legitimate investigation when Kevin Sands went over the stern of the *Winning Hand*.

No one except me, apparently. So many of the things I thought and learned about George since his death have clouded my memory of him. I learned he had gotten Kevin Sands out of jail. George had put up the bail. Why had he done it? I can only imagine he wanted to follow Sands to the money and Ewers's body, but when he had the chance to search the *Naked Horse* he seemed disinterested. Had George bailed Kevin out so he could then follow him and kill him? And after killing him, did he intend to shift the blame to me?

But George was part of the honored dead now, and he would not answer, so I could afford to be generous. I think Doggy probably just ended his life in unfamiliar territory. He was frightened and caught up in circumstances he couldn't control, like so many of the men from whom he had coaxed confessions.

I just don't know how to judge Doggy's guilt or innocence.

It seems strange to be in the position at all, so I'll just leave it at this: George Doggy loved my family and he wanted to help me. That's all that matters to me now.

But I had to be charged with something. I was the last one left standing in some demonic party game. These were the directions which came down from above: I had to be found guilty of something. So the district attorney eventually took a case against me to the grand jury. It was for negligent homicide in connection with the death of Kevin Sands. I could have come up with more creative charges against myself, but the D.A.'s office was playing it safe.

Troopers had worked the ballistics on all the guns and had reinterviewed everyone involved in both the Sands brothers' deaths and Patricia Ewers's police killing. They revealed the DNA evidence they had from the bathtub in Richard Ewers's hotel room in Ketchikan, where the investigators had found "significant trace evidence of blood along the edges of the tub." But it wasn't until they took the plumbing apart and found clots of bloody tissue in the traps of both the sink and bathtub that they were able to say with some confidence that Richard Ewers had been cut up for transport in the hotel bathtub. So eventually a coroner's jury found that Richard Ewers had died by an unspecified homicide. The troopers tested ballistics of the AK-47 young Sean Sands had been carrying when he had been gunned down and found that it "could not be excluded" as a possible source for the slug fragments that had been found years ago in the *Mygirl* killings. One expert stated that there were enough similarities between the test slugs from the AK-47 and the lands and grooves found in the badly misshapen slug fragments found in the four burnt bodies to make a positive identification, whereas another expert said there were clearly not enough similarities. None of it mattered to me. I believed Jonathan Chevalier had used Albert's own rifle, the one with the *No Doubt* sticker on the stock, to kill Albert himself. Then he gave his brother's rifle to Sean knowing it would loop the Sands brothers into the killings if suspicion ever came down on him. Sean Sands had simply not wanted to throw the weapon away, no matter that it had been used to kill his family. Later, when Jonathan felt the pressure of George Doggy tracking him down, Jonathan had told Sean to get rid of the rifle. Sean said he was going to turn the gun in to the police officer who visited his school. It was in that second that Jonathan decided to tip Doggy about the young schoolyard shooter.

Why didn't Sean put the rifle down when Doggy had commanded him? Perhaps all the years of passively viewing his violent dreams made him want to finally take things into his own hands. Guns feel good in a young boy's hands. A gun gives the illusion that he is in control of his own destiny, and there is some truth in that. Sean must have known his own destiny, from the moment his playmate Albert had made him an orphan. Perhaps that made Sean put the old man in his sights.

I had actually killed Jonathan Chevalier, but that was too sloppy for the D.A.s. The ballistics were against them and pointed toward a "defense of others" argument. Also there was Doggy's own tape, which was fairly conclusive. I hadn't been around for Patricia Ewers's or Sean Sands's deaths, so the D.A.'s office was left with Kevin's death as their best opportunity to convict me of murder. Jane Marie was scheduled to testify, after they forced her to take an immunity deal so she didn't have the option of taking the Fifth. I was asked to appear before the grand jury although the request was given in the form of a "target letter," which is the official warning that I was the target of a grand jury investigation and I might also find the Fifth Amendment to be useful.

I got Harrison Teller to represent me even though he could have been a witness against me. He said he'd cross that bridge if the D.A.s were stupid enough to try and make him cross it, but he claimed he wasn't all that concerned. I, on the other hand, was very concerned. The reason most cases settle before trial is that everyone familiar with the system knows that juries are unpredictable. Many lawyers would rather settle litigation by cutting cards.

But I was most worried because I frankly had no real clear memory of how Kevin went over the back deck of the

Winning Hand. All I could remember was the tiny bundle of my daughter in his arms, the gun in Doggy's hand, and Blossom's skin turning blue as Kevin held her. I also remembered the time we waited before we started looking for Kevin in the water.

My worry was building to a nearly manic pitch when Todd finally got a bunch of his film back and discovered, rather casually, a week before the grand jury was to convene, that he had filmed the entire incident on the back deck of the *Winning Hand* in spectacular, color-soaked 8mm.

That first time we watched it, I was a swirl of anxiety, for it was shot clearly and all the action was visible. We were struggling. Kevin was obviously holding the baby as some kind of hostage. Doggy had his gun, and we were all backing Kevin up against the rail. Lips moved. Hands jerked around, and then Kevin was gone. Glinting sun dogs seared into the old camera lens. Todd had then focused on Blossom, back in Jane Marie's arms, Jane Marie crying and stroking the baby's head. Then he'd stopped shooting. The next image was of the Coast Guard helicopter, taken many hours later.

My first impression of the film was ambiguous. When we slowed it down, we could pay more attention to the gestures and each individual movement: my right arm had been around Kevin's back, apparently trying to prevent him from going over, or at least that was what we would argue at trial. Doggy seemed to be holding Kevin by the shirt and pulling up just before Kevin handed Blossom over to Jane Marie. Teller forwarded a copy of the film on to the D.A., along with a written notice that we fully expected the film to be shown to the grand jury as exculpatory evidence.

The D.A. showed the film, and all the jurors saw was a baby in peril. They "no true billed" the case in record time. This meant I was out from under the charges, though later the district attorney threatened me with an obstruction of justice charge, which he never got around to taking to a grand jury.

Several weeks later one of the grand jurors came up to me in line at the grocery store and, although the juror had sworn not to discuss the case with anyone, he pulled on my coat and whispered, "I would have drowned the fucker." He bagged his own cigarettes, gave me a thumbs-up and walked out the automatic doors.

All of us were relieved, of course. The secretary at the prosecutor's office said the D.A. had been pressured to take the case. "But still," she said, "you should be a little more careful next time, Cecil."

Jurors love photographic evidence, and somehow they like to think the truth is there. Of course the whole truth is no more on a piece of film than it is in one bloodstain or one statement uttered in a lockdown cell.

One image from Todd's film floats to the surface with eerie clarity for me. Just as he is aware that his body weight is pivoting toward the water, Kevin Sands's face surrenders to us. I'm holding his back, George is pulling on his shirt, and Kevin is a child, wanting nothing more than to be rescued. His eyes are wide and beseeching, he is holding the baby out toward Jane Marie's arms mouthing the words, "Take her, take her," and for the briefest moment there is gentleness and concern. This could be seen only in the slightest flicker in his eyes when the film was slowed down frame by frame. When he releases the baby, you can clearly see me forgetting about Kevin and letting him go. He tilts backwards, his head drops and his feet fly up.

I don't know. I try and replay these events in my mind and I think: I could have saved them—Kevin, Patricia, young Sean and George Doggy. I don't know how, or how saving one might have changed the others, but I can't shake the feeling that I could have helped them somehow, and I'm wearing that feeling now, even on the warmest summer days.

Later that fall, Gary managed to get Paul deLay to town and the big harmonica player from Portland, Oregon hit Sitka, Alaska like another storm. We had just gotten the news about the grand jury decision, and Jane Marie had convinced me we should go out dancing.

"You can't hide out in this town, Cecil. You know that. People will think whatever they want, but you should make them look at you while they're thinking it." Jane Marie wore a soft velvet dress and had her hair combed back off her face. We had arranged to have her sister baby-sit Blossom, but she backed out at the last minute. We don't ask Todd to baby-sit, so we tried to talk Toddy into coming out with all three of us to hear the live music.

"No, thank you," he said, as he pored over the list of garage sales he was planning to hit early in the morning. "I believe my time would be better spent in preparing for my morning tomorrow. I'm going to be looking up the street addresses and making sure we have a proper schedule. Besides, I have never been particularly adept at dancing to modern music."

"That's only because you haven't tried," Jane Marie said, as she draped her bare arm over his shoulder. A necklace of silver and lapis lazuli glittered on her neck, she was wearing a dark shade of lipstick, and her ancient, glittering eyes were gay. "You can do whatever you want, but if you decide to come I want to be the first to dance with you," she said to him, though he was staring down at his paper.

"Yes," he said, "I suppose I would dance with you if I were going to dance with anyone." Todd looked up briefly, amazed at the very thought of that, then went back to the paper.

We agreed the bar would be too smoky and loud for Blossom, so one of us would stand outside with her. The bar had an awning over the sidewalk and on all but the worst evenings the sidewalk was the preferable place to listen to loud bar bands anyway.

First came Blossom's clean diaper and then the tiny cotton shirt. Then I zipped her up into some fleecy hooded jammies, then some bag-like contraption with yet another hood, and finally our daughter looked like a bale of fabric with her face peeking out of the top. I think she knew we were going to a party though, for her eyes darted around expectantly, and she smiled as she chewed on one end of her hood string.

"You are a needle in a haystack," I babbled to her as I zipped up the last zipper and hefted her into my arms.

We walked down the street to the bar. I was dressed in my woodcutting jacket, T-shirt and canvas pants as I carried Blossom in my arms. Jane Marie looked like a movie star.

As we left the house she grabbed a beautiful silver bracelet Dave Galanin had carved for her in trade for some of her whale photographs. Now the bracelet glittered on her slender wrist. The outlines of her hips and waist were in parallel motion as we walked together arm in arm. She was as beautiful as a sunny morning with steam rising off the ground.

The fat dachshund was sleeping in his little house and the wind was calm on this night. Stars salted the sky above the narrow street. We could hear the band preparing for its first number as we crossed the street: the drummer hit the snare a couple of snaps and a harmonica moaned out through the cracks in the crowd noise. Jane Marie was about to hop the curb to head into the bar when she turned and threw one arm around my neck and the other hand she placed on our daughter's well-padded head.

"You have any money?" she asked.

I reached into my pants pocket and took out one of the soft and frayed hundred-dollar bills I had been saving all summer long and gave it to her.

Jane Marie held the bill in her hand and stared at it. For a moment there was a shadow of sadness across her face. But then someone opened the door and music swept out on the sidewalk. She kissed me, then her daughter, turned and skipped into the clatter of the crowded bar.

Blossom and I stood outside with the underage bar crowd, the street kids and the others who had been forever banned from going inside. Matt was there talking to someone about fishing regulations. Larry drove by slowly in his ancient Saab with the two kayaks permanently attached to the roof. Nels and Bob stopped to listen out on the sidewalk. Pirate Ron was there. Davey, Lisa and Shannon were all dancing together. As the music thumped out into the evening, the sidewalk filled up. Nita, Walt, Carol, Tory, Preston, Mark, Nancy, Jim and

Lynne all arrived eventually. Some were gossiping in the darkest corner under the eaves near the back door, some were dancing, but all of us were crowding under the awning, for miraculously it had started to rain. We laughed and joked as they asked about Blossom. No one mentioned the shootings or the grand jury. No one wanted to. Someone offered me a drink from a plastic bottle in a paper bag, which I declined, and it occurred to me that I didn't have to worry about this story of my life and what to bring with me, for it was finally dawning on me that I am not the sole author of this story of my life, and that all my luck, both good and bad, will follow the lay of the land.

This was fine with me because on this night I was surrounded by friends outside the bar and we were all dressed for the weather.

I peeked in to see the band. Gary was standing in his usual corner. The great Paul deLay was next to him, a large, large man with a gravelly voice and powerful lungs. The Screaming Love Bunnies counted off the first number. Paul deLay lifted his harmonica to his lips and blew a squall of blues through the crowd.

Out on the sidewalk we danced and moved and bumped into one another while Paul deLay sang about love and misery, going to jail and getting out. Blossom cooed and laughed in my arms as deLay played twisting and unexpected riffs, rising and falling, sometimes a saxophone, sometimes an organ line. We all spun and danced and felt as if we were floating above a hole in the street. Gary smiled and smiled watching his bandmates play until Paul deLay asked him to come up and take a solo and we cheered. Then Jay played a guitar solo, and we all cheered again. The spinning dancers spun and the awkward dancers clumped around. The watchers watched and all of us were smiling. Jane Marie came outside and we danced on the sidewalk together, her arms around my neck as we held on to Blossom cooing and laughing at the noise and the lumbering motion of the ride. We danced that way until a fisherman cut in and I stood in the gutter watching the rain blow like a torn curtain through the light above the fish plant.

* * *

Two days after the dance, Bob and Nels would be surfing on the outside of Kruzof Island and would find the spine, rib cage and skull of a human being tossed up above the drift line of the beach. The bones would be tangled in the laces of some waterlogged but unworn sneakers. There would be only faint traces of flesh on the bones, and the eye sockets would be scoured clean by the small crabs and sand fleas. The cartilage would be sparkling white in places, but the bones would be a slick grayish tone. Other than the shoes, there would be no trace of clothing near the partial corpse. The surfers would find bear scat nearby with some gray bone chips in it. Bob and Nels would then wrap the rancid skull and piece of torso in a plastic bag and bring it to town. Two weeks later, the coroner would identify the remains through the dental records. This was Richard Ewers, my client.

Even though it was impossible, I already knew it. Standing outside the bar as the guitar cut through the cool wet air, I knew somehow that Richard Ewers was lying on the beach entangled in shoes and rubbery strands of kelp. I shuddered, as if God were reaching back from the future and tapping me on the shoulder. I remember feeling the strange rise of a storm within me, as if I were back out to sea.

I turned to Jane Marie, who was dancing with the bear-like fisherman. He was wearing a dirty white cap and a wet wool coat, which smelled equally of mildew and diesel fuel. Jane Marie cradled our daughter in her arms and when I touched her shoulder, she turned toward me looking up with a wide and crooked smile.

The sight of her, as it always does, took me by surprise. "I hope this is what Myrna Loy still looks like in heaven," I thought stupidly. The fisherman tugged on his beard, mad, probably, at losing the most beautiful dance partner on the island. He scowled at his feet for a moment, then laughed and lumbered down the street.

I wanted to tell Jane Marie how I felt about walking away

from all the people I had loved and watched die. I wanted to tell her something urgent and complex, something that took in the shapelessness of my guilt and the giddy rising of my relief, but I couldn't find all the words.

The music stopped, someone laughed, then broke a bottle on the pavement, and as the storm sank away in my heart, I pulled my collar up against the rain and realized there were only three words I could think of: grateful, grateful, and even more grateful.

Author's Note

This book is a work of fiction. I have drawn a few details from actual incidents in which boats have burned and lives have been lost, but the characters, motivations and events portrayed here came directly from my imagination. Anyone looking for clues to Alaska's unsolved mysteries will be disappointed. All of the characters involved in either crime or law enforcement in this tale are fictional. I know this for a fact, because I created them.

There are real people who walk through this story. If you come to Sitka and spend enough time you could find Gary Gouker and the members of the Screaming Love Bunnies. You might also be able to recognize some of the people Cecil encountered while hitchhiking. I included them here because they represent my strange and invigorating town as well as any characters I could make up.

My thanks too go out to The Island Institute, a nonprofit arts and humanities organization here in Sitka, for their inspiration early on and for their continued support.

Paul deLay appears in the story because I've seen him play in Juneau and I want him to play a gig in Sitka. Here's hoping.

I also have to acknowledge the help of Dr. Bob Klem, Tory O'Connell, James McGowan, Nita Couchman and Marylin Newman for their counsel and advice along the way. Carol Price Spurling, of Old Harbor Books, was an invaluable assistant and friend. My debt to her is immeasurable.

Finally to Jan, Finn and all the people on my daily "trap line." *Cold Water Burning* turned out to be a long journey through tough country and was only possible because of their love and friendship.

About the Author

JOHN STRALEY lives in Sitka, Alaska, with his son and wife, a marine biologist who studies whales. He is the Shamus Award–winning author of *The Angels Will Not Care, The Woman Who Married a Bear, The Curious Eat Themselves, The Music of What Happens,* and *Death and the Language of Happiness.*